TAKEN

LISA STONE

HarperCollins*Publishers*

HarperCollins*Publishers* Ltd
1 London Bridge Street,
London SE1 9GF

www.harpercollins.co.uk

HarperCollins*Publishers*
1st Floor, Watemarque Building, Ringsend Road
Dublin 4, Ireland

First published by HarperCollins*Publishers* 2020
6

A catalogue record for this book is available from the British Library

ISBN: 978-0-00-837882-0

This novel is entirely a work of fiction.
The names, characters and incidents portrayed in it are
the work of the author's imagination. Any resemblance to
actual persons, living or dead, events or localities is
entirely coincidental.

Typeset in Sabon by Palimpsest Book Production Ltd, Falkirk, Stirlingshire

Printed and bound in the UK by CPI Group (UK) Ltd, Croydon CR0 4YY

MIX
Paper from
responsible sources
FSC™ C007454

This book is produced from independently certified FSC™ paper
to ensure responsible forest management.

For more information visit: www.harpercollins.co.uk/green

A big thank-you to my readers for all your wonderful comments and reviews. They are much appreciated. Thank you to my editors, Kathryn and Holly, my literary agent, Andrew, and all the team at HarperCollins.

ONE

It was not a safe place for a young girl.

Colin Weaver looked through the window of his third-floor flat at the children's play area below. She was there, as she was most nights after school. Leila Smith, eight years old, alone and vulnerable. He had a good view from up here, apart from the dirt on the outside of the glass, which he couldn't clean. Tenants could no longer open their windows wide enough to clean the outside since the council had fitted cable restrictors after a child had fallen from the seventh floor and died.

Sad, indeed, but shouldn't the parents have been keeping watch on their child?

That was the problem with parents today, Colin thought, not for the first time, as he watched Leila gently rocking on the swing. Too many absent fathers and self-centred mothers oblivious to the needs of their children. Not like *his* mother, he reflected grimly. She'd wanted to know exactly where he was and what he was doing every minute of the day, until he couldn't stand it any longer and had left ten years ago, aged thirty-eight.

As he watched Leila the sun began to set behind the block

of high-rise flats, its shadow falling across the play area and casting another corridor of gloom. As if there wasn't enough gloom here already: grey tower blocks and rooftops, cables strung between pylons, unemployment, and the steady rumble of the city line reminding residents that a better life lay a train ride away. Children used the play area on the Hawthorn Estate during daylight hours. It was a small oasis of fun, laughter and innocence in an otherwise bleak and depressing landscape. But once darkness fell it was a different matter and most children knew they had to return home straight away.

Apart from Leila.

She was there long after the other children had gone, because her mother didn't give a damn.

As Colin watched, the sun continued its descent until darkness fell. The only child left in the play area was Leila. Her mother, Kelsey Smith, had never told her she needed to be home so she was safe and warm. She didn't care, and Colin knew it was doubtful she even noticed when her child was missing, since she was so often off her head on drink and drugs or entertaining clients. That was Kelsey. Nearly everyone on the estate knew about Kelsey and that she wasn't fit to be a mother. If something happened to her child, it would be her fault.

Leila was still gently rocking on the swing, her silhouette just visible in the small light coming from the lamplight, dimmed by the council to save electricity. Rocking herself was probably the only comfort the poor child had, for there'd be none at home, Colin thought bitterly. She was pretty, with dark hair and big round eyes, but those eyes had seen more than they should for a child her age, which gave her a hard, streetwise look. Colin found this very sad. Children should be innocent for as long as possible.

Leila and her prostitute mother lived in the flat directly above Colin's. He had to listen to their comings and goings, so he knew when they were in or out, when Kelsey was entertaining clients and when Leila was left home alone. He heard her crying and her mother losing her temper and shouting at her for not cleaning the flat, shopping or cooking. The child was only eight, for Christ's sake! That bloody mother needed to be taught a lesson.

To his shame, Colin had fancied Kelsey when she'd first moved in, before he'd found out what she was really like. Now he was disgusted with her and with himself for making such a gross error of judgement. The woman was all tits and tattoos, flashing her eyes with a come-on expression at every bloke she passed. It was probably her tactics that had fooled him at the start, he thought. He'd be the first to admit he was ignorant when it came to women, shy, having only his mother as an example. But then he'd come to his senses and realized what she was like and felt sorry for the child.

What the social services were doing leaving Leila with her mother Colin had no idea. Her older kids, four in all, had been taken into care and then adopted years ago. Probably for the best, he thought. She'd told him this when she'd first moved in, and that she was being given another chance with Leila because she was clean – off booze, drugs and the game. That was laughable! It didn't take much to see she was lying, and the situation couldn't be allowed to continue. Kelsey's sister, Sharon, agreed. He'd seen her going into the flat and had stopped her and voiced his concerns. They'd agreed Leila needed help, and fast. But what to do for the best?

Leaving the light off in his living room so he couldn't be seen from outside, Colin kept watch on the play area. Leila continued to gently work the swing in the gloom as two teenage lads rode in on their mountain bikes. Aged about thirteen, they were known on the estate for selling drugs for their rich dealer. Kelsey bought her stuff from them. Colin knew that residents had largely given up on calling the police. It was a waste of time and created bad feelings, as the mothers of the boys lived on the estate too, as did most of their customers. If the police were called, the lads were usually tipped off and had long gone by the time they arrived, pedalling at speed down the alleyways that linked the estate, where the police car couldn't go. He'd watched it happen from his window. It was a game to them, although the one having the biggest laugh would be the dealer who was making big money out of these runts.

The lads took up their usual place in front of the row of sheds where the bins were kept, standing astride their bikes so they could clear off quickly if necessary. A man appeared from the shadows, hoodie up, money at the ready. The deal was done in seconds and he hurried off again. A minute later the next customer arrived and then the next, a steady procession of druggies desperate for their next fix. It was no place for a child, Colin thought again, his anger and concern growing. Most of the customers ignored Leila, but a few didn't and she was forced to fend off their unwanted attention as best she could.

Colin had seen enough. Grabbing his keys from the table and stuffing them into his pocket, he left the flat. It was time to act.

TWO

Kelsey heard the front door of the flat below slam shut. The walls, ceilings and floors were so thin you could almost hear someone having a shit. She guessed most of her neighbours could hear the goings-on in her flat, but what the hell. That was her business. In the small light coming from the hall Kelsey looked at the man lying next to her in bed, whose name she couldn't remember, if she ever knew it. He was proving difficult to get rid of and had become angry and aggressive when she'd told him it was time to go.

She'd managed to pacify him with more rough sex and thankfully he'd fallen asleep and was now flat on his back, snoring like a pig. But she still had the problem of getting rid of him. Just because they paid, some clients thought they could do what they wanted, which they could within reason – consenting adults and all that – but it didn't mean they could stay for as long as they wanted. Once the job was done and their time was up, she couldn't get rid of them fast enough. Some took liberties. A few guys just wanted to talk after having sex, which was a pain but manageable. But the big blokes – alpha males – could easily become abusive if they didn't get their way. Too much testosterone, Kelsey thought. Fine for getting it up, but not so good for putting it away and going home. This one would need some help.

Careful not to disturb him, Kelsey slipped quietly from the bed. He grunted and turned over but stayed asleep. He'd overrun his time by nearly an hour, so she was entitled to some overtime pay, she decided. Picking up his trousers from where he'd thrown them on the floor, she carefully slid out his wallet and removed two twenty-pound notes. There were three left so hopefully he wouldn't notice two were missing until he was long gone. Added to the sixty pounds he'd already paid her, she now had a hundred quid, which was plenty to buy some more coke and something to eat. She was craving both. Starving, shivering, her head throbbed and she felt cold, exhausted and anxious, a sure sign she was withdrawing and needed another fix. The lads, Mike and Jason, would be in the play area dealing by now. She'd get some stuff and then buy fish and chips. But first she needed to get rid of the pig in her bed.

After carefully returning his wallet to the pocket of his trousers, Kelsey pulled on her jeans and T-shirt and crept from the bedroom. She needed Leila's help to send this one on his way. She didn't want to risk another beating. Leila was good at getting rid of unwanted guests – she had perfected her act, and it hadn't failed them yet. On cue from her mother, Leila would pull off her top and run screaming into the bedroom, pointing at the man and shouting that he'd raped her, closely followed by Kelsey, phone in hand, threatening to take a photo and expose him online as a paedophile. It was a hoot and it always worked. The guys couldn't get out of the flat quick enough, and she and Leila had a laugh after. But where the hell was the child?

'Leila? Are you here?' Kelsey whispered in the hall.

She hadn't heard her come in, but that wasn't surprising given the noise the pig had been making with his groaning and expletives. Funny what some guys cried out as they came. She had to bite her lip to stop herself from laughing sometimes.

Kelsey flicked on the light switch in Leila's bedroom, but she wasn't in there. Used clothes, discarded crisp and biscuit packets and general mess lay everywhere. Left where they had fallen. Like mother, like daughter, Kelsey thought, and opened the living-room door. Sometimes the kid fell asleep on the sofa watching television, but the television was off and she clearly wasn't in here. Just more mess. Pizza boxes, fizzy-drink bottles and empty cans of beer – hers, not Leila's. She supposed they'd have to make an effort and clear up before the social worker's next visit, which must be due soon.

It seemed Leila hadn't come home yet, which, although not unusual, was a pain. The pig still had to be got rid of, and Kelsey was feeling increasingly unwell from the effects of drug withdrawal and no food. Cold, irritable and running out of patience, she decided it was time for plan B. Unplugging her phone from where it had been charging in the kitchen, she held it to her ear and then ran into her bedroom, flicking on the light switch as she entered.

'Get up! Quick!' she shouted, panic-stricken, shaking the pig awake. 'You have to go! Now. My partner's found out you're here. He's on his way with six of his mates! They're armed with chainsaws and machetes. You don't stand a chance!'

Wide awake in an instant, he was straight out of bed and frantically struggling into his clothes. 'How long have I got?' he panted.

'Five minutes max. Run for your life!' Kelsey shouted. 'Finish dressing as you go!'

Trousers on, he grabbed his sweatshirt, socks and trainers and fled the room. Kelsey opened the front door and watched him go – running along the corridor and dressing as he went, then disappearing down the stairwell. Returning inside, she laughed as she crossed to the living-room window and looked down onto the estate. A few seconds later the pig appeared, jumped into his car and drove off.

Now to find the kid and buy some coke, although not necessarily in that order.

With the hundred pounds held tightly in her hand, Kelsey left the flat. The lift was on an upper floor so she used the stairs, which as usual stank of stale piss and disinfectant. It was cold even here and she realized she should have worn her jacket, but she wouldn't be long. Reaching the exit, she half expected to find Leila hanging out with some of the older girls from the estate and sharing a smoke, but she couldn't see her.

'You seen Leila?' she asked them.

'Nah,' came a reply.

'Leila?' she called as she headed towards the play area. 'Leila? Can you hear me?'

The kid was often hanging around the estate, although she knew she wasn't supposed to because some nosy parker was sure to see her and phone the social services again. Worst of the bunch was that Mrs Goodman. 'Gawping Goodman' Kelsey had nicknamed her, because she was always watching – gawping. She lived in a ground-floor maisonette on the other side of the play area and didn't miss a thing. She took pride in taking in local kids, giving them a meal, then phoning social services and reporting their parents for neglect. Bitch. Leila had been there plenty of times, although Kelsey wished she hadn't.

'Leila? Where are you?' Kelsey called. There was no reply, so she had to assume she'd wandered off the estate, which Kelsey had told her not to do. She'd come back when she was ready. The little madam was strong-willed, but she could take care of herself. It briefly crossed Kelsey's mind to knock on Goodman's door to see if Leila was there, but she decided equally quickly she wouldn't give the old cow the satisfaction of another lecture and phoning social services. Four kids taken from her was enough. She needed to keep Leila; she was all she had.

Kelsey continued to where Jason and Mike stood laughing and sharing a joint with some other lads.

'Hello, boys,' she said, joining them. 'What have you got for me tonight?'

'How about a nice big cock to suck?' Kevin Bates, one of the older lads and a local thug, quipped. The others guffawed.

'Well, that rules you out,' Kelsey returned, equally sharply. 'I hear you were at the back of the queue when they gave out cocks and brains.'

The others laughed again.

'Fuck you,' Bates snapped, immediately angry.

'Hey, Kev,' one of the other lads said, 'yours must be the only cock in Coleshaw she hasn't sucked.'

'Very funny,' Kelsey replied, and concentrated on Jason who was still grinning. 'How much a gram?'

'Forty-five, same as last night,' he said. 'It's good stuff.'

'It better be at that price. Give me two grams.'

Kelsey handed over ninety pounds, turned and was about to walk away when Kevin Bates blocked her path.

'You're too old for me,' he snarled in her face, 'but that daughter of yours ...'

He didn't get any further. Kelsey slapped his face hard. She heard the sound of her palm on his cheek, felt the sting of flesh on flesh, and knew straight away she shouldn't have done that. But she was withdrawing fast – her body ached and she wasn't thinking straight.

The others had fallen silent. Bates was staring at her, eyes cold and hard. 'You'll be sorry you did that, slag,' he snarled, spitting in her face, and pushed her.

Kelsey staggered, regained her balance and, stepping around him, hurried back towards her flat, praying he would just let it go. Kevin Bates was a nasty piece of work, as were his family. No one crossed them, not if they knew what was good for them. The silence behind her erupted into laughter and one of the lads shouted, 'How much for a mother-and-daughter double act?'

Kelsey's eyes filled. She would never have wished this life on her daughter. Never in a million years. Perhaps the child would be better off without her – adopted like her older kids, or living with her sister, Sharon. Sharon had offered enough times, but if Leila went, what would she have left to live for? Nothing. There'd be no reason to carry on. The rest of her life was shit. Leila was the only reason she got out of bed. Perhaps she should really try to turn over a new leaf and get clean like she'd told the social services and her sister.

Once in her flat, Kelsey took the half-drunk bottle of vodka from the kitchen and settled on the sofa with the coke. If it was good stuff like Jason had said then one gram should last all evening and she could save the other for tomorrow. She always bought extra when she had the money. She was sensible like that.

Taking a swig of vodka, she set to work on the coke, rubbing some on her gums and then snorting it for immediate effect. A few seconds later, her mind and body relaxed as the alcohol and coke took effect. Any thoughts of hunger went, as did those of missing Leila. Another few snorts of coke and swigs of vodka and Kelsey had forgotten most things from the real world and was floating high on a cloud of euphoria, confidence and opportunity, where anything and everything seemed possible.

THREE

Strange, unsettling dreams, noises, sensations and raised voices floated into Kelsey's thoughts. She heard distant footsteps in the corridor outside and doors opening and closing. She dreamt she heard Leila laughing, possibly at her, which made her sad, and a man's voice that seemed familiar, though she couldn't place it. Her eyes shot open and suddenly she was awake. She was lying on her side on the threadbare sofa, her mouth bone dry and craving something sweet.

Shit. She'd overdone it again. 'Leila!' she shouted. 'Get me a drink of water, will ya?'

There was no reply. The flat was quiet and the only light seemed to be coming from the lamp she'd left on in the living room. There was no bulb in the main light, as it had blown ages ago and she'd never got around to replacing it.

God, she felt rough. She really shouldn't have drunk all that vodka with the coke. The bottle was empty and the coke had been strong stuff as Jason had said. She'd only used a gram, and with the vodka her life had become OK for a few hours, but now she felt awful.

What time was it? She groped for her phone and found it on the floor. 3.20. How time passed when you were having fun, she thought bitterly. Leila would be asleep, having let herself in with her key and put herself to bed. She'd have to get her own bloody drink of water – in a minute, though, when the room had stopped swaying and she could stand without falling over.

Scrolling down her phone, she saw the last text message she'd read was sent at 10.05 p.m., so she'd been out for over five hours. Well-deserved respite after the shitty day she'd had yesterday, she thought: two clients not showing, one not paying and then that pig taking advantage of her. Well, she'd shown him! He'd paid her for overtime. She smiled to herself, then gingerly turned onto her back and read the other messages. One was from a regular client, Alan, who visited her during his lunchtime while Leila was at school, asking if she was free today. He always paid well, never wanted extras, gave her a tip and left on time, so today was already promising to be better.

Time to get up, she thought. Dropping her phone on the sofa, Kelsey lowered her feet and then hauled herself upright and slowly stood. Her head spun and it took a moment for her to get her balance. No, she really shouldn't have had that vodka as well as the coke. She walked unsteadily into the kitchen, which was off the living room. It was still a mess! The kid hadn't touched it. Typical! She must have come in late and gone straight to bed.

Kelsey leant against the sink and poured herself a glass of water, drank it straight down and then peeled off a couple of biscuits from the open packet on the drainer and ate those. Her stomach cramped from lack of food. Now the vodka and coke were wearing off she felt hungry and sick. Perhaps the kid had left something for her to eat. She did sometimes if she'd been to the fish-and-chip shop or the Burgers-For-All café on the main road. She bought extra for her mother and left it in the oven for her. Leila was good like that, taking care of her. But when Kelsey opened the oven door she saw it was empty and stone cold. With a stab of guilt, Kelsey wondered if Leila hadn't had enough money to buy food. Hopefully she'd had the sense not to go to Goodman's again for something to eat.

Kelsey drank a second glass of water and then badly needed a piss. By the light of the lamp she went slowly down the hall. Leila's bedroom door was open, which was odd. She always closed it when she came in. She liked her privacy, and if there was a stranger in the house she bolted the door too. Kelsey had fitted the bolt herself to keep her daughter safe when she had clients in.

She stepped into Leila's bedroom and in the half-light couldn't see a lump in the bed. She flicked on the main light. The bed covers were thrown back and the bed was empty. Where the hell was she? 'Leila!' she cried, an edge of panic in her voice. Perhaps she was asleep in Kelsey's bed, although she'd never done that before.

Kelsey took the couple of steps down the hall to her own bedroom and switched on the light. Her bed was empty too, and just as she'd left it after getting the pig out: crumpled and with the bottom sheet spotted with her blood. But where was Leila? Ridiculously, Kelsey crossed to the wardrobe to see if Leila was in there. Sometimes, when it was just the two of them, she hid in there as a game and then jumped out to scare her mother, but not at 3.30 a.m. She opened the wardrobe door to find it empty apart from Kelsey's miserable selection of clothes.

'Leila!' she called again. 'Where the hell are you?' The only room she hadn't looked in was the bathroom and she needed a piss more than ever now.

Opening the bathroom door, she pulled on the light cord. It was obvious straight away Leila wasn't in there, and from the look of it she hadn't used the bathroom the previous evening. There was no towel or face flannel dumped in the bath and her toothbrush was dry. What the hell was the kid playing at?

Kelsey took a piss, the warm stream of urine giving her some relief. Once she'd finished, she checked the kid's bedroom again and then the living room, as if by magic Leila might suddenly have reappeared. There was nowhere else in the flat she could be. Had she been back at all yesterday after she'd left for school in the morning? Kelsey wondered. She couldn't remember but didn't think so. There was no sign of food having been eaten and her school bag wasn't here. So where the hell was she?

Kelsey picked up her phone and checked the texts again. There were no new messages and anyway Leila didn't have a phone of her own. According to the school, kids her age weren't old enough to have phones. Kelsey had gone along with it because she needed to do what the school said, as they sent a report to the social services every term – not just about Leila, but about Kelsey's parenting skills: things like if Leila was on time and looked clean, with her hair brushed. Well, this just showed how much they knew! Her daughter was missing and she had no way of contacting her! She should have followed her gut instinct and given Leila a phone. She could have kept it in her bag for emergency use only, although deep down Kelsey knew the temptation to show her friends or text in class would have been too great.

As the last of the numbing effect of the coke and vodka completely disappeared it was replaced by the depressing realization that her daughter hadn't come home, and instead of getting into bed Kelsey was now going to have to go out and look for her. How thoughtless was that!

Annoyed and irritated, Kelsey picked up her leather jacket from the clutter on the floor of the living room, tucked her keys and phone into her pocket and left the flat with a feeling of self-righteousness. This was what good mothers did if their kids were missing, wasn't it? Go out on a cold night and look for them. Even so, she didn't think she'd be telling the social worker what had happened.

It was freezing; a frost had settled and she could see her breath in the air. Leila wouldn't be outside in this for sure. She hated the cold and was always complaining her coat wasn't warm enough. Perhaps she was staying the night at a friend's house. That's what kids her age did, Kelsey thought. They had sleepovers, although Leila had never been invited to one before, and if she was sleeping at a friend's house why hadn't the parents phoned to let Kelsey know? Perhaps Leila had pretended she'd told her and was now teaching her a lesson for being a crap mother. Yes, that fitted. It seemed a reasonable assumption. Had she known who her daughter's friends were she could have phoned them and checked Leila was there. But she didn't have a clue who her daughter associated with or even if she had any friends. The kid just got on with her life as she had to.

Kelsey continued across the estate, which was poorly lit and now eerily quiet in the early hours of the morning. She was still half-expecting Leila to suddenly appear, perhaps having been watching her from one of the flats. She looked up at the windows she passed for any sign of a child looking out, but nearly all the flats were in darkness, and no face appeared. A police siren sounded in the distance and a lone dog barked. The cold was seeping through her clothes and into her bones, making her miserable and her teeth chatter.

Suddenly she needed to crap. That was the trouble with coke: it gave you the squits that couldn't be ignored. Ducking behind a wall where the refuse bins were kept, Kelsey squatted down, did her business, then took a tissue from her jacket pocket and wiped her bum. Straightening, she zipped up her jeans and continued to search the estate for her daughter.

Kelsey had known all along that at some point she was going to have to knock on Gawping Goodman's door. If Leila wasn't there, Goodman would probably know where to find her. Her maisonette looked straight onto the play area where the kids gathered. Goodman spent most of her waking hours looking out, and she knew better than most of the parents on the estate where their kids were and what they were up to. If the police came looking for someone or if there'd been an incident on the estate, they usually asked Goodman if she had any information, and she was always pleased to assist. When a teenage girl fell pregnant, which they did quite regularly around here, Goodman knew first, and who the father was, long before anyone else did, even the girl's mother. As well as being the eyes of the estate, she was also its ears. The kids seemed to confide in her, probably because there was no one at home to listen to their problems. Granny Goodman, the kids called her, while the adults – resenting but needing her help – called her plenty of other things.

Kelsey continued along the perimeter road that ran all around the edge of the estate and saw no one. Feeling she'd done everything she could, she retraced her steps. As she approached the play area she was sure she could smell the dump she'd taken earlier lingering in the cold night air. Goodman's maisonette was in darkness and her curtains were closed, but as usual the porch light was on. The old bat made a point of leaving it on every night, telling the kids it was a light in their darkness, a beacon of hope for them to come to, or some such rubbish.

Kelsey stared at the doorbell, reluctant to press it. She was sure to get a lecture before the witch told her where Leila was. She didn't think she could stomach it right now. She was

16

tired, cold and hungry and she needed to find Leila and get into bed. With a small flash of hope she checked her phone again, but there were no new messages. The time showed 4 a.m. She glanced up at her own flat on the other side of the play area – the lights were on as she'd left them. She wondered if Leila could have returned in her absence, but realistically the chances of that were slim. And if she had returned, she would have used the landline to call her to find out where she was. Kelsey either had to press Gawping Goodman's doorbell and listen to her lecture, or tell her sister or the police that she couldn't find Leila. She didn't fancy doing either. Sharon would be even more angry and holier-than-thou than the last time, and the police were sure to notify the social services, who would take Leila away from her. Leila had a habit of disappearing, but she always turned up eventually.

Shivering from the cold and with mounting nausea, Kelsey pressed the doorbell. A Big Ben chime rang pretentiously in the hall. She waited but not for long. The net curtain in the window beside the door twitched and Goodman peered out. She must have been awake.

'Open up,' Kelsey mouthed, pointing at the door. 'I need to talk to you.'

Goodman rolled her eyes disapprovingly and let the curtain drop. A moment later the door chain rattled, a bolt slid and the door opened. Goodman, wearing a floral fleece dressing gown buttoned up to her neck and with her grey hair clipped down for the night, didn't try to hide her censorious expression. Kelsey forced herself to stay calm and not give her a mouthful. She needed her help.

'Yes?' the old bat asked. 'What do you want at this time of night, Kelsey?'

'Is Leila with you?'

'No, she isn't. Children rarely stay overnight. Their parents come to collect them eventually.'

'Do you know where she is?'

'No.'

'Did you see her yesterday?'

'Yes, in the evening when she should have been at home.'
Here we go, Kelsey thought. Just stay calm. 'You never learn,
do you, Kelsey? God was kind enough to bless you with
children. And you have wasted his precious gift. Women like
you don't deserve kids. If I had my way, I'd—'

It was too much for Kelsey in her fragile state. 'Will you
shut the fuck up and tell me where Leila is? I'm not feeling
well and I'm worried about her.'

'Really?' Goodman asked cynically.

'Yes, really.'

'And you honestly can't remember where she is?'

'No. Sorry. It seems to have slipped my mind,' Kelsey
snapped sarcastically

'Your bloke took her. Well, I assume that's who he was.'

'My bloke? What are you talking about?' Kelsey stared at
her.

'Your new fancy man, latest boyfriend, client, whatever
you call him. He came to the play area around six-fifteen
and took her. Just as well, otherwise the poor child would
have been there all night for all you care.'

Kelsey continued to stare at her, trying to make sense of
what she was being told.

'A man took my Leila?' she asked, shivering.

'And you can't remember!'

'Who was he?'

'I don't know. I can't be expected to keep track of all your
fancy men.'

'He's not my fancy man!' Kelsey exploded. 'Will you stop
saying that! You're doing my head in. I didn't send anyone
to collect Leila.'

Mrs Goodman held Kelsey's gaze. 'You wouldn't know

even if you had. You're so out of it most of the time. I can't help you and I'm getting cold standing here. Go home. I'm sure your daughter is being looked after by him. Goodnight.' The door closed.

FOUR

Pulling her jacket closer around her to keep out the cold, Kelsey headed back across the dark, deserted play area towards her flat. Leila had gone with a man – her boyfriend, the old witch had said – but Kelsey didn't have a boyfriend. She hadn't sent anyone to collect Leila, she was sure of it. Or was she? Goodman knew most things and the old cow was usually right. Kelsey knew her own mind was so messed up from years of drink and drug abuse that she forgot stuff all the time. But could she really have forgotten that she'd asked someone to fetch Leila from the play area? Was it possible? Yes, her brain was in such a state, she had to admit it was.

As Kelsey walked, she struggled to think back, but once she'd started on the coke and vodka her mind had become blank. That was the point of it – to block out her miserable life and make things seem better for a while. She remembered she had vaguely heard a man's voice in the distance and Leila laughing, but it was all indistinct, like in a dream. She hated to admit it, but Gawping Goodman was probably right. Hopefully Leila had now returned to their flat or was being looked after by the man who'd collected her. But who was

20

he? Certainly not Leila's father. He'd disappeared as soon as she'd told him she was pregnant. And hadn't she searched the flat before she'd come out? Perhaps she hadn't searched it properly.

The lift doors clanged shut, reverberating down the empty corridor, and the lift began to rise with a harsh grating noise. A printed notice inside the lift asked residents not to use the lift late at night or early in the morning as it woke others, but there was no way Kelsey was going to climb three flights of stairs in her state. Exhausted, with her head throbbing and feeling sick, she just needed to get into her bed. The lift juddered to a halt and the doors opened. For a moment as she went down the corridor towards her flat she wondered why she'd been out at all, then she remembered.

'Leila?' she called as she let herself into her flat. 'Are you here?'

Silence. She checked her bedroom, then Leila's room, then the bathroom and living room. There was no one here. No man and no Leila, so the old witch Goodman was wrong! Now what? She hadn't a clue. She wondered if she should be really worried as Leila was still missing, but she didn't think it was necessary just yet. Goodman had said a man had taken her, but it had to be someone Leila knew because she would never have gone off with a stranger. She was too streetwise and savvy for that.

But where was she? Who knew Kelsey well enough to do her a favour like that? Their immediate neighbours were both single mothers. Brooke Adams, who lived in the flat to the right of hers, had helped her out in the past, but she'd said she wouldn't do it again and had told Kelsey to get herself sorted before it was too late.

Kelsey flopped on the sofa and tried to think of someone who might have collected Leila from the play area and could now be looking after her. No one came to mind. Bone weary – it was now 4.30 a.m. – she rested her head back on the sofa and closed her eyes. She could really have done with a smoke, but she didn't have anything apart from the remaining gram of coke and she was saving that for later. If she used it now, she'd have nothing to look forward to. She'd save it for as long as she could.

But what to do about Leila? Perhaps the man who was looking after her would return her soon. Or maybe he would take her directly to school in the morning. That's what Brooke had done. She'd seen Leila alone in the play area, collected her, and then pushed a note through Kelsey's door to say Leila was there with her and that she'd give her breakfast and take her to school with her own kids the following morning. No one had been any the wiser, but after that Brooke had said enough was enough and that she wouldn't do it again. Next time, she'd said, she'd report her to the social services for neglect.

Kelsey sat upright with a jolt. Of course. That's what had happened! She should have realized sooner. She wasn't so daft after all. Brooke had seen Leila in the play area and had reported her to the social services. The man who'd taken Leila was their social worker, Peter Harris. That's why Leila had gone with him: she knew him. Too fucking well – from all his visits, the interfering git. But this was solvable.

Peter had taken Leila and put her with a foster carer for the night like they'd done with her other kids when they'd been living with her. By tomorrow she'd have to come up with an excuse for Leila being out late on the estate. She'd phone Peter as soon as the office opened at 9 a.m. and go on the attack. Blast him for taking Leila without telling her and all the worry he'd caused her. She'd threaten to report him, for she knew that not even a social worker could take a child without informing the parents. He wouldn't want more aggravation from her, and Leila would be sent home. Problem sorted, Kelsey now felt she could stop worrying and go to bed.

What the hell was that? Ringing? She'd only just dropped off to sleep. Was it the doorbell or her phone making that bloody noise? It couldn't be her client, Alan, already, could it? What was the time?

Kelsey struggled up in bed as her phone stopped ringing and bleeped with a text message. She reached for her leather jacket, which was dumped on the floor where she'd left it, and took out her phone. There was a missed call and a text telling her she had a voicemail message. The time on her phone showed 9.30 a.m. Drat. She'd overslept. She'd intended to phone the social services at 9.00 but she hadn't yet come up with a reason for Leila being out so late. Best wait until she'd had a strong black coffee to get her brain into gear, she thought.

Getting out of bed, Kelsey pulled on her jumper over her bra and pants and padded barefoot to the kitchen, retrieving the voicemail message as she went.

'Mrs Smith, it's the school secretary here. Leila isn't in school. Can you phone us and confirm she is unwell? Otherwise we'll have to mark it as an unauthorized absence.'

Kelsey stopped where she was and replayed the message, thinking she might have misheard. But she hadn't. Leila wasn't in school. That was strange. In the past the foster carer had taken her children to school unless they were ill or had played up and refused to go. Whatever. The social worker should have told her – the parent – Leila was in care.

Five minutes and a cup of black coffee later, Kelsey sat on the sofa and called Peter Harris's office number. The caffeine had given her the boost she needed, and, fired up and aware of her rights, she was ready for a fight.

'Peter Harris, children's services,' he said, answering straight away.

'It's Kelsey Smith here.'

'Hello, Kelsey. How are you doing?'

'I was doing all right until you stuck your nosy beak in. Lots of kids play out. I've told you before I can see Leila from my flat window so I can keep an eye on her.'

'Kelsey, can you calm down and tell me what's happened?' Peter said in a conciliatory tone that infuriated Kelsey even more.

'You stuck your bleeding nose in and took my Leila! That's what's happened! I've been doing all right until now. You'd no business taking her without telling me. I want her back with an apology or I'm reporting you.'

There was a moment's pause before he said, 'Kelsey, I haven't seen Leila since I visited you both four weeks ago. Are you saying you don't know where she is?'

Kelsey went cold. She'd been certain he'd taken Leila and put her with a foster carer. 'Of course I know where she is,' she said, and cut the call.

If Peter Harris hadn't taken Leila then who the hell had? Suddenly Kelsey was very worried, very worried indeed.

FIVE

Leila was scared. What had started off yesterday as a sort of game wasn't fun any more. She was thinking she really shouldn't have gone along with it. But he'd been so nice at the start – kind and caring. He'd said he was worried about her and told her she was pretty. Her mother called her plain. He'd said a young girl like her shouldn't be out all by herself after dark. It wasn't safe and it was very wrong of her mother not to look after her properly, which Leila sort of knew. He'd said he would take care of her and together they'd teach her mother a lesson. He'd given her chocolates – really posh ones with soft centres – and told her he'd bought her a beautiful doll and it was waiting for her in his flat. It wasn't like she was going with a stranger – she would never have done that. She knew him, so did her mother, which made it OK.

His flat was warm and tidy – not like hers – and to begin with it had all felt really cosy and nice. He'd talked to her about the bad life she'd led with her mother and how he could put it right. She deserved much better, he'd said: pretty clothes, good food, holidays and a visit to Disneyland, all of which he'd promised would happen if she did as he said.

But when she hadn't liked the dinner he'd cooked and asked for chicken nuggets and chips instead, he'd got moody and raised his voice, which frightened her. 'You can't keep eating that muck! It's bad for you,' he'd yelled. 'From now on you'll eat proper meals, the ones I give you, and you'll be grateful.' She'd gone quiet and said she wanted to go home, so he'd apologized and said it was early days yet, and he had a lot to learn.

Now Leila sat on the bed and held Buttons, her teddy bear, very tightly to her chest. Colin had gone out this morning and left her locked in the bedroom. He'd told her it was very important she kept quiet and that no one must find her here or she'd be in very big trouble. That the social services would take her away like they had her older half-brothers and -sisters and she'd never see her mother again.

She believed him, but she hated being locked in. It was like at home when she had to lock herself in her bedroom when her mother brought men back, so they didn't hurt her. They hurt her mother and would hurt her too if they got a chance, her mother told her. She tried to be out when her mother had men in, but that wasn't always possible, so she slid the bolt her mother had fitted on her bedroom door. But that bolt was on the inside of the door, so she could open it if she wanted to. This one was on the outside, so she was locked in. Trapped. Colin had bolted the door when he'd left for work and said he would unlock it when he returned. It was for her own good, he said, but it didn't feel like it.

Anxious and sad, Leila propped herself on the pillow and picked at the loose threads of the bedspread. It was an old-fashioned bedspread like the ones at Granny Goodman's. The furniture in the room was old too, and so was the bed. It creaked every time she'd turned over in the night and the pillow smelt of old people. Perhaps someone had died here, she thought with a shudder, and threw the pillow on the floor. It narrowly missed the potty. She'd already had to do a wee in it once, although she hadn't wanted to. Potties were for babies and she was a big girl, as her mother kept telling her. She'd held on to her wee for as long as she dared, until she'd been bursting and her stomach had ached. Then she'd been so desperate she'd missed the potty and some of her wee had gone on the floor. She hoped Colin wouldn't be angry like her mother was when she made a mess. There wasn't anything in the room to mop it up with.

Leila was hungry but the sandwich he'd left for her smelt horrible. Salmon and cucumber. Yuck. She pushed it off the bed and its contents spilled over the floor. She'd eaten the crisps he'd left and drunk the juice, but she was still hungry. If she'd been at school she would have been given a school dinner, and if she'd been at home she could have gone to the chip shop. Her mother didn't care what she ate, not like Colin. He seemed to fuss over food and what he called 'good hygiene practice', which involved him repeatedly washing his hands, the work surface in the kitchen and the chopping board. She'd had to wash her hands too before she ate.

He'd left her puzzles, games and books to keep her amused while he was out at work, but they too were now scattered across the floor. She'd tried to do a puzzle but had quickly lost patience and given up, and she never read books or played games. She watched television when she was at home and the hours whizzed by, but now time was dragging. She wondered what her class was doing at school. She didn't like school but at least the time passed quickly there and she wasn't locked in and had a hot meal – food she liked.

With mounting frustration and anger, Leila picked up the doll Colin had bought her and threw it on the floor with the other stuff. It landed head down with a nasty crunch, its china face shattering. Leila stared, horrified. Colin had said it was expensive and he'd chosen it especially for her. She'd have to lie and say it was an accident. It was no loss to her. She hadn't liked it anyway. She loved Buttons, her teddy bear. She talked to him and told him things she couldn't tell anyone else. Buttons went with her everywhere. She'd had him for as long as she could remember and called him Buttons because he had two rows of buttons on his coat that she liked to undo and do up again.

Suddenly the doorbell rang and she froze. Had someone heard the doll smashing on the floor? Keep calm, she told herself. She knew what to do if someone came to the door. Colin had shown her and made her practice, reminding her of the consequences if she didn't do as he said. Now this was for real! The doorbell rang again. Grabbing Buttons by the arm, Leila slid quietly from the bed and then climbed into the storage compartment beneath it. She drew the sliding door to and kept very still and quiet. Colin had said no one else had keys to his flat, so hiding was a precautionary measure to keep her safe. She was to do this whenever anyone came to the door, whether he was in or not.

But it was dark and cramped in the strange compartment beneath the bed and Leila didn't like it. She began counting off the seconds as Colin had told her. 'Count to sixty, that's a minute,' he'd said. 'If it's all quiet and the caller doesn't ring again, it means they're likely to have gone and you can get out. But don't make any noise just in case.'

She counted steadily to sixty, then carefully slid open the compartment door, clambered out, stood still and listened like he'd told her to. Suddenly she was startled as the bell rang again. She stood still, wondering if she should return to the cupboard beneath the bed, but then she heard footsteps going along the corridor in the direction of the lift. Thank goodness. She breathed a sigh of relief. Colin would be proud of her.

Leila sat on the bed and thought of her mother in the flat

above. What was she doing? She'd heard movements earlier, about an hour after Colin had gone. Did her mother know she wasn't at school? And if so, was she worried she was missing? Probably not. From what Colin and Granny Goodman had told her she had a very bad mother, negligent and selfish, and she would be better off without her. But it wasn't as simple as that. She loved her mother despite all the wrong things she did, and she hoped this would teach her a lesson to take better care of her in the future. Locked alone in this strange room, and having to hide from callers, Leila thought she might be better off at home. But that wasn't an option now.

SIX

'Sharon, it's me, Kelsey.'

'I know who you are,' Kelsey's sister, Sharon, replied curtly. 'I'm at work. What do you want?'

'I'm sorry to bother you,' Kelsey said, her voice tight. 'But I've got a problem.'

'So what's new? I can't talk now. I'll phone you this evening as soon as I'm home.'

'I don't think it can wait that long.'

'Why not?' Sharon sighed. 'What's happened now?'

'It's Leila, I'm not sure where she is.'

'What do you mean, you're not sure where she is? She's either at school or at home with you, isn't she?'

'That's the thing. She's not here and she's not at school.'

A pause, then: 'Just a minute, I'll have to go out of the office to talk. I hope this isn't another wild goose chase. After all, Leila has run away before.'

'No, I don't think it is.'

Kelsey heard muffled voices in the background and her sister's stiletto heels clipping purposefully across the office floor as she made her way out. She knew she was a pain in her sister's arse, but there was no one else she could turn to.

Sharon had helped her out before, and although she'd be angry, she'd know what to do. She always did.

'Well?' Sharon demanded, coming back on the phone. 'Hurry up, Kelsey, it's freezing out here, and I've stacks of work on my desk.'

'I'm sorry,' Kelsey said, acutely aware of her own inferiority. 'The thing is, I let Leila play out last night, perhaps a bit later than I should, but you know how it is.' She heard her sister sigh. 'It got late so I went to get her, but I couldn't find her, and that nosy cow Goodman said the social worker had taken her, but when I phoned him he said he hadn't, and she's not in school.'

'Just a minute,' Sharon said. 'Let me get this straight. Mrs Goodman told you a social worker had taken Leila, but he says he didn't?'

'Sort of. Goodman said a man took Leila, so I thought it must be the social worker because she doesn't know any other men, but it's not him.'

'This was when?'

'Yesterday evening.'

'And you haven't seen Leila since?'

'No.'

'So, what have the police said?'

'Well, that's the thing, I haven't told them yet. I wanted to speak to you first.'

'Jesus, Kelsey! Are you telling me that Leila has been missing all night and you haven't reported it to the police yet? She's eight years old! She could be anywhere! What's the matter with you?'

'I'm sorry. I thought she would come back like she did before.'

'And she's definitely not at school?'

'The secretary left a message on my phone.'

'Call the police now. The chances are she's run off again

31

and will come back, but better to be safe than sorry. I'll try to get the rest of the day off work and come over, but phone me if she returns.'

'I will. Thank you. I'm sorry for being a pain.'

'I know.'

SEVEN

Detective Constable Beth Mayes parked the police car where they would be able to see it from Kelsey's flat window. The last time they'd left the car unattended on the estate they'd come back to find all the windscreen wipers snapped off and *PIGS GRUNT* sprayed in red gloss paint along both sides of the car. Beth turned to her colleague, DC Matt Davis. 'Gently does it with Kelsey,' she said. 'She's had a hard life.'

'So her kid has to suffer too,' Matt sighed. 'Leila is probably back with her mother now, sitting in filth but watching television, just like the last time.'

'But if she's not then we need to treat it with the same priority we would any other missing eight-year-old.'

But they both knew that wasn't going to happen. A child who suddenly vanished with no history of running away would be prioritized as high risk and all available police resources would be deployed straight away. But that was expensive, and given Leila's history of disappearing and then reappearing, they would be exploring other avenues as well.

'I spoke to their social worker,' Beth said as they entered the lift. 'He thought Kelsey had been doing OK.'

Matt took a sharp breath. 'Really? And what planet is *he* on?'

'Kelsey knows how to play the system,' Beth said. 'She will have told him what he wanted to hear, and social services are underfunded and stretched to the limit.'

'Just like us then!' Matt returned.

The lift juddered to a halt and they stepped out. As they approached Kelsey's flat, number 417, the door suddenly opened and a man came out – short, partially bald and almost cowering in his wish not to be seen.

'Hello,' Matt said, stepping into his path and flashing his ID. 'You've just come from Kelsey Smith's flat?'

'Yes, why? What do you want?' he replied nervously, clearly wanting to be on his way.

'Can I have your name, please?' Matt asked.

'Alan.'

'Alan what?'

'Stevens.'

'Are you a friend of Kelsey's?'

'Sort of. Why?'

'She's reported her child missing,' Beth said.

'Oh. She didn't mention it to me.'

'Any idea where she could be?' Matt asked.

'No, of course not. The kid's usually at school when I visit.'

'How well do you know Kelsey?' Beth asked.

'Not very. I see her for an hour every so often.' His cheeks flushed red.

'We may need to talk to you again,' Matt said, taking out his notebook and pen. 'Full name and contact details, please.'

'Do I have to?' Alan asked Beth. 'My wife doesn't know I'm here.'

'Naughty boy,' Matt said.

'If we do need to call you, we will be discreet,' Beth reassured him, and waited as he reluctantly gave his full name, address and mobile number to Matt. 'Thank you.'

'Goodbye, Alan,' Matt said, watching him scuttle off to the lift. Then to Beth, 'Unbelievable! Her kid is missing and she's still having punters in.'

'I know.' Beth shook her head.

The door to Kelsey's flat had remained open and Kelsey now came out. 'I thought I heard voices. Have you found Leila?'

'Not yet,' Beth replied. 'Let's go inside and we'll have a chat and take a few details.'

'But I told the woman on the phone everything I know. You should be out looking for Leila, not talking to me.'

'We are looking for her,' Beth said. 'But it will help if you can give us some background information. You know the routine by now.'

Kelsey sighed, and led the way into her flat.

'You didn't bring Alan in here then?' Matt said dryly, surveying the mess in the living room

'None of your business,' Kelsey replied. 'I've still got to earn a living.'

Beth shot Matt a warning glance. She'd worked with him before and they got on well, but subtlety wasn't his strong point, which was why she usually led the questioning in sensitive cases such as these.

'Is there anyone else in the flat?' Beth asked, moving clutter off the sofa so she could sit down.

'No. Just me.'

Matt positioned himself by the window so he could see their car. Kelsey looked dreadful, Beth thought – worse than she had the last time she'd seen her, when neighbours had reported a domestic incident.

'Can I make you a cup of tea?' Beth offered.

'Nah, I just want you to find Leila,' Kelsey said pitifully. 'I'm sure something bad has happened to her this time.'

'What makes you say that?' Beth asked. 'I mean, she has gone missing before.'

'But not for this long, and this time she's gone off with a man. I don't know who he is.'

'OK. Let's start from the beginning,' Beth said, taking out her notebook and pen. 'When was the last time you saw Leila?'

'Yesterday, I think.'

'When yesterday?'

'Morning, I think.'

'But you're not sure?'

'No.' Kelsey rubbed her finger over her forehead, leaving an impression on her dry skin. 'The thing is, if I'm asleep Leila knows to get herself off to school, so I don't always see her in the morning.'

'Was she in school yesterday?'

'I think so.'

'She was,' Matt replied. 'I checked.'

'So if you're not sure you saw her in the morning, when did you last see her?'

'The evening before, I guess. Yes, I'm sure she was in all evening and so was I.'

Beth made a note while thinking that an eight-year-old should be in every evening, especially in winter when it was cold and dark out. 'And how did Leila seem the last time you saw her?'

'OK, I guess.'

'Was she happy or did she seem quiet? Maybe worried about something?'

Kelsey shrugged. 'She seemed normal to me.'

'Talk me through the last time you saw Leila,' Beth said.

'The little buggers!' Matt shouted and opened the window. 'Clear off! Or I'll be straight down to arrest the lot of you!'

Beth returned her attention to Kelsey, who was clearly struggling to remember. 'I think Leila went to school yesterday as normal but didn't come home. She likes to play out, so I wasn't worried to start with.'

'Where were you?' Beth asked.

'Here. I had a client in if you must know, so it was better Leila stayed away from the flat.'

'OK,' Beth said non-judgementally. 'What time were you expecting Leila home?'

Kelsey shrugged. 'When it suited her, I guess, but not ever so late.'

'Five o'clock? Six? Seven? Later?' Beth prompted.

'Yeah, I guess around seven.'

'But you're not sure?' Matt put in.

'No. The thing is, I lose track of time and I don't always remember things right.'

'Were you using yesterday?' Matt asked.

Kelsey looked at Beth as she replied. 'A bit. I'd had a bad day, so I needed something. I remember now. I went down to buy some stuff as soon as the lads were there. So it would have been around seven o'clock. I asked them if they'd seen Leila, but they hadn't.'

'Then what?' Beth asked as she wrote.

'I came back here.'

'And?' Beth prompted.

'I used some stuff, had a glass of vodka, then I must have crashed out around ten. I had a rough night. I dreamt I heard Leila laughing and a man's voice that sounded familiar, but when I woke she still wasn't here. That's when I got worried and went out looking for her. It was very cold.'

'So what time was that?' Beth asked, glancing up from writing.

'Four o'clock,' Kelsey admitted quietly.

'Four in the morning?' Beth asked, unable to hide her shock. Kelsey nodded. 'You didn't think to call the police then?'

'No, I thought Leila was staying out to punish me.'

'Why would she do that?' Matt asked, keeping one eye on their car below.

'Because I'm a crap mother,' Kelsey snapped, 'as you well know.'

Beth felt sorry for her. However lacking Kelsey was, she hadn't intended her life to be like this. There were so many on the estate like her struggling with addiction. 'So at four o'clock this morning you went out looking for Leila. Where?'

'Around the estate. I walked all round the ring road. I couldn't see her, so I knocked on Goodman's door. You know, that old bat whose home overlooks the play area. She doesn't miss a thing.'

Beth nodded. She knew Mrs Goodman. 'Did you speak to her?'

'Yeah. She was in her dressing gown, but she answered the door pretty quickly, so I guessed she was already up. She gave me a lecture and then said she'd seen Leila in the play area go off with a man a little after six. I wasn't worried to begin with. I knew Leila wouldn't go with a stranger, so I guessed Brooke had reported me to the social services like she'd threatened, and it was our social worker, Peter Harris, who'd taken her. But when I phoned him this morning he said he hadn't seen Leila.'

'We've spoken to Peter Harris,' Beth said. 'Who's Brooke?'

'My neighbour, Brooke Adams.'

Beth nodded as she made a note and then looked up. 'Can you think of anywhere Leila might have gone?'

'Nah, that's the thing. If Leila isn't in school and our social worker hasn't taken her, I don't know where she can be. I found her on the estate before. I wondered if she could be at a friend's house.'

'We'll be speaking to the school again,' Beth said. 'Do you know the names of her friends?'

Kelsey shook her head.

'What was Leila wearing?'

'Her school uniform, I guess. I didn't see her leave, but she must have it on. It's not here.'

'Has she taken anything else with her? Clothes, money, her hairbrush, toothbrush?'

'I don't think so.'

'Have you checked?'

'Not really.'

'We'll have a look together in a moment,' Beth said sensitively. 'We'll need to have a look around anyway.'

'She's not here,' Kelsey said.

'I know, but we need to see for ourselves. Then, once we've finished here, DC Davis and I will speak to Mrs Goodman and other neighbours. A lot of flats overlook the children's play area so hopefully others will have seen Leila and may even know where she is. We'll also talk to the lads you bought from last night. They might have seen or heard something. Mike Doherty and Jason O'Leary, was it?' It was their patch.

'Yeah. That ugly bastard Kevin Bates was there too, giving me grief. He said nasty things about Leila.' All these lads were known to the police.

'What did Kevin Bates say?' Beth asked as she wrote.

'That I was too old for him but Leila wasn't. I don't think he meant anything by it – he's not like that – he was just being his usual nasty self.'

'We'll speak to him,' Beth said. 'But try not to worry. I'm sure Leila will turn up soon. She usually does.'

Kelsey shrugged despondently. 'That kid gives me a lot of trouble, but I do miss her.'

'I'm sure you do,' Beth said. 'Let's have a look around the flat now then.'

'I'll stay here and keep an eye on the car,' Matt said.

Beth checked the kitchen first, opening and closing the

cupboard doors, as Kelsey looked on. Then she went down the hall to Leila's bedroom. Beth knew the layout of the flat from being here before. As well as Leila going missing in the past, neighbours had reported disturbances coming from Kelsey's flat. Kelsey seemed to attract trouble like a magnet. It really was no place for a kid.

Leila's room was in just as much of a mess as the rest of the flat and Beth had to step over the rubbish on the floor. Crisp and biscuit packets, empty cartons of Pot Noodles, fizzy-drink cans and other stuff that should have been thrown away, all left where they had fallen. As Kelsey watched, Beth opened Leila's wardrobe door, but apart from a broken child's scooter dumped in the bottom, it was empty. The few clothes Leila possessed seemed to be scattered on the floor and bed.

'Was she wearing a coat over her school uniform?' Beth asked.

'She must have, it's not here. It's a navy zip-up jacket.'

'And her school bag?'

'Yes, she must have that too.'

Beth's thoughts flashed back to her own mother, who had lovingly seen her off to school at the door every morning with a hug and a kiss even when she was a teenager. This poor child just had to get on with it.

To the right of the wardrobe was a small chest of drawers. Beth pulled open the top drawer. It was crammed full of packets of sweets and chocolate novelties, doubtless stolen. The second drawer contained packets of unopened biscuits and three new ladies' watches.

'Well, I can't keep tabs on her the whole time,' Kelsey said defensively.

Beth didn't comment. They could check out the watches another time. Completing the missing persons' procedure was their first priority. The bottom drawer contained a torn colouring book, a small packet of crayons and a couple of broken plastic dolls, their limbs separated from their bodies. It was a sad reflection of the poor kid's life, Beth thought – stealing, squirrelling away food, with a nodding glance at childhood.

'What shoes was she wearing?' Beth asked.

'Black trainers, same as usual. That's the only pair that fit her.'

'Has she taken her nightwear?'

'No, it's there.'

'So apart from her school uniform, coat, trainers and school bag, you can't see anything else missing?' Beth asked, turning to Kelsey.

But Kelsey was preoccupied, pulling the covers off the bed, checking under the pillow and on the floor, looking for something. 'Her teddy bear, Buttons, isn't here,' she said anxiously.

'Perhaps Leila took it to school with her.'

'Nah, they're not allowed toys in school.'

'Could it be in one of the other rooms?' Beth asked. The flat was in such a state you'd be hard pushed to find anything.

'No. Leila always kept it on her bed. She can't go to sleep without it.'

'Let's check in the other rooms anyway,' Beth said, taking the missing bear seriously. If Leila had taken the bear with her, it suggested that her leaving had been premeditated, which raised the search to a whole new level. She could be miles away by now. 'What does the bear look like?'

'It's about this big,' Kelsey said, moving her hands apart, 'and it has a red coat with lots of buttons on it.'

'Matt!' Beth called as they crossed the hall to Kelsey's bedroom. 'Can you have a look in the living room for a teddy bear wearing a red coat?'

'Will do,' he returned.

Beth found that Kelsey's bedroom was much tidier than

the other rooms – possibly, she thought, because this was the only room the clients saw. Kelsey straightened the duvet as Beth checked in the wardrobe and then under the bed.

'There's no bear in here,' Matt called from the living room. 'In fact, there aren't any toys at all.'

'Thank you,' Beth replied, then said to Kelsey, 'So we'll assume Leila has the bear with her when we put out her missing-person appeal.'

'But it doesn't make sense,' Kelsey said, rubbing her forehead again. 'Leila would never have taken it to school because she'd know it would be confiscated until the end of the day. She must have come back for it, but when? And then what happened?'

'That's exactly what we're hoping to find out,' Beth said.

EIGHT

'We'll speak to Mrs Goodman first, then go to the school, and on to see Bates,' Beth said as she and Matt returned to their car. 'Perhaps the children in Leila's class know something. Kelsey is adamant that Leila must have returned to the flat at some point and taken her teddy bear. Leila may have confided in a friend at school what she was up to.'

'But if Leila was planning to run away, surely she would have taken other things too – clothes and money? She's pretty savvy and would know a bear wasn't going to get her very far.'

'Matt, she's eight years old. Kids her age don't think like that. She will have homed in on her most treasured possession, especially if she was short of time. Kelsey says Leila always sleeps with the bear. It's comforting for her. It would have been her main priority.'

Beth started the car and pulled away. Although Doris Goodman's flat was only on the other side of the play area – a two-minute walk – it made sense to keep the car close. School finished soon and teenagers unleashed from a day of having to do as they were told liked nothing better than to vent their frustration on a police car.

'From the timescale Kelsey gave us,' Beth continued, 'Leila must have returned to the flat and taken the bear between ten o'clock on Tuesday evening and four this morning while Kelsey was asleep. Either that or she returned to the flat while her mother was out looking for her, but I don't think that's likely. It would suggest Leila was close by all that time, watching her mother and waiting for the opportunity. A child of her age wouldn't have that sort of patience.'

'I don't know much about kids,' Matt said.

'No,' Beth agreed and threw him a look. 'So for now we'll go with the assumption that Leila returned to the flat between ten and four while Kelsey slept, which means she was still in the area.'

'Unless the bear vanished ages ago and Kelsey just didn't notice, like she didn't notice when her daughter was missing,' Matt said.

'It's quite possible,' Beth conceded.

Doris Goodman's clean and recently painted front door opened even before Beth had finished parking. It was one of the few properties on the estate that had been bought by the tenant and was therefore privately owned and maintained. 'She doesn't miss much, does she?' Matt said.

'Hopefully not. At present she's all we have, and the last person we know to have seen Leila.'

'Good afternoon, Mrs Goodman,' Matt said as he and Beth crossed the narrow strip of grass that separated her maisonette from the road.

'I've been expecting you.'

'Have you?' Beth asked, mildly surprised.

'I assume you're here about the break-in at number fifteen. Unfortunately I can't be of much help. I heard the glass break but that was all. I didn't see anything.'

44

'Uniform will be dealing with that,' Matt said. 'We'll pass on what you said. We're actually here about Leila Smith.'

'Oh really?' Mrs Goodman looked surprised.

'Can we come in?' Beth asked. Most residents on the estate wouldn't be seen dead talking to the police and couldn't get them inside quickly enough, but Doris revelled in it. She liked everyone to know what a good relationship she had with the local police and that if anyone crossed her, they'd feel the full force of the law. It seemed to work, for despite her maisonette being on the ground floor, it had never been burgled, unlike many on the Hawthorn Estate.

Beth and Matt followed Doris into her living room. It was at the front of the property and reserved for adult guests only. As usual it was spotlessly clean and meticulously tidy: scatter cushions were aligned on the sofa, the glass-topped coffee table gleamed and dozens of china ornaments sparkled in the display cabinet. The children she made meals for weren't allowed in this room but ate and played in the kitchen-diner at the rear, where there was a dining table, chairs and bean-bags. Matt and Beth had seen the rest of the property when they'd had to search it last year. Another kid had run off and her father was adamant Mrs Goodman was harbouring her, which she wasn't.

Matt took the armchair by the window so he could watch their car.

'Leila Smith is missing,' Beth said, sitting at one end of the sofa as Mrs Goodman sat at the other. 'We've just come from seeing her mother, Kelsey. It appears you were the last person to see Leila.'

'So she really is missing?' Doris asked, clearly shocked.

'It would seem so. Did you doubt it then?' Beth asked, opening her notebook.

'I assumed she would be back by now. She's never gone missing for this long before.'

'No. Kelsey said you saw Leila in the play area yesterday evening and that she left with a man.'

'Yes. It would have been around six. I assumed it was her mother's boyfriend or a client and she couldn't be bothered to collect her daughter herself.' She pursed her lips in disapproval.

'Have you ever seen this man before?' Beth asked.

'No.'

'Can you give us a description?'

'He was of average height and build and was wearing a coat. Sorry, it was dark, and I didn't really take much notice.'

'Approximate age?' Beth asked. Doris shook her head. 'Was he in his twenties? Thirties? Fifties or older?'

'Early fifties I would say, but I'm not sure.'

'Was he wearing a hat, scarf or gloves?' Beth tried, making a note of what Doris had said.

'I don't think so.'

'Was he carrying anything?'

'Not as far as I could see, but it was dark. The lighting there is very poor. It's something the council needs to address.' She fidgeted with the cuffs on her cardigan as Beth wrote.

'Did Leila appear to go with the man willingly or was she reluctant?'

'He said a few words to her and she went off – happily, I thought.'

'In which direction?'

'I don't know, I just saw them leave the play area.'

Beth nodded. 'How long was Leila in the play area for?'

'She arrived at the end of school just after three-thirty, as she often does, and was there until that man took her at six-ish. It was cold and I went out a few times and asked her if she wanted to come in and have something to eat. She said she wasn't allowed to. Her mother had told her that if she did, I'd phone the social services and she'd be put into care. That's what I call selfish, and I'm not the only one who thinks that around here.'

'What was Leila doing all that time she was in the play area?' Beth asked as Matt flicked the net curtain for a better view of their car.

'Same as usual,' Doris replied. 'Rocking on the swing, sitting on the roundabout, talking to the older lads. I worry Leila will end up like some of the others here: pregnant at fifteen.'

'Did Leila have anything with her?'

'Just her school bag. You know, one of those reading folders with the school's logo on it. All the kids from the school seem to have one.'

'She wasn't carrying a teddy bear?' Beth asked.

'Not that I could see. Why?'

'It's missing.'

'Perhaps it was in her school bag.'

'It's too big.' Beth paused. 'You said you assumed the man who took Leila was known to Kelsey, and that she'd sent him to collect Leila. Has she ever done that before?'

Doris thought for a moment. 'No, not as far as I can remember.'

'So why would you think that was the case yesterday evening?' Beth asked, puzzled. Matt looked at her.

Doris Goodman seemed to falter and took a moment to reply. 'I'm not sure, really. It was just something that crossed my mind.'

'Interesting,' Matt said. 'I wonder why you'd make that assumption rather than being worried that Leila had gone off with a complete stranger.'

'I suppose because Leila was smiling as if she knew the man. If she'd been reluctant to go with him, I would have obviously been worried and called the police immediately.'

'Yes, of course,' Beth said as she finished writing. 'Thank you.'

47

'Will that be all?' Doris Goodman asked. 'Only I have to go out shortly.'

'Yes, for now. If you do remember anything else, please call us straight away.'

'I will.' Doris stood and saw them out.

The door closed quickly behind them.

'I think she's losing her touch,' Matt said as they returned to the car. 'She could see the emblem on Leila's school folder and that she was smiling, but she can't give a description of the guy beyond average height and build.'

'In fairness to her it was dark,' Beth replied. 'But at least her account confirms what Kelsey told us. And it seems Leila knew her abductor.'

'Or he used the ploy of telling her he was a friend of her mother's and she'd sent him to collect her,' Matt suggested.

'Yes, indeed,' Beth agreed as they got into the car. 'Next stop the school, then check the sex offenders' register for those living in the area, including Kelsey's client, Alan Stevens.'

'I'll update the boss,' Matt said. 'Uniform will need to start knocking on doors.' He glanced up at the rows of windows overlooking the play area as Beth started the car. 'Someone in those flats must surely have seen Leila leave with that guy.'

'Let's hope so,' Beth said. 'We haven't got much to go on at present.'

NINE

Colin could smell excrement as soon as he walked into his flat. The stench was unmistakable, and it wasn't coming from dog shit on his shoe. Dropping the carrier bags of groceries in the hall, he unlocked the bedroom door.

'Jesus! Couldn't you have waited until I got back and used the bathroom?' The smell was overpowering.

'No!' Leila shouted angrily. 'I had to go and there was no toilet paper. I hate being shut in here. I want to go home now! I don't want to play any more.'

She was off the bed in a second and running towards the door. He grabbed her just in time and held her fast as she struggled and lashed out, surprisingly strong for a child. 'I want to go home!' she cried.

He put his hand over her mouth. 'Shut up. You can't go home. Your mother doesn't want you.'

She bit his hand.

'Ouch, you little cow!' He went to slap her face, but she pulled out of reach.

Still struggling, she began to scream and he clamped his hand over her mouth again. 'Shut up!' he hissed. 'Someone will hear you.'

She kept struggling, then suddenly she went floppy. He took his hand from her mouth and she gasped for breath. 'I couldn't breathe, you idiot!'

'So don't scream.' Perhaps he'd overdone it. She'd gone very pale. 'Sit on the bed and take a few deep breaths,' he said more gently.

He guided her to the bed and waited until her breathing eased and the colour returned to her cheeks. Cupping her chin with his fingers he raised her head so she was looking directly up at him. 'Leila, you need to learn to do as I say. It's for your own good. Do you understand?' She stared back at him, wide-eyed and fearful. 'You're not living with your mother now. You've been saved from that life, it's ended, but we need a few ground rules here. Are you listening to me?'

She managed a small nod.

'Good. No kicking, screaming or biting,' he said. 'Only animals bite. You will do as I say while I am acting as your parent. I am all you have for now. Consider yourself lucky you have this chance of a new start. In future you will use the bathroom before I go to work and then again when I come home. Understood?'

'But what if I can't wait?' Leila asked, her voice slight.

'You're a big girl, you can wait. It's not nice for me to come home and find this disgusting mess, so it won't happen again.'

Leila gave another small nod. 'Excellent. Good girl. You will empty the potty. Clean it well. I made a mistake in buying that. But I am learning about looking after children, just as you are learning what it is to have a responsible parent. Once the potty is clean, you can clear up the mess in this room. I don't want to come home and find it like this again.'

'What's my mummy doing?' Leila asked in the same small voice.

'I've no idea. Why would you want to know that?'

50

'I heard her crying before you came in.'

He glanced up at the ceiling. It was quiet up there now, but if Leila had heard her mother then it was possible Kelsey could hear Leila.

'You didn't make any noise while I was out, did you?' he asked with a stab of fear. 'I warned you what would happen if you did.'

'No, but someone came to your door so I hid under the bed like you told me to.'

His lips curled into a smile. 'Good girl, you've done well. But how did that doll get broken?' His gaze went to the smashed doll and his smiled vanished.

'I dropped it by accident,' Leila stammered.

'Are you sure? You wouldn't tell me a lie, would you?'

'No. Really.'

'And you didn't make a noise all day?'

Leila shook her head.

'Good. Because if you do make a noise, I'll have to tape your mouth shut and tie you up each time I leave the flat, and that wouldn't be very nice for either of us, would it?'

'No.' Her voice trembled.

'Excellent. Now off you go. Empty that potty and then clear up in here while I make us dinner.'

Leila obediently went to the potty. 'Careful you don't slop it,' he called after her. 'Or you'll have more cleaning to do.'

He followed her out of the bedroom and, as she went into the bathroom, he turned the key in the front door and put the key into his trouser pocket. Just in case she had any more thoughts about leaving. He wasn't sure he could trust her any more. Picking up the carrier bags, he went through to the kitchen and began unpacking the groceries. The toilet flushed and then he heard water running as Leila washed out the potty. He'd give it a good clean with disinfectant later to make sure. He couldn't stand the thought of dirt or germs.

Perhaps he was expecting too much of the child, Colin wondered as he began preparing dinner. It was early days for both of them. They had a lot of adjusting to do and he should try to be more patient and understanding. Once they'd eaten, they'd feel better. Roast chicken, potatoes and fresh vegetables – a proper meal, like the ones his father used to cook for him. But unlike his father he wouldn't force Leila to eat every last scrap – even the fat and gristle on the meat, which had made him gag.

Once they'd eaten, they would play the games he'd bought specially: Scrabble, cards and Cluedo. They'd have fun. He could picture it. Unlike in his home where there'd been no games or laughter, just routine and discipline. As an only child, most of his free time had been spent in his bedroom playing by himself. In his imaginary games he cast himself as the hero rescuing lost and lonely children. And now he was doing it in real life. The irony didn't escape him. To finish the evening, he'd read Leila a bedtime story and tuck her into bed. The perfect ending to what eventually would become another perfect day.

Strange the way things worked out, he thought as he placed the meal in the oven. Who would have ever guessed that at his age he'd find a partner and have a family!

TEN

'You should eat something,' Sharon said with a sigh, placing the tray on her sister's lap. 'It used to be your favourite. Cream of tomato soup with bread in it.'

'It's not food I need,' Kelsey said wretchedly. 'I need something to help me get through this.' Her fingers shook as she steadied the tray.

'You're not using while I'm here,' Sharon said sharply. 'You know my views on drugs. And supposing the police look in again later like they told you they would and find you're off your head. That would end any chance of you keeping Leila.'

'I've had my last chance and I blew it,' Kelsey said wretchedly. 'When they find Leila she'll go straight into care and then be adopted like my other kids, and that will be the last I'll see of her.'

'You don't know that for certain,' Sharon said. 'You can't be held responsible for a man taking Leila away.'

'Oh, come off if,' Kelsey snapped. 'Get real. I left Leila in the play area all evening and didn't realize she was missing until fucking four o'clock this morning! Then what do I do? I go back to bed and don't report her missing for another

53

six hours! Nice of you to be on my side, sis, but it's not helping. This really is the end of the road for me being a mother. And I don't want this soup either.' She put the tray on the floor. 'All I wanted was to have a family and give my kids what we didn't have. But I've made a complete fuck-up of it. You've got a career, your own house and car.'

'But no children,' Sharon pointed out.

'You didn't want any, did you? I mean, I know you've offered to take Leila in the past, but that's just you being nice, isn't it?'

'To be honest, after what our step-father did to you I was too wary to let any man close enough to start a proper relationship, let alone have kids with them,' Sharon said.

'Clearly I wasn't,' Kelsey replied cynically, with a humourless laugh. 'I had the men and kids easy enough, but then I needed drugs to shut out the past.'

'I'm sorry,' Sharon said, touching her sister's arm. 'I know we agreed not to talk about it, but I do feel responsible. I always have. It's a massive burden for me to carry because I know deep down you must resent me. You put up with his abuse for all those years so he would leave me alone.'

'Of course I don't resent you, you daft cow. You were my little sister. Mum didn't want to know what was going on and there was no one else to take care of us. You'd have done the same for me.'

There was silence before Sharon said, 'And now I can repay you. I have the feeling this is going to turn out better than you think.'

'I doubt it,' Kelsey said. 'It's going to take more than your wishful thinking to bring Leila back and wipe out everything I've done wrong. Where do you think she could be?'

'I don't know, but I'm certain she won't come to any harm.'

A knock sounded on the door and Sharon stood to answer it.

'If it's one of my clients, tell them I'm not open for business right now,' Kelsey called after her.

She heard the door open and then a male voice say, 'DC Matt Davis and Beth Mayes.'

'I'm Kelsey's sister. Any news?' Sharon asked. 'Come in.'

They appeared in the living room.

'Sorry, we've interrupted your meal,' Beth said, seeing the bowl of soup on the tray. Matt positioned himself by the window. 'I take it Leila hasn't been in touch?' Beth asked.

'No, and she hasn't got a phone. The school saw to that!'

'She could have got a friend to call you,' Beth suggested.

'Well, she hasn't.'

'Won't you sit down?' Sharon asked, making room on a chair.

'Thank you. We won't stay for long,' Beth replied. 'I just wanted to give you an update. And to let you know we're doing everything we can to find Leila.'

Kelsey snorted with derision while Sharon said a polite 'Thank you'.

'We've spoken to Miss Baker, the Head of Leila's school,' Beth continued. 'If Leila hasn't been found by tomorrow, she will address the whole school in assembly, and explain that Leila is missing and if anyone knows where she might be or has seen her to tell a teacher.'

'I hope that old bat of a Head is feeling guilty,' Kelsey snapped. 'If she'd let Leila have a phone in school none of this would have happened.'

'Sshh,' Sharon silenced her sister.

'Well, it's true,' Kelsey retaliated.

'We've got officers knocking on doors all over the estate,' Beth continued. 'Many of the flats overlook the play area so it's likely someone else saw Leila leave with the man, apart from Mrs Goodman. Unfortunately her description wasn't that detailed.'

'What did she say?' Sharon asked.

...ly that the man who took Leila was of average height and build and wearing a coat. However, the important part is that Leila appeared to know him. Can you think of anyone it could be?' Beth asked, looking at both sisters.

'No,' Sharon said, 'but I don't know many people around here.'

'He might not be from here,' Matt put in.

'I don't know any of my sister's friends,' Sharon corrected. 'And that description could fit thousands of men.'

Beth concentrated on Kelsey. 'What about you? Can you think of someone who might fit that description?'

Kelsey shook her head. 'Like Sharon says, it could be anyone.'

'We'll need a list of your clients with their contact details,' Beth said to Kelsey.

'You've gotta be kidding me!'

'No. We're working on the assumption that the man Leila went with was someone she knew, so it's important you're honest. We're especially interested in the men who visited you here at the flat so very likely know you have a child, maybe have even met Leila.'

'I don't keep the blokes' names and addresses,' Kelsey said. 'I'm lucky if they give me a first name.'

'So how do they get in contact with you?' Beth asked.

'They text my mobile,' she said.

'So can you provide us with a list of their phone numbers?' Kelsey looked sceptical.

'Yes, we will,' Sharon said. 'I'll see to it.'

'Thank you,' Beth said. 'We won't contact them yet. Most missing persons are found within forty-eight hours, but if Leila isn't found tomorrow, we'll escalate the search. We'll put out a missing person's appeal on the news with a description of what she was wearing and the missing teddy bear. We'll use her recent school photograph – Miss Baker gave us a copy. I assume the bear hasn't turned up?'

Kelsey shook her head.

'We're going to speak to Mike Doherty and Jason O'Leary shortly and see what they know. Are you staying with your sister?' Beth asked Sharon.

'Just for the evening, then I have to go home. I work full-time, but Kelsey knows she can call me whenever she wants.'

Beth nodded and looked at Kelsey. 'Would you like a family liaison officer to stay with you for support?'

Kelsey stifled a laugh. 'A copper staying in my flat! That'll be good for business.'

Sharon rolled her eyes and sighed.

'It's something you can think about,' Beth said evenly. 'Here's my card.' She handed it to Kelsey. 'Call or text me if you think of anything that might help.'

'We will,' Sharon said, taking the card from her sister. 'Thank you for your time.'

As Sharon saw the officers out, Kelsey checked her phone, then pushed the tray of food out of reach with her foot. It was even more unappetizing now it was cold. The remaining gram of coke hidden in the bathroom was far more appealing: a small break from an otherwise shit life. But before she could have the coke, she'd have to get rid of her sister.

ELEVEN

On leaving Kelsey's flat, Beth and Matt took the stairs, as the lift was stuck at the top floor. 'Probably jammed open by vandals again,' Beth said as they continued to walk down.

As they passed the corridor of the second floor they saw a uniformed officer knocking on residents' doors. Seven in the evening was generally a good time to find people in, as those who were employed had usually returned from work and those with kids were home for the evening.

They nodded hello to the officer as they went by but didn't speak. He was talking to a woman who'd just answered her door. They'd be told straight away if anything significant came to light, otherwise they'd be updated at the daily management meeting in the morning.

One of the lights in the stairwell wasn't working, adding another layer of gloom to the flats. Outside it wasn't any better. The estate was shrouded in a dank November mist.

'Now to have a chat with Mike Doherty and Jason O'Leary,' Matt said.

They were in their usual place on the other side of the play area, out of view from the entrance to the flats and the road but visible from the higher-level flats. Matt had seen them from Kelsey's window. Their regulars knew where to find them. 'We'll leave the car here so we have the element of surprise,' he added.

'Agreed,' Beth said.

Instead of walking in a straight line across the play area where their approach would be seen, Matt and Beth took the path that led to the left and came in behind the sheds housing the bins, in front of which Jason and Mike were dealing. The mist also helped conceal their arrival and, Jason and Mike, facing away and busy dealing, didn't look round and see them until it was too late.

'Gotcha,' Matt said, grabbing Jason, the larger of the two, and forcing him into an arm lock up against the wall. 'Shouldn't you be at home doing your homework?'

Beth similarly forced Mike up against the wall. The other lads scattered and an approaching punter saw what was happening and turned and fled.

'Get off, you're hurting me,' Jason groaned.

'Sorry,' Matt said, keeping on the pressure. 'Would you like to empty your pockets or shall I?'

'I'll do it! Just get the fuck off me! You're gonna break me bleeding arm.'

Matt released the pressure and turned Jason around so they were face to face, keeping his hands on his shoulders in case he tried to make a run for it.

'Have you got anything on you?' Beth asked Mike.

'Nah.'

'You won't mind if I take a look then.' She patted him down and took several packets of white powder out of his pockets. Matt was removing more drugs and a roll of bank notes from Jason's pockets.

'Why do you keep picking on us?' Jason moaned. 'The boss is gonna kill us this time.'

'Nothing personal,' Matt said. 'It's just that you're on our patch and we don't like what you do.'

'Can I go now?' Jason asked as Matt bagged up the drugs and money to take to the police station. 'I promise I won't do it again.'

Mike sniggered.

'So you think it's funny?' Beth asked.

'You know the procedure,' Matt said, his hands still on Jason's shoulders. 'I'll caution you and then we'll take you to the police station and call your parents. But before we go, what do you know about Leila Smith's disappearance?'

'Nothing,' Jason said with bravado.

'What about you?' Beth asked, turning Mike around to face her.

'I don't know nothing about anything,' he replied.

'Very true,' Matt said dryly. 'But you were both here last night around the time Leila went missing. You must have seen something – possibly saw her leaving with someone.'

'No,' Jason said. 'Didn't see a thing.'

'Neither did I.' Mike nodded in agreement.

'And what about Kevin Bates?' Matt asked, his hands still firmly on Jason's shoulders.

'Who?' Jason asked, feigning ignorance.

'He had a run-in with Kelsey last night,' Matt said.

'Did he? Wouldn't know. Didn't see anything,' Jason returned.

'Nah. That's right,' Mike agreed. 'We didn't.'

'Do you know where Bates is now?' Matt asked.

'At home, doing his school work,' Jason replied cockily. Mike sniggered again.

'Got more sense than you two then,' Beth said. 'You're off for an uncomfortable night in the police cell.' She began cautioning Mike as Matt did the same with Jason. 'You do not have to say anything. But it may harm your defence if you do not mention when questioned something which you later rely on in court. Anything you do say may be given in evidence.'

TWELVE

As Mike Doherty and Jason O'Leary were being arrested, Colin sat in his flat, disillusioned and deep in thought, an unread newspaper on his lap. The kid was hard work, he had to admit. Far more demanding than he'd ever imagined a kid of her age could be, especially a girl. He'd assumed Leila would be grateful for a warm home and decent meals – somewhere she was safe and well looked after. Not so. She was sulky and uncooperative, and complained about everything: having to clear up, not being able to watch television, not liking the dinner he'd made. She'd refused point blank to help him wash the dishes or play the games he'd bought specially for her.

He felt hurt after all the trouble he'd gone to and had told her so – that he'd looked forward to the two of them sitting together like father and daughter and playing a game. She'd laughed, which had made him angry, so he'd grabbed her by the arm and shouted that she was an ungrateful brat and it was little wonder her mother didn't want her. She'd started to cry then, and he had felt bad. It brought back unhappy memories of the times his father had hit him and made him cry.

He'd tried to make it up to her and went to give her a

cuddle, but she'd pulled away and called him a pervert. That had made him even more angry – some of the kids on the estate called him a pervert – so he'd slapped her. Not hard, but enough to leave a red mark. She had to learn! That was the problem with children today. No discipline. Spare the rod and spoil the child had been his father's motto, and he hadn't spared Colin at all.

He'd sent Leila to her bedroom for a cooling-off period and to give him a chance to read the paper as he liked to do in the evening. But he couldn't concentrate. He turned a page, then started as a knock sounded on his front door. A firm and insistent knock that expected a response. He glanced at his watch. It was seven-thirty. Who on earth could it be? He never had visitors, just salespeople trying to sell him something. Hopefully they would go away.

He kept very quiet and still, praying Leila wouldn't make a noise. She knew what would happen if she did. There it was again. Another knock as firm as the first, then a female voice: 'Police. I'd like to talk to you. You haven't done anything wrong.'

His heart began drumming loudly and sweat pricked the back of his neck. What to do? The lights were on in his flat. He couldn't just ignore them and sit it out.

He stood and took a couple of steps across the living room. The police – yes, it would make sense that they were knocking on all the residents' doors, asking them what they knew. He'd seen them on the estate when he'd come back from work. If he didn't answer they would come back later or another day when only Leila was in or wasn't so quiet. Better to deal with it now.

He glanced around the living room, checking nothing of Leila's was in view from the door, and went down the hall. 'I'm coming!' he called. 'Just a minute, I was in the shower.' Was his voice steady? He thought so.

He quietly opened Leila's bedroom door. She was standing in the centre of the room, staring at him, petrified. 'Don't tie me up,' she pleaded. 'I won't make a noise, I promise.'

'So you know what to do when someone comes to the door. Come on, hurry up,' he hissed.

Leila immediately dropped to her knees and scrambled under the bed, sliding the door of the storage compartment closed. He went over and adjusted the bed covers so they were over the doors. He picked up Leila's teddy bear and nightwear and threw them in the wardrobe. If the police did come in, he'd say his niece stayed with him sometimes. With a final glance around he went quickly into the bathroom where he rubbed cold water into his hair to make it look as though he'd been in the shower. Taking a deep breath to steady his nerves, Colin opened the front door.

'Sorry to keep you waiting. I was having a shower. How can I help you?' He smiled politely at the uniformed officer as she flashed her ID.

'We're making door-to-door inquiries in connection with Leila Smith. She's eight years old and went missing yesterday evening. She lives in the flat above you.'

He shook his head. 'Sorry, I don't know her. I'm out all day at work.'

'Were you in yesterday evening?'

He paused to think. 'Yes, from about five-thirty.'

'Your flat is one of those that directly overlooks the play area from where Leila went missing. Do you remember seeing a child there, maybe talking to older children? She was wearing her school uniform and carrying a school bag and possibly a teddy bear.'

He shook his head slowly as if trying to recall anything that might be of help. 'Sorry, no. I didn't see her. I close the blinds once it's dark outside.'

The police officer nodded. 'OK, thank you. If you do

remember anything, please contact Coleshaw Police Station.'

'I will. I hope you find her safe and well soon. It must be very upsetting for her mother.'

'It is.' The officer paused.

What now? Had he said something wrong?

'So you know the child's mother is a single parent?'

'Not really,' he said with only the briefest of hesitations. 'I just made that assumption. They're mostly single mothers around here, so I assumed she was too.'

The officer nodded, apparently accepting this. 'Thank you for your time. If you do think of anything, please get in touch.'

'I will.'

Colin closed the door and leant against it, his heart racing and his knees weak. It was a stupid mistake to make, one that could have easily given him away – mother instead of parents. Another slip like that might jeopardize everything. Take it as a warning, he told himself, and be more careful in future. You've planned this in detail; don't mess it up now. Thankfully he'd had the presence of mind to think on his feet and deal with it. He waited by the door a few moments longer and when he heard the officer leave his neighbour's flat and move on again, he opened Leila's door.

'You can come out now,' he said, taking a step in.

The doors beneath the bed slowly slid open and Leila crawled out and stood. 'They're looking for me,' she said. 'I heard. You said Mummy didn't want me any more, but I think she does. The police are looking for me. I hate you. I want to go home now.'

'Not possible,' Colin said. 'As I've told you before.'

'I won't tell anyone I was here. I promise. I'll just say I ran away like I did before. They'll believe me.'

Her plaintive, whiny voice irritated Colin.

'Forget it. You're not going home now or ever. You are part of my plan. You are going to have a much better life far away from here, and so am I. You'll have a proper two-parent family who will take care of you and teach you right from wrong. In the meantime, it would be better if you and I got along, so do as I say. Understand?'

Leila gave a small nod.

'Good, now let's play one of those games I bought for you, like a proper father and daughter.'

He saw a look of defiance briefly cross Leila's face, but only for a moment and then she clearly thought better of it. She gave another small nod.

'Excellent, good choice. You see how much easier it is for us both when you do as you're told? You'll learn in time. We don't want you ending up like your mother, do we?'

THIRTEEN

In the flat above Colin's, Kelsey had succeeded in getting rid of her sister and was now looking forward to the remaining gram of coke to help ease the pain of everything that was wrong in her life. Worryingly for her, it would be her last until she could work again, and at present there was sod all chance of that happening. She was sure that none of her regulars would visit the flat while the police were swarming all over the estate. And she could hardly go out and work her usual patch under the bridge on the canal in case she was spotted or the police came back to find her gone. Decent parents didn't give blow jobs while their kid was missing; they stayed at home waiting anxiously for any news. But, of course, she wasn't a decent parent, as she'd been told plenty of times. Did she have anything more to lose? Probably not.

Kelsey looked at the packet of white powder and savoured the moment. Snort, smoke, ingest or inject it? The choice was hers. If it was as good as the last one, she'd be out of it for hours. Welcome to oblivion. She couldn't wait. She picked up the packet and began to open it carefully. Her phone, on the sofa beside her, bleeped with a text message. Probably Sharon checking on her again to make sure she wasn't using. She'd only been gone half an hour and she'd already texted twice.

But no, as Kelsey looked at her phone she saw the text wasn't from her sister. The caller's number hadn't been recognized by her phone, so it wasn't in her list of contacts. But the message was clear and just what she needed. *On my way up now. Hope you're ready for me!* ☺

Wonderful, she thought. Money on its way. It must be a client; it couldn't be anyone else. Clearly she'd forgotten she was seeing someone tonight – not surprising with the worry of Leila going missing. Slightly odd that he wasn't in her contact list, though. Perhaps he'd got a new phone. He clearly knew who she was and where she lived and had braved the police on the estate to come and see her. Must be keen, she thought, and her spirits rose. They were usually generous when they were desperate, and a bonus would be if he'd brought some coke with him to share. Some of her regulars did.

The doorbell rang – a short, firm blast. Tucking the small bag of white powder behind a cushion – she wouldn't be sharing hers – Kelsey stood and smoothed her clothes. She would have liked to have showered, changed and cleaned her teeth first. She knew good hygiene and sexy clothes were important to most of her clients, but there wasn't time for that now.

Going quickly down the hall, she went into her bedroom and straightened the duvet. The old sheets were still on, stained with blood and semen from the pig's visit, but with the lights down low and what her client had on his mind, hopefully he wouldn't notice. The bell rang again and Kelsey peered through the security spyhole. As often happened, her visitor was out of view. If they stood to the side, they weren't in range. Setting her face to a seductive smile, Kelsey began to open the door.

It didn't get wider than a few inches before it was slammed back into her face. Her nose burst and she staggered sideways. A man came in, looming large above her. Shit! She was in trouble now. It was the pig, her last client, the one she'd stolen money from.

'No husband or mates on their way?' he growled, kicking the door shut behind him. Kelsey turned to run but he grabbed her by the hair. She cried out in pain. 'I doubt you even have a husband. Who'd want you? Slut! But we'll check the flat to make sure.'

He was a big bloke, built like a house, his face scarred from his boxing days. He dragged her by the hair in and out of the rooms, checking the flat was empty. Kelsey tried to follow his movements by bending her neck to ease the pressure on her scalp. She had to take little running steps to keep up and held her hair to stop it from coming out.

'This place is filthy, like you,' he spat.

'Sorry.'

He paused as they entered Leila's bedroom and did a double take. 'So you have a child. The poor kid. Where is she now?'

'Missing. The police are looking for her. They could come back at any time.'

'Yeah, and I'm the tooth fairy.' He dragged her into the living room and threw her on the floor.

'Didn't you see all the police cars as you came in?' she asked in desperation.

'Shut up!' He kicked her in the stomach and she squealed in pain.

'Make a fool of me, would you? Forty quid you stole from me. Where is it?'

'I haven't got it, honest. You can check my purse.'

He grinned malevolently. 'No need. You're going to pay it back in kind, and with interest. It may take a while, and

I like rough sex as you already know. But this is going to be rougher than you could ever imagine. I hope you're up to it, but then again I'm not bothered if you're not.'

Forcing Kelsey to her knees, he pulled the leather belt from his trousers and bound her arms tightly behind her back. He stood in front of her – legs slightly apart – and unzipped his trousers. 'Payback time. Open wide. Deep throat.' She gagged and tried to pull away, but he held her fast. 'No one gets the better of me,' he said. 'As you're about to find out.'

FOURTEEN

Leila was in bed, petrified, with the covers pulled up over her face, trying to block out the sounds coming from her mother's flat above. She knew her mother was in trouble as soon as the noises started. She'd told Colin her mother was being hurt and that she needed to help her, but he'd said it wasn't her problem any more, and that her mother was an adult and could take care of herself. She'd made a fuss and said she had to go and help, but Colin had got very angry and sent her to her room.

Now, two hours later, she was still wide awake, listening to the sounds coming from the flat above, more worried than she had ever been in her life before.

Leila knew what the noises meant and guessed Colin did too. That's why he'd looked embarrassed. The grunting, gasps, cries, slaps, and then her mother's screams, growing louder until she'd begged the man to stop. Leila recognized some of the sounds from when her mother had brought men home, but this was far worse than anything she'd heard in the past and it seemed to go on forever. If her mother couldn't deal with a man and Leila was at home, she'd cry out for her help. 'Leila! Come quickly!' Then she would dash into

71

her mother's bedroom and accuse the man of raping her. It didn't matter what time of day or night it was. If her mother needed her help, she would be there for her. But now all she could do was listen and will it to stop.

She wiped away a tear. She felt guilty. It was her fault her mother was being hurt. If she hadn't agreed to come here with Colin, she would have been at home now and able to help her. Her mother had warned her not to trust men and she was right. Colin had been kind when he'd seen her on the estate and had talked to her nicely, with respect. He'd given her pretty things, bought her food, listened to her problems and said he understood her. He'd said she deserved better than the life she led. If she'd known what he was really like she would never have agreed to come to his flat. Never!

There was something about him now – the way he looked at her. It reminded her of the way some of the men her mother brought home looked at her, but at home she could lock herself in her bedroom to stay safe. Now the bolt was on the outside of her door, which didn't make her feel safe at all. In fact, she now doubted Colin was any better than many of the men her mother had brought home.

A loud crash sounded on the floor above, together with her mother's piercing scream. Then it went quiet. Leila waited and listened, hardly daring to breathe.

'Mummy?' she asked in a small voice, aware her mother wouldn't be able to hear her. 'Are you all right?' She got off the bed and looked up at the ceiling and waited. Nothing, not a sound. 'Mummy?' she called more loudly. Then she shouted, 'Mummy!'

She listened again, but it remained quiet in her mother's flat. What had happened to her? She ran to the bedroom door and rattled the handle, then banged on the door with her fists. 'Let me out! Colin! I want to go to my mummy. She's hurt. Colin, let me out!' She banged again, harder still.

Suddenly Colin's voice came from the other side. 'Shut up. Someone will hear you.'

'No! I want to go to my mummy. She's hurt.'

'You're not going. She's not your problem. Get back into bed and stop making a noise or something bad will happen to you too.'

'I'll shout until someone hears me,' she cried, made brave by concern for her mother.

The bolt slid open on the outside of the door and then Colin stood before her, his face bulging with anger and a silk scarf pulled tightly in his hands. 'Any more noise and I'll tie you up and gag you.'

She looked at the scarf and didn't move.

'I mean it.' He took a step towards her and raised the taut scarf. 'Be quiet and go back to bed or else.'

At that moment the doorbell rang. Colin started in horror. 'Now look what you've done! Get under the bed.'

She hesitated.

'Now! Or you'll be sorry.' He came towards her, his jaw set, twisting the scarf as if about to use it.

Leila dropped to the floor and scrambled under the bed, pulling the door to behind her. The doorbell sounded again.

Hot and sick with fear, Colin looked at his watch. It was nearly ten o'clock. Surely it wasn't the police again at this time?

'Not a peep or you'll be sorry,' he hissed, and kicked the bed to emphasize the point.

No sound came from under the bed. Satisfied, he left the room, bolting the door behind him. Another small tap on the front door, then a voice he recognized. 'Colin, it's me. Open up. Quickly.'

He took the front door key from his trouser pocket and unlocked the door. 'What do you want?' he asked anxiously as Doris Goodman stepped in. 'You weren't supposed to come here. There are police everywhere.'

'No one saw me. They've gone now, although doubtless they'll be back in the morning. You're going to have to move Leila tonight.'

'Why? That wasn't the plan.'

'And neither was you returning to the flat to get her teddy bear! That was stupid. Thanks to you the police are working on the assumption that she's still in the area. Why the hell didn't you buy her a new teddy bear like you did all her clothes?'

He stared at her. 'She wanted that one,' he said pathetically. 'She made such a fuss – someone would have heard her. Don't blame me. You were the one who told Kelsey you'd seen Leila go off with a man.'

'Because I knew it was likely someone else saw you in the play area, and the lads certainly saw me watching from my window. It wouldn't have taken much for the police to find out I was lying and that I must have seen something. Calm down. We can sort this out. Where is she now?' Her gaze fell to the twisted scarf Colin still held tightly in his hands. 'Where is she?' she asked again, desperation in her voice.

'Locked in her room. I haven't used this. What do you think I am? I just threatened to gag her if she made a noise. You told me she'd be happy to stay with me, but she's not. I'll go to prison for a long time if the police find her here.'

'Stop panicking. You'll give yourself away,' Doris said sharply. 'You can move her earlier than planned – tonight. The cottage is empty, and the police are bound to up their search of the estate tomorrow. You have a choice, Colin: either leave tonight or sit it out as we planned if you think you can cope with that.'

'Supposing she won't go?' he asked nervously.

'Don't be silly! She's eight years old. She'll do as she is told. Do you want me to talk to her?'

'If you think it will do any good.'

'Kids trust me. Pack what you need and I'll speak to her. There is nothing to link her to you, but make sure you take all her stuff to be on the safe side and give the place a good clean.'

More agitated than ever, Colin disappeared into his bedroom as Doris unbolted Leila's bedroom door and went in. 'Leila?'

The door below the bed opened and Leila climbed out, her expression a mixture of surprise and fear. 'What were you doing in there?' Doris asked.

'I have to hide when anyone comes to the door.'

She sighed. 'I suppose he knows what he's doing. There's nothing for you to worry about, but we do need to have a chat. Come and sit beside me on the bed.' She took Leila's hand and drew her to sit next to her.

'Colin is a good man,' Doris began.

'No, he's not. I don't like him. He's horrible to me.'

'What makes you say that?' Doris asked, suddenly concerned.

'He gets angry with me. He wouldn't let me help Mummy and makes me do things I don't want to.'

'What sort of things?' Doris asked suspiciously.

'He makes me play games and clear up the mess I make.'

Doris gave a small laugh. 'Colin doesn't know much about children and what it's like to be a father. He's having to learn. Just as you're having to learn how to be a good daughter.'

'Am I his daughter?' Leila asked, surprised.

'Yes, in a way.'

'Why?'

'You need proper parents, a new start. Leila, we've been watching you and your mother for some time and know the sort of life you have and it's not right. You told me yourself you weren't happy and sometimes wished you could be adopted. Trust me, this is for the best. But you must help Colin by doing what he says.'

'I'm worried about my mummy,' Leila said, her voice small. 'Someone was in our flat hurting her. I told Colin and he wouldn't let me go to help her.'

'That was the right decision,' Doris said calmly. 'Your mother isn't your responsibility. Would it help if I went to check on her?'

Leila nodded.

'And then you'll be a good girl for Colin?'

'Yes.'

'Excellent.' She rubbed Leila's arm reassuringly. 'You stay here then and try to get some rest. I'll speak to Colin and then I'll see your mother. You're going on a long journey tonight.'

'Am I? Where?'

'It's a secret,' Doris said, putting her finger to her lips.

'Are you coming?'

'No. But I will see you again, I'm sure.'

'What about Mummy? Will you tell her where I am and that I love her?'

'Of course. Now try to get some sleep. And Leila, whatever happens I want you to forget I came here and that we had this conversation. Do you understand?'

'Yes.'

'Good girl.'

Having settled Leila in bed, Doris left the room and went to find Colin. He was in his bedroom, agitatedly throwing clothes and other essential items into a suitcase.

'She's fine now,' she said, watching him. 'Calm down. You're not leaving yet. It's too early. Wait until later, after the pubs close and the estate clears.'

'I should never have agreed to this,' he cursed. 'It was madness.'

'But we both know why you did, and I doubt it was because of an altruistic urge to save the child.'

Colin stopped what he was doing and glared at Doris. He was about to say something but changed his mind.

'You're too far in now to get out,' Doris said. 'Treat the kid right and she'll cooperate. And remember, don't phone me or anyone else until all this calms down. The police are bound to start monitoring calls of any suspects before long.'

'But they don't suspect me,' he said.

'No, and there's no reason for them to as long as you don't panic and give yourself away.'

Doris watched him a while longer as he anxiously dropped items into the case, only to take them out and repack them again a moment later. He was his own worst enemy, she thought.

'Stick to the plan and you'll be fine,' she told him again. 'Goodbye, Colin, and good luck.'

He didn't answer. She turned, left the room and let herself out of the flat. Of course the child would play up to start with; Colin should have been prepared for that. He was so naive and spineless. Going back for that teddy bear had been downright stupid. He'd panicked. Another mistake like that might be their undoing. He'd known from the beginning what was involved, and these first few days would be the most difficult part. If he got through this, the rest should fall into place.

Doris continued down the stairs and headed across the play area towards her flat. She wouldn't check on Kelsey now. It was too risky. There were still plenty of people out and about on the estate at this time. She'd taken a chance going to see Colin, but she'd had to warn him. Kelsey could take care of herself. She always had in the past. It was the child who needed saving and that's exactly what they were doing.

FIFTEEN

Colin sat nervously by the window in his living room with the curtains parted and the light off, staring across the estate. It was raining, the steady drizzle of a cold November night, with a cloud-laden sky threatening more. Most of the flats were in darkness now, including Doris Goodman's, apart from the porch lamp that she left on all night. He would leave at exactly 1 a.m., he'd decided, when the estate was at its most deserted on a weekday. At that time good folk were asleep in their beds and the druggies and alkies had disappeared for the night.

He'd thoroughly cleaned the flat, bagged up and thrown out all their rubbish, and Leila was at last asleep in her bed. She was still in her day clothes, so all he had to do was wake her and get her out the door and into his car without her making any noise. She seemed a bit more compliant now Doris had spoken to her, so hopefully that would continue. If not, he'd have the scarf at the ready to gag her if necessary.

He'd packed a couple of changes of clothes for him, toiletries for them both and all of Leila's belongings, apart from her coat and shoes, which were ready in the hall. Everything else of his was staying. He'd buy new things once they were safely in the cottage, ready for his new life. But he mustn't forget that bloody teddy bear, which had caused him so much trouble and Leila insisted on sleeping with.

Colin had no regrets about leaving his council flat and dead-end job. He'd grown to hate both. A new life beckoned in a way he could never have imagined a year ago, and as long as he didn't panic or make another slip-up, their plan should work. Pity he had to put up with the child, he thought; she'd become the fly in the ointment. He'd never really liked kids and this one was proving less endearing than most. He supposed he could get used to her in small doses when he wasn't solely responsible for her. She was a means to an end. But right now she was hard work and stressful. If things didn't improve, he certainly wouldn't let her get in the way of his future happiness. Plenty of kids disappeared abroad and were never seen again.

Colin studied his watch as it gradually approached 1 a.m. The time had come. He stood and, with trembling fingers, propped the suicide note he'd written on the coffee table so it would easily be seen if and when someone came into the flat. He checked the living room and kitchen one last time for anything that was out of place, incongruous with him having left without any intention of returning, then went to Leila's room. While she'd slept, he had removed the bolt from her bedroom door and made good the screw holes as best he could. He was sure they wouldn't be noticed among all the other scuff marks on the door.

By the light coming from the hall, he crossed to Leila's bed. She was fast asleep on her back, hair spread out on the pillow, her face relaxed. She looked pretty like this, he had to admit, as a child should, without the harshness that usually blighted her features and innocence.

'Leila, time to wake up,' he said, tapping her shoulder.

She gasped and sat bolt upright. 'Get away from me!' she shouted, immediately on guard. Grabbing the bed covers, she clasped them to her chest.

'Sshh, be quiet,' he hissed, clamping his hand over her mouth. 'Be quiet. It's time to leave.'

She blinked, dazed, and then nodded. He removed his hand. 'Come on, get up, we have to go now.'

She rubbed her eyes. 'Did Granny Goodman see my mummy?'

'I expect so. Get up quietly and put on your coat and shoes.'

'I need the bathroom.'

'Go then, but hurry.'

Leila clambered off the bed and took Buttons with her as she went to the bathroom. Colin stripped the bed, stuffed the bedding into a black sack he had ready and looked around, checking to make sure he hadn't missed anything. He thought it looked like a spare room should now – ready for a guest, with a few bits of furniture but no personal items. It shouldn't raise any suspicions if the police eventually broke in. He could imagine the chain of events when he didn't show for work. His manager would ask his colleagues if they'd heard from him or knew where he might be, which they wouldn't, as he didn't have anything to do with them outside of work. Human Resources would then try to phone him, but his mobile would be off and his landline would go unanswered. At some point they'd become concerned enough to notify the police, who would eventually break in and find an empty flat and his suicide note.

Doris was right: if he kept his nerve and didn't panic, it would all work out.

Colin heard the toilet flush and went into the hall. 'Put on your coat and shoes,' he told Leila as she came out of the bathroom, holding her teddy bear.

He checked the bathroom for any stray items and then

put on his own coat and shoes. 'So remember, not a sound until we are in the car,' he warned her. She nodded seriously. He threw the holdall over his shoulder, picked up the suitcase and bin bag, and let them out. Leila gave a small cough. 'Sshh.' He glared at her and she put her hand to her mouth.

He kept close by her as they walked along the corridor, with her clutching her teddy bear. Her mother's flat was only a flight of stairs away, within easy reach if she made a dash for it. But she was still half asleep and yawning, and she walked compliantly beside him down the stairs – the lift would have made too much noise – and then outside into the cold, wet night.

'I don't like the rain,' she moaned.

'Sshh, be quiet,' he hissed, pushing her towards the car. 'Don't say another word.'

A motorbike could be heard entering the estate, then accelerating around the perimeter road. He'd heard it before on other nights – a few laps to wake the residents, then off again before the police arrived.

'Get in,' Colin whispered, opening the rear door of the car.

Leila did as she was told. Colin closed her door, then went to the boot where he put in the suitcase, holdall and bin bag, which he would dispose of en route. Once in the driver's seat, he felt slightly better and pressed the internal locking system. He saw Leila looking out of her side window and up towards her mother's flat. The sooner they were away, the better. Fastening his seatbelt, he turned the ignition. The engine whimpered and cut out. Shit! He tried again with the same result. It was an old car and sometimes played up in damp weather. He should have come down earlier and got it started and given the engine time to warm up, as he did when he used it for work in winter.

Colin glanced anxiously up at the windows of the flats,

81

praying no one would hear them and look out. The motor-bike began a second lap.

'Won't your car start?' Leila asked.

'What does it look like!' he snapped. His stomach was knotted into a tight ball and he was sweating profusely despite the cold.

Calm down, he told himself, and gave the ignition another try. This time the engine spluttered into life. 'Thank god.' He touched the accelerator to give it some gas. He should really sit here for a while and let the engine run – otherwise it might cut out again – but he daren't take the risk. It was imperative that no one saw them leave.

Gripping the steering wheel with his right hand, he gingerly engaged first gear and eased up the clutch, hoping the engine wouldn't stall. The car slowly pulled away, gradually leaving their block of flats behind.

'When will I see my mummy again?' Leila asked from the back.

'Never, if you're lucky.' He glanced in the rear-view mirror and saw she was clutching her teddy bear closer still.

He stopped at the T-junction that led onto the perimeter road. 'Get down!' he shouted, as the motorbike appeared. It flashed by, the rider briefly turning his helmeted head in their direction. Had he seen Leila? He couldn't be sure. But even if he had, he doubted anything would come of it. A night-time joyrider was unlikely to be interested in or suspicious of them.

'Stay down,' he told Leila as he pulled onto the ring road that would take them off the estate. There were no other vehicles apart from the motorbike. He heard its engine roar again and it appeared in his wing mirror, its single headlamp dazzlingly bright. It quickly gained on them and sounded its horn as it roared by.

'Idiot,' Colin shouted.

'I feel sick down here,' Leila groaned.

He concentrated on the road ahead. It was a filthy night and the windscreen was misting up. A minute later he was at the exit of the estate and pulled onto the main road. The car engine was warming up and running more smoothly now, and the road was pretty much deserted.

'You can get up now,' he said.

In the rear-view mirror he saw Leila reappear on the back seat. 'Shall I put on my seatbelt?' she asked.

'Yes, of course, you're not stupid.'

Calm down, he told himself. Everything will be all right. Only fifteen minutes to the motorway and then a steady three-hour drive to Heath Cottage, where they would be safe. He never did more than sixty miles per hour on the motorway, as his car was old and could easily overheat. A new car was something he promised himself once they were settled and had some money. Something nice and smart that would fit with his new, smart lifestyle. His spirits began to rise.

'Where are we going?' Leila asked after a few minutes.

'To Doris Goodman's cottage,' he replied convivially.

'What's a cottage?'

'A small house out in the middle of nowhere.'

'Will Granny Goodman be there?'

'No, she won't.' Jesus! Didn't the child ever shut up?

'I didn't know she had a cottage,' Leila said.

Neither had he until a few months ago when it had formed part of the plan to take Leila. She'd told him it was an old crofter's cottage that she'd lived in until she'd got married and moved south. She'd inherited it when her parents died and had continued to use it as a holiday cottage until her husband had passed and the journey and the cost of the upkeep had become too much. Sometimes others used it, but only in summer. It had fallen into disrepair but was isolated and remote, so it was ideal for their purpose – a hideaway until they could leave the country.

The windscreen wipers continued their steady rhythm back and forth as the motorway signpost appeared. Colin glanced in the rear-view mirror again and saw that Leila had started to doze. He began to relax. It would be fine as long as he stuck to their plan and kept his nerve. He had no regrets.

SIXTEEN

'Nothing so far from the door-to-door,' DC Beth Mayes said, thinking aloud as she drove.

'No, and as the DCI said, no one on the estate is likely to want to get involved,' Matt pointed out. 'Apart from Mrs Goodman, of course. But she's not much help with this one. Perhaps we'll have better luck today.'

It was 10.30 a.m., two days after Leila had gone missing. Beth and Matt had not long come out of the management meeting led by Detective Chief Inspector Aileen Peters. They were now on their way to Hawthorn Estate to see Kelsey and update her on the police investigation. Mike Doherty and Jason O'Leary had spent the night in the police cells, having been charged for possession, and had eventually been collected by their parents, who were in no hurry to have them home again.

'So we're still working on the assumption that Leila is in the area, though not necessarily on the estate,' Beth said, consolidating what they had been told. 'Uniform are continuing the house-to-house inquiries in the streets around the estate.'

Matt nodded. 'And the DCI has given us the go-ahead for visiting the three registered sex offenders living locally, although they're bound to see it as harassment.'

'There might be some more on Kelsey's phone list who don't live in the area,' Beth said. 'Her sister has sent it in and it's been checked now. So we know Alan Stevens isn't a registered sex offender, but the DCI wants us to speak to him anyway at some point.'

'As well as any other clients who may have visited Kelsey's flat,' Matt pointed out. 'Assuming Kelsey is going to be more cooperative today and tell us who they were. Otherwise we'll just have to work our way through the contact list from her phone and eliminate them one by one. Although it may be that after all this the man who took Leila wasn't known to them.'

'I wonder if the Headmistress of Leila's school has had any luck?' Beth said as she navigated the traffic. 'She was going to talk to the children in assembly this morning.'

Matt's phone started ringing and he answered it. He listened for some moments with only the occasional 'I see', then ended with, 'Thanks for that.'

'Wonder no more,' he said, glancing at Beth. 'Miss Baker, the Head of Leila's school, has phoned in. She spoke to all the children in assembly and also to some of them individually. A few say they saw Leila in the play area straight after school, but no one saw her leave. They were home by then. The Head said she would send a letter out with all the children asking parents to contact her or the police if they know anything that might help find Leila and also asking them to be vigilant. Apparently the parents were talking about it when they dropped off their kids this morning. They're worried their child might be next. But the Head also said that Leila wasn't a popular child and didn't have many friends. I guess she's the sort of kid parents warn their children not to associate with.'

'Poor child,' Beth said. 'She didn't stand a chance.'

'No,' Matt agreed. 'Alone and vulnerable, with a mother

like Kelsey, she would be easy prey. Their social worker, Peter Harris, has also phoned in and asked to be kept updated on the police investigation. It was likely that Leila would be taken into care before long, and possibly she picked up on this, which raises the possibility that Leila has run away to avoid going into care.'

'Apart from the fact that she was seen leaving with a man,' Beth pointed out.

'Unless Doris Goodman was mistaken,' Matt said. 'No one else saw Leila leave with a man.'

'No one else saw anything!' Beth exclaimed sceptically. 'Of course, there is another scenario – that Kelsey is at the bottom of this and has hidden Leila to stop her being taken into care. In which case, she probably had the guy – whoever he was – collect Leila from the play area.'

Matt agreed. 'It wouldn't be the first time a parent has legged it with their child when they were about to be taken into care.'

'So if we're right, when we get to Kelsey's we'll probably find she's disappeared too.'

Ten minutes later Beth parked the car outside the block of flats where Kelsey lived. She and Matt got out and made their way up the stairs. A baby could be heard crying in one of the flats, a television was on loud in another and dogs barked in another. The sounds of everyday life continuing in the flats despite the enormity of what was unfolding outside. Some of the doors they passed had children's bikes parked outside, although it was doubtful the kids would be allowed out alone until Leila was found. Some of the flats had patterned doormats and the occasional potted plant, taking the edge off the grey concrete. Not Kelsey's, though. There were no homely extras, just a badly scratched navy-blue door in need of a good wash and a repaint.

'Here we go then,' Matt said, pressing the bell. 'Place your bets as to whether she's scarpered.'

They waited but the door remained unanswered and Matt pressed the bell again. 'Kelsey, it's DC Matt Davis and DC Beth Mayes,' he called, knocking on the door. There was no reply. He tried again.

'Looks like we were right then,' he said.

'Or she could just be out – you know, buying milk or something,' Beth said.

Matt threw her a doubtful look. 'More like out cold from whatever she took last night,' he said.

'If she has disappeared, we'll need to update the DCI straight away,' Beth said. 'The missing person's bulletin is going out later. It'll need to be amended to say that Leila is thought to be in the company of her mother. We should have a photograph of Kelsey on file; she's been brought in enough times for possession of drugs and soliciting.'

Matt took out his mobile phone, ready to call in and update their boss as Beth tried the doorbell one more time. 'Kelsey. It's the police.'

Kelsey's neighbour, Brooke Adams, who they'd spoken to the day before, came out of her flat. 'There was another domestic there last night,' she said. 'I was going to call you, but then I heard him go.'

'There was a man here last night?' Beth asked, surprised.

'Yes, as I say, I was going to call the police, but then he left.'

'What time was that?' Beth asked.

'I don't know when he arrived, but the shouting started around ten o'clock, then it was off and on for ages. I guess he went around midnight. It's happened before and it's not nice for my kids to have to listen to all that sex and stuff. It was obvious what was going on.'

'Do you know if Kelsey left with the man?' Beth asked.

'I've no idea. It's possible, I guess. It's been quiet in there ever since.'

'I don't suppose you know who the man was?'

'I haven't a clue. She has a lot of male visitors.'

'Kelsey didn't say his name then?' Beth asked. 'I know the walls in the flats are thin.'

'I heard him calling her names, but I didn't hear her use his name.'

'And there were no sounds suggesting Leila was there?'

'God, no, I hope not. I didn't hear her. I haven't heard her since she went missing. You haven't found her then?'

'No, not yet.'

Beth thanked Brooke for her help and she returned indoors.

'That's worrying,' Beth said.

'Kelsey!' Matt shouted, banging on her door again. 'Are you in there?' There was still no reply. 'So I'm guessing we break in,' he said. 'I can force that lock.'

'Just a second,' Beth said. 'Listen.'

A small noise came from the other side of the door.

'Kelsey, are you in there?' Beth tried. 'It's the police – Beth and Matt.'

Another noise like a groan and then the door slowly opened.

'Jesus!' Beth gasped, catching Kelsey as she collapsed against her. 'Matt, call an ambulance.' She steadied Kelsey and then helped her back inside the flat and to the first room, her bedroom. 'Sit down,' Beth said, easing her onto the bed. The poor woman could barely stand from the beating she'd received. Her face was so badly bruised that one eye was nearly closed. Her lip was split and swollen and there was dried blood around her mouth, on her cheeks and jeans and matted into her hair.

'Don't call an ambulance,' Kelsey pleaded, wincing as she spoke.

'We have to,' Beth said. 'You're badly hurt. Who did this to you?'

Kelsey shrugged.

'You must know, love,' Beth said. 'Brooke told us she heard a man in here knocking you about last night. Look at the state you're in. He could have killed you.'

'Can you just get me a drink of water, please?' Kelsey asked, touching her lip.

Beth went into the kitchen, rinsed a glass under the tap and filled it with cold water. As she returned Matt came into the flat. 'The ambulance is on its way,' he said, following Beth into Kelsey's bedroom.

'I'm not going to hospital,' Kelsey said again. Beth passed her the glass of water.

'That's your right,' Matt said. 'But we would strongly advise you to get checked over. You look in a bad way to me.'

'And that's the bits you can see,' Kelsey said, trying to smile. 'The bastard. But I won't be pressing charges.' She took a sip of the water and grimaced as it stung her lip. 'I owed him some money. He got what he came for. I'll be more careful in future. Have you found Leila?' She looked up at them imploringly.

Beth's heart went out to her and she felt guilty for thinking she could have played a part in Leila's abduction.

'Not yet,' she said. 'But we've got a lot of officers working on it.' She perched on the edge of the bed next to Kelsey. There were no concerns about her contaminating DNA evidence as Kelsey wasn't pressing charges – she never did. It wasn't the first time a client had turned on her, but it was definitely the worst beating Beth had seen. 'Kelsey, did you know the social services were thinking of taking Leila into care?' she asked gently.

'Not for sure, but I guessed it wouldn't be long.'

'Did Leila know?'

'Maybe. I don't know.'

'Do you have any idea where she might be?'

'No. Honest.' She winced again. 'I'm worried sick. I know I should have taken better care of her. I just want her back.'

'And you have no idea who the man was who was seen with Leila?'

'None.'

'Do you think it's possible she might have run away because she didn't want to go into care?' Beth asked.

'Yeah. I wondered that, but Gawping Goodman said she'd seen Leila go with a man.' The glass she was holding shook.

'I know, but we're wondering if Mrs Goodman could have been mistaken. No one else saw Leila leave with anyone.'

Kelsey shrugged. 'If she's mistaken it'll be the first time. The old bat is usually right.'

An ambulance siren could be heard pulling onto the estate and Matt stepped into the corridor to wait for the paramedics while Beth stayed with Kelsey. Presently they appeared from the stairwell and Matt showed them into the flat.

'Sorry, guys, I'm not going with you,' Kelsey said as soon as she saw them.

'I'm Dave and this is Simon,' the lead paramedic said. 'It's Kelsey, isn't it?' She nodded. 'You've taken a bit of a beating, love. Can we at least check you over here?'

'Yeah, I guess.'

Beth moved out of the way and waited with Matt by the door as the paramedics took Kelsey's blood pressure and pulse, and then examined the cuts and bruises that were visible on her face, neck and arms.

'You've had a nasty bang on the head,' Dave said. 'Did you lose consciousness?'

'I don't think so.'

'Do you have any injuries anywhere else?' Dave asked.

'Yes, but I'm not showing you, it's private.'

'I think we should take you to hospital so all your injuries can be checked,' Dave said. 'You could have internal injuries too.'

'No. I'm fine.'

'You don't look fine,' Dave replied, and waited, hoping Kelsey would change her mind.

'Sorry, I'm not going,' she said.

'OK, we can't force you, but we will need you to sign a form saying we advised you to go to hospital and you refused.' He gave Kelsey the form and a pen. She set her glass of water on the floor and carefully wrote her name. Her hand trembled as she passed the form and pen back.

'If you do feel ill, dizzy or nauseous, or you have any concerns about your health, please seek medical treatment,' Dave said, tucking the form into his pocket.

'Thanks, guys,' Kelsey said.

Saying goodbye, the paramedics left, closing the front door behind them.

'Will Sharon come and sit with you?' Beth asked Kelsey.

'She's at work, but don't you worry about me. I'll be all right. You just concentrate on finding my Leila.'

'We are,' Beth said.

'So we were wrong,' Matt said as they made their way down the stairs to exit the block of flats. 'She's certainly a tough cookie.'

'She's had to be,' Beth replied grimly. 'Kelsey's had a hell of a life, and to top it all her last kid goes missing, then she gets beaten up because she owes some lowlife money. I wish she'd give us his name so we could bring him in.'

'Perhaps she'll change her mind.'

'I doubt it.'

They crossed to their car. Matt was driving today so Beth got into the passenger seat. 'Let's go to Doris Goodman's first and check her version of events for the night Leila went missing,' Beth said.

Matt started the car. 'She may also have seen something going on last night. She doesn't miss much on the estate.'

A couple of minutes later, Matt parked the car outside Doris Goodman's ground-floor maisonette. Her front door opened immediately and she appeared.

'Good morning,' Beth said, going up the short path.

'Any news of Leila?' Doris asked, concerned.

'Not yet.'

She showed them into her living room, which was neat as usual. Matt sat by the window where he could see the car and Beth took the sofa.

'We've just come from seeing Kelsey,' Beth said. 'I'm afraid she's in a bad way. Someone beat her up last night.'

Doris gasped. 'I'm so sorry to hear that. The poor woman.'

'A neighbour thinks her attacker arrived around ten and left around midnight,' Beth continued. 'We were wondering if you saw anything of the disturbance?'

'No.' Doris shook her head.

'You can see the entrance to the flats and Kelsey's living-room window from here,' Matt said, pointing.

'Yes, if I were to look out of my window, but I was watching television for most of the evening and then I went to bed around ten o'clock.'

'Thank you anyway,' Beth said. 'It was a long shot.'

'Is that all you wanted?' Doris asked, apparently unusually eager to end their visit.

'There is something else,' Beth said.

'Yes?' Doris cocked her head.

'When we spoke to you yesterday you said you saw Leila leave the play area with a man, although you couldn't give us a description and you weren't sure in which direction they were heading.'

'That's correct.'

'Did you actually see Leila leave with him?'

Doris seemed as though she was about to confirm this, then hesitated and appeared to change her mind. 'I'm not sure. Why?'

'Because no one else saw Leila leave with a man, and if she didn't then it raises the possibility that she wasn't abducted but has run away.'

There was a short silence as Doris considered this thoughtfully. Beth and Matt looked at her and waited. 'It's important,' Beth prompted.

'Do you know,' Doris said after a moment, suddenly making eye contact, 'now I come to think of it, I remember seeing Leila talking to a man, but I didn't actually see her leave with him. I saw her get off the swing as if she was about to go with him, then I must have turned away from the window, because when I looked again she and the man had gone. I just assumed she'd left with him. But of course it's far more likely Leila has run away as she has before. How silly of me. I am sorry.' She threw them a self-depreciating smile.

Beth nodded. 'Mistakes happen and it was dark,' she said.

'I guess that changes things then, doesn't it?' Doris asked. 'I mean, you won't be looking for a man with a child now, just a child alone.'

'We won't rule out the abduction theory completely at this stage as a man was seen talking to Leila. But yes, it does alter our lines of inquiry. Thank you for your time, Mrs Goodman.'

'You're very welcome.'

SEVENTEEN

It was almost laughable, Colin thought. Doris Goodman had warned him not to use his phone, but there was no bloody signal anywhere in the cottage! And no landline. The time on his phone showed 11.15 a.m. and the low-battery signal was on. How was he supposed to charge it with no mains electricity? He couldn't be expected to live like this. It was ridiculous.

He threw back the blanket, got off the couch and looked around the one main room. A wintry light crept in through the thin curtains. It was no less grim now than it had been when they'd arrived in the dark, at 4 a.m. The fire that would have once burnt peat for heating and cooking was boarded up, and gas canisters now fuelled a small heater in the living room and a stove in the kitchen.

They had arrived, exhausted, under a dark, moonless sky, having bumped along Fern Lane – a rough, unlit road – for nearly two miles. He'd had to leave the car's headlamps on, pointing at the front of Heath Cottage, to find the key Doris had said was hidden under some stones, and then grope for the battery-powered lamp hanging just inside the door. She had told him the cottage was basic, but nothing could have prepared him for this. It was grim beyond belief and he was completely pissed off.

Leila had started playing up as soon as they'd walked in and she'd discovered the state of the place and that there was no television. He'd quickly lost his temper and shouted at her. She'd shouted back in a voice that sounded very much like her mother's. But the cottage was so remote no one could hear them. She was still asleep in the only habitable bedroom. The other bedroom was unusable due to a badly leaking roof that Doris had either omitted to mention or been unaware of. Colin had slept on the sofa in the living room and had given Leila the bed. Not out of chivalry, but because he wasn't going to leave her alone in the room that had the only door in and out of the cottage. Doubtless she was as pissed off as he was and would scarper given the opportunity. He'd checked the window in her bedroom and it was stuck closed from layers of paint added over the years. Thankfully, the bedding had been stored in sealed polythene bags to keep out the damp. Even so, he'd been cold and unable to stretch out his legs on the sofa, so he'd hardly slept a wink. Now he was going to have to boil water on the camping stove to wash and make a hot drink!

He opened the curtains that covered the small casement windows and his spirits sank even further. A thick mist had rolled in from the moors, reducing visibility to nil. He'd have to wait until it lifted before venturing out. The nearest village with a grocery store was three miles away and Doris had warned him to use it only if he really had to. Strangers appearing outside of the tourist season were sure to spark interest in the locals. If they were asked where they were staying, which was highly likely, he should say they were just passing through. Doris had told him to drive into Marsborough, the next big town, for provisions, but that was fifteen miles away! He clearly wouldn't be doing that yet. Aside from the fog, if he got in the car in his present mood he was unlikely to return.

The bedroom door slowly creaked open and Leila appeared, clutching her teddy bear. Like him she'd slept in her clothes to keep warm. 'I'm hungry,' she said. 'And cold. This place is creepy.' Her gaze went past him to the window and the fog outside. 'I don't like it here. I'm scared. It's like a horror movie.'

'And if you don't behave yourself, the fog monster will get you,' he said, baring his teeth in a grimace.

He began searching the cupboards in the small kitchen for cooking utensils. If he could make something to eat, he might start to feel a bit better.

'I want to go home,' Leila whined, watching him from the doorway.

'So you keep saying.'

'You and Granny Goodman told me my life would be better if I came here with you, but it's not, it's got worse.'

Colin felt a stab of sympathy for her. They were in this together. 'It will get better,' he said more gently, turning to look at her.

'When?' she asked.

'When you stop asking questions. If you want to make yourself useful, fetch one of the cans of food from the holdall.' He'd found a pan and was now trying to work out how to use the bloody stove. Doris had said there would be enough gas in the canister to see them through a couple of days and then he'd have to buy more from Marsborough.

Out of the corner of his eye he saw Leila go to the holdall, rummage through it and take out a can of beans and sausages. She placed it on the small wooden table beside him, then walked over to the door and leant nonchalantly against the wall as if she hadn't a care in the world. He smiled to himself.

Cute, but he wasn't that daft. It seemed the fog monster outside held more appeal than staying with him. A few moments later she'd grabbed the door handle and was trying to open it.

'It's locked,' he said, and laughed as he emptied the can of beans into the pan. 'As if I'd go to all the trouble of bringing you here only to have you vanish! You're my passport to the future, so you'd better get used to it. And after we've eaten, I'm going to cut your hair short.'

'Why?' She stared at him in horror.

'To make you look different so I can take you out.'

'I don't want it cut. I don't want to go out. I want to go home.' Her bottom lip trembled.

'Going home isn't an option, so cheer up. I really don't like miserable children. In fact, now I've spent time with you, I don't think I like them at all.' He laughed mirthlessly.

EIGHTEEN

Kelsey and Sharon sat to attention on the sofa as the missing person's appeal for information appeared on the television. 'About bloody time,' Kelsey said as Sharon raised the volume.

A picture of Leila in her school uniform was now on the screen as the news presenter spoke. 'Police are appealing for information on the disappearance of Leila Smith, who went missing four days ago from a play area on the Hawthorn Estate, Coleshaw.' A shot of the play area flashed up and then the screen returned to the photo of Leila as the presenter continued. 'Leila is eight years old, has long brown hair and blue eyes and is of average height and build. When she was last seen she was wearing her school uniform with a navy zip-up jacket and black trainers, and was carrying her school bag. She may have a teddy bear with her similar to this one.' A picture of the once-popular bear appeared on the screen and was then minimized as the presenter continued. 'Leila was last seen at approximately six o'clock in the evening on Tuesday, the thirteenth of November, talking to a man in his early fifties. Police would like to speak to that man and anyone who may have information about Leila's disappearance. Concern for her safety is growing. Please call the number below or contact your local police station.'

The appeal ended as abruptly as it had begun, and another news item started. Sharon pressed the remote to silence the television.

'Is that it?' Kelsey asked, disappointed. 'It wasn't very long.'

'It's probably long enough to jog someone's memory,' Sharon said flatly.

'Why did they say Leila *may* have her teddy bear with her?' Kelsey asked. 'She must have it. It's not here.'

'Because the police can't be a hundred per cent certain.'

'I told them she had it. Don't they believe me?'

'It's difficult,' Sharon replied carefully. 'I mean, you get confused sometimes, and Beth said it's unlikely Leila returned to collect her teddy bear.'

'So where is it?' Kelsey demanded, her eyes flashing. 'It certainly isn't here. I've turned the place upside down.'

'It's possible it went missing some time ago,' Sharon offered.

'And I didn't notice! Well, fuck you, Sharon!' Kelsey jumped up and confronted her sister. 'Time for you to go before I say something I'm going to regret.'

Sharon stood. 'It's impossible to talk to you when you're like this. I'll go if that's what you want. I've left you a micro-wave meal in the kitchen for your dinner tonight and there are others in the fridge.'

'Thank you,' Kelsey said tightly.

Sharon hesitated. 'Are you sure you won't come and stay with me for a while?'

'Yes. I prefer my own company and I want to be here if Leila comes back.'

'You won't let anyone in, will you?'

Kelsey shrugged and Sharon knew the answer was probably yes, that even after the beating Kelsey had received and from which she was still recovering, she would put herself at risk again to obtain money for drugs.

'I'll leave you fifty pounds if you promise you won't let anyone in.'

'You're kidding me?'

'No.'

Kelsey stared in disbelief as Sharon took the cash from her purse and handed it to her. 'I really don't understand you. You know what this will be spent on.'

Sharon shrugged. 'That's your choice. I'll see you tomorrow. It's Saturday and I'm not working, so I'll come over mid-morning.'

'OK.'

Kelsey watched her sister leave, unable to fathom her. Sharon had known her hard-earned money would go on drugs or alcohol, yet instead of another lecture she'd given her the money to buy them – to keep her safe. Was she doing her a favour? Kelsey really didn't know. Her head was full to bursting. Leila was missing and the longer it went on the less chance there was of finding her alive, and it was all her fault. Sharon knew that, yet she was still willing to support her. She should be grateful she had a sister like her.

NINETEEN

Colin was starting to feel a bit better now he was back in civilization. It had been the right decision to drive into Marsborough. It was Saturday and the shopping centre was heaving with families, so a middle-aged man with a child didn't stand out. He'd bought groceries and other provisions and now Leila was amusing herself in the children's play area provided by the shopping centre, while he sat nearby enjoying a second cup of coffee and a croissant. His phone and laptop were charging at the courtesy power point at his table, so life didn't seem so bad now. If he could come here every couple of days then he could probably face staying in that god-forsaken cottage as planned until all the fuss had died down.

He took another sip of coffee and glanced over to where Leila was playing. She was barely recognizable with her hair cut short. That had been a good move. Clever. He moved his cup and saucer to one side and opened his laptop while it continued to charge. He began going through the emails in his inbox. It was surprising how many had accumulated since he'd last been able to log in – at his flat – even though he didn't know that many people. There were two official emails from HR at work, a less formal one from his boss and a friendly one from a work colleague, although Colin couldn't ever remember giving the man his email address. They all said pretty much the same thing, only differently: where was he? When would he be returning to work? And he needed to get in touch straight away. The short answer was no, he wouldn't be going back or getting in touch. Ever. He was supposed to be dead. He smiled to himself. They'd find out eventually when the police broke into his flat and found his suicide note.

He deleted the junk email and then read the notice of the standing order for his rent. It was due to be taken at the end of the month. He couldn't cancel it or any other standing order for the same reason he couldn't contact work or access his bank account. If anyone checked, it could give him away. He'd gradually withdrawn most of his money in cash during the months leading up to his departure. He assumed that once his bank account was empty the standing orders would be refused, so it would sort itself out. Having been meticulous in managing his money all his life, never getting into debt or going overdrawn, he now felt an irresponsible devil-may-care lightness and a wish to be free of it all. It buoyed up his spirits even further.

Emails read, Colin closed his inbox, then tapped the keypad to bring up the online news. The national news headlines appeared first, but he wasn't interested in those. He scrolled down the page – through the state of the economy and trouble in the Middle East – until he found what he was looking for: *Appeal for Missing Child*. He'd been expecting something, so it wasn't a shock. Of course the police would put out an appeal to try to find Leila. It was usual when a child went missing.

Leaning in and tilting the screen slightly towards him so those passing or sitting at nearby tables couldn't see, he began to read: *Police are appealing for information on the disappearance of Leila Smith, aged eight, who was last seen on*

Tuesday, 13 November, playing on the Hawthorn Estate, Coleshaw ... There was a photo of Leila in her school uniform, but now she was dressed in the clothes he'd bought for her and had her hair cut short she looked completely different. He read on ... *She was last seen talking to a man thought to be in his fifties, of medium height and build* ... That didn't give much away, although he was only forty-eight, he thought churlishly. *And she may have a teddy bear with her similar to this one,* the article continued.

His heart stopped. There was a picture of a bear identical to Leila's. Newer and less used, but distinctive and recognizable. Fuck! Where the hell was it? Did she have it with her now? He looked over to where she was playing, then stood for a better view. He couldn't see the bear, but he doubted she'd left it at the cottage or in the car. That bloody bear went everywhere with her and it could be their undoing. Had she brought it into the shopping centre? He couldn't remember. He looked under the table and then lifted her coat, dumped on the seat next to his. To his utter relief the bear was there.

Quickly covering it over again he glanced around, made sure no one was watching him, then checked Leila wasn't looking in his direction and carried the bear in the coat to the nearest bin. Reaching under the coat, he furtively stuffed the bear into the bin as far down as it would go. He checked that no part of it was visible above the other rubbish and then returned to his table, relieved. He should have got rid of it at the start. In fact, he should never have gone back for it in the first place. It was the one mistake he'd made, and he needed to make sure it was his last.

'I'm hungry,' Leila whinged, arriving back at the table. 'Can we have McDonald's? We passed one on the way in.'

Colin sighed. He was trying to read the rest of the news. 'We'll eat later.' The kid was always hungry and asking for food. It was an obsession with her, although she was skinny.

'We've been here ages,' she moaned.

'And you've been having a good time, so go and play some more.' He could have sat there all day drinking coffee – the place was warm and comfortable, not like the cottage.

'I'm bored,' Leila whined, still standing beside him.

He tried to ignore her. She was often bored. Without a television in the cottage, she didn't know how to amuse herself. To stop her moaning all day and bothering him, he'd taught her some simple paper-and-pen games like noughts and crosses and hangman. She'd learnt surprisingly quickly and had stopped complaining and enjoyed playing – so had he, if he was honest. They'd almost had fun. But while he'd been sitting here, he'd taken the opportunity to use the shopping centre's Wi-Fi to download some children's films. When they returned to the cottage, if she was good, she could watch those on his laptop.

'I'm hungry!' she said more loudly. A man with his partner and two children at the next table looked over.

Colin closed his laptop. 'OK. We'll go to McDonald's,' he said amicably, loud enough for them to hear.

'Yippee!' Leila cried, clapping her hands.

The man at the next table threw him a smile, empathizing with his situation. Colin doubted he would feel much empathy if he knew the truth.

He packed his laptop, phone and chargers into his briefcase and picked up their coats.

'I want a six-piece chicken McNugget Happy Meal,' Leila said, and gave a little jump of delight.

'I would like ...' Colin corrected as they walked away and the man nodded approvingly.

It was only once they were outside, crossing the car park and heading towards McDonald's, that Leila realized she didn't have her teddy bear.

'Stop!' she shouted, coming to an abrupt halt. 'I've left

Buttons in there!' She immediately turned and began running back towards the entrance.

Colin ran to catch up with her and grabbed her by the arm. 'It's not in there. I'll get you another bear.'

'He is in there. I left him on a chair,' Leila cried. 'I don't want another one! I want Buttons!' She pulled against him, struggling to free herself from his grip.

'You can't,' he hissed. 'The bear's gone, so shut up.'

'I want Buttons!' Leila cried louder.

Others passing by were looking at them now, their attention drawn by the commotion Leila was making. Then one woman with two young children stopped. 'Are you all right, love?' she asked Leila. Colin glared at her. Interfering cow.

'I want Buttons,' Leila appealed to her, tears springing to her eyes. 'And he won't take me back to get him.'

'She's lost her teddy bear,' Colin explained, still holding Leila tightly by the arm. 'I'm going to buy her another one.'

'Oh dear,' the woman sympathized. 'I know how attached they can get to their soft toys. Well, good luck.' Then to Leila: 'Dry your eyes, pet, Daddy is going to buy you a new teddy bear.'

'He's not my—' Leila began, but Colin was already pulling her away, smiling and apologizing to the woman as they went.

'This way to the toy shop,' he said loudly, drawing her across the car park towards the car.

'I don't want another bear, I want Buttons!' Leila wailed and kicked his shin.

He quickly opened the rear car door and pushed her in, then ran round and jumped into the driver's seat, pressing the central locking system so she couldn't escape.

'You stupid girl!' he cried, turning the ignition key. Thankfully it started first time.

'I want Buttons!' she screamed, trying to open the door, then hammering on the window.

'Shut up!' he cried.

'Let me out! I hate you! I want to go home. I want my mummy!'

'No, you don't!' Colin gripped the wheel and concentrated on navigating out of the busy car park. He was aware that not only those passing could see a distraught child at the car window, crying to be let out, but very likely it was being recorded on CCTV too. 'Get down in your seat!' he yelled.

'No. You can't make me! I want to go home.'

'Get down if you know what's good for you!'

TWENTY

Kelsey sat alone in her flat, staring into space. It was Sunday, twelve days since Leila had gone missing, and her thoughts were unusually clear. She hadn't taken anything all weekend. Partly because she'd run out of money again and partly because Sharon had got angry with her – really angry – and said Kelsey's brain was so messed up from alcohol and drugs that she'd been unable to help the police find Leila, suggesting it was Kelsey's fault Leila was still missing. That had hurt. Kelsey respected her sister's opinion. Sharon was smarter and cleverer than her and had led a good life. But to blame Kelsey for Leila not being found – that was unfair! She'd been doing her best to help the police, but she honestly couldn't remember any more than the little she'd already told them. That was probably because of the drink and drugs, though, so Sharon was right – again.

It had taken a lot for Kelsey to let Sharon download her contacts list from her phone and send it to the police. It was laying bare her dirty, sordid life, and it hadn't produced anything yet. She doubted it would. Her clients weren't paedophiles (as far as she knew), but men who couldn't get regular sex, or who wanted something different from what their wives or partners were prepared to give them. Usually rough, oral or anal sex. But Kelsey hadn't told Sharon that. She would have been even more disgusted with her than she was already. Sharon's world was clean, neat, regular and normal: work, paying the mortgage and going to church on Sundays. Sharon hadn't a clue about the kind of men who inhabited Kelsey's world and used slappers like her. 'Why don't you have any female contacts in your phone apart from me?' Sharon had asked. 'Surely you must have some friends?'

But Kelsey didn't have any friends, because who would want to associate with someone like her? She'd made up an excuse to Sharon that she knew her friends' numbers off by heart, although she doubted Sharon had believed her. She knew her too well.

Kelsey continued to stare, unseeing, across the room, acutely aware of how miserable and disgusting her life was compared to her sister's. Perhaps she should have let Leila live with her – Sharon had asked enough times. But Kelsey had been holding on to Leila for all she was worth. The child was her last hope; all the others had been taken away and given new families. Clearly she hadn't held on tightly enough, though, or she'd still be here.

Had Leila really run away as the police were suggesting? Kelsey wondered. It was *one* of their lines of inquiry, they'd said. The other being that someone had taken her. Kelsey didn't hold with the running-away theory; it didn't feel right. Leila was a survivor and streetwise and would have taken clothes and some money, not just Buttons – although the police were doubtful that Leila had taken the bear, and thought Kelsey had simply forgotten it was already missing, as she'd forgotten so many things. But if that was true then surely Kelsey would have some memory of Leila kicking off when she'd discovered her bear was lost? She would have made a right fuss, but try as she might, Kelsey couldn't picture that scene. She could recall plenty of other scenes when Leila had got angry and upset, but not one relating to Buttons. Also, and more worryingly, hadn't she heard Leila and a man's voice the night she'd gone missing? Although she'd be the first to admit she might have imagined that. She had been out cold for hours and often hallucinated and heard and saw strange things when she passed out from drink and drugs.

Surely someone must know where Leila was? Kelsey thought. Besides, she couldn't just sit here and do nothing. She picked up her phone and began scrolling through the text messages, trying to decide if any of her clients were capable of taking Leila. Their texts were short, sharp and to the point. They only texted when they wanted to see her, with a date and time. She never initiated conversation either by text or by phone in between visits – it wasn't what they wanted – and she only replied to confirm the arrangements. That was the extent of their contact with her outside of the actual sex.

Kelsey continued to scroll down. Her clients were in her contacts list by first name only – the name they'd given her, which may or may not be their real name, as she'd told the police. It didn't matter to her what they called themselves as long as they paid. Kelsey was nothing if not realistic and had no expectations of more, either from her clients or life in general. There would be no fairy-tale *Pretty Woman* ending for her.

Some of her clients had refused to give a name at all, so their text messages just showed their mobile number, apart from the ugly bastard who'd beaten her up, who she'd entered in her address book as PIG – a reminder to have nothing to do with him, no matter how desperate she was. Was he capable of taking Leila? He'd come back seeking revenge – only now had her bruises completely faded and her cuts healed. Could snatching Leila be part of his revenge? She didn't think so. Leila hadn't been in the flat either time he'd visited. And the second time – when he'd dragged her around the flat before beating her to a pulp – he'd seemed genuinely surprised that Kelsey had a child at all. 'So you have a child. The poor kid,' he'd said. 'Where is she now?'

Kelsey stood, wandered over to the window and looked out. Her body was still withdrawing and it made her restless. Outside, the light was fading fast as the evening drew in. The play area had cleared of children and the teenagers were grouping together. Bored and in destructive mode, they were now amusing themselves by tying the swings in knots and graffitiing the roundabout. Doris Goodman appeared at her window and banged on the glass. They looked over and ran off.

Gawping Goodman, self-appointed custodian of the play area and people's morals. She'd been so certain a man had taken Leila, even ridiculing Kelsey for not knowing who he was – 'Your latest fancy man,' she'd said. Kelsey had gone home convinced Goodman was right and that she'd forgotten she'd sent someone to collect Leila. But then it turned out that Goodman could be wrong, although she doubted she'd ever get an apology.

As Goodman's curtains closed again the lads returned to the play area. Leila had been there with others on the night she'd gone missing, yet according to the police no one had actually seen her leave. Or, more likely, someone had and they weren't saying. Kevin Bates? Was he the reason no one on the estate was willing to talk? She knew the police had already spoken to him, but without any results. It was agonizing just waiting. Perhaps she should speak to Bates and appeal to his better nature. As the thought came, so it went, for the likes of Bates didn't have a better nature. All she was likely to achieve was another beating.

TWENTY-ONE

'You'd have thought the poor child could fly, given the number of simultaneous sightings from all over the country,' Matt said dryly, leaning back in his office chair and stretching. It was 5.45 p.m. and nearing the end of another long day.

'And not a single one verifiable,' Beth said, glancing at him over the top of her computer screen.

'No,' Matt sighed. 'Not one, after all these leads.'

Since the appeal had been shown on television the investigating team had been inundated with possible sightings of Leila, but so far none of them had led anywhere. The house-to-house had given no clues either and the men on the sex offenders' register living in the area had all been seen and eliminated, having had sound alibis for the night Leila had gone missing. Alan Stevens, the client of Kelsey Beth and Matt had met on his way out of her flat, had also been interviewed and eliminated. He'd been at home with his mother, wife and children that night from five o'clock. The list of phone contacts from Kelsey's phone that Sharon had sent in had virtually been exhausted too. Most of the phones were pay-as-you-go, so there were no registered details of the owner. The few who had contract phones weren't on the

sex offenders' register, although two had served time in prison
– one for breaking and entering, and the other for grievous
bodily harm. Those who had answered their phones or
responded to the voicemail messages usually began by saying
they had no idea why Kelsey should have their phone number
and ended by pointing out that it wasn't illegal to use a
prostitute.

Tomorrow it would be two weeks since Leila Smith had
disappeared and the chances of finding her alive now were
very slim indeed. The theory that she had run away was
losing credence, because a runaway of her age would have
reappeared by now, unless someone had taken her off the
streets. In which case she could be anywhere by now and
very likely deceased. If they were honest, they were waiting
for a call to say a child's body had been found, rather than
a plausible sighting of her alive.

'We could interview Mrs Goodman and Kelsey again, to
see if they remember anything new,' Beth suggested, also
leaning back in her chair and flexing her shoulders.

Matt grunted a half-hearted agreement. 'If you like.'

The general office phone rang and DC Tom Hilt, whose
desk was directly behind Beth's, answered it. He listened and
Beth heard him say, 'OK, someone will come down.' Replacing
the handset, he announced to the office, 'Another helpful
member of the public in reception with information about
the disappearance of Leila. Whose turn is it?'

A collective sigh went up. Since the appeal had been aired,
not only had members of the public been phoning and filling
in the web form with information, but they'd been arriving
at the police station too. So far none had anything useful to
add to the inquiry and some were just plain silly or time
wasters. One elderly gentleman, Mr Ley, stopped by most
days on his way to the grocery store and claimed Leila was
much older now, married with kids, and living in the same

street as him. He said he was getting her shopping. They'd notified adult social care, but it hadn't stopped him coming in.

'It isn't our Mr Ley, is it?' Matt asked.

'Not this time,' Tom said. 'It's a Mrs Kelly. Don't all rush at once.'

'I'll go. I need to stretch my legs,' Beth said, standing. A small cheer went up. She smiled as she made her way out of the office. You needed some lighter moments even in an inquiry as worrying as a missing child. As Beth entered the reception she was surprised to see Mike Doherty and his mother. She hadn't made the connection when Tom had said Mrs Kelly. Mike's mother had changed her surname when she'd remarried. The last time she'd seen her was when Mike had been discharged into her care after he and Jason had been found to be in possession of class-A drugs on the Hawthorn Estate. She was looking very worried, Beth thought, but what could she contribute to the Leila Smith inquiry?

'Hello, Mrs Kelly, Mike,' Beth said, going over to them. 'I believe you've asked to speak to someone in connection with the disappearance of Leila Smith?'

'He needs to,' Mrs Kelly said, standing and nodding at her son.

Mike was staring at the floor and couldn't meet Beth's gaze. Gone was his usual bravado and in its place was a look Beth recognized as guilt. Beth braced herself for what she was about to hear. They already knew Leila had been seen hanging around Mike, Jason and other older lads, although Mike had denied seeing her the night she went missing. Now Beth was sure he was going to say he, and possibly other lads, had sexually assaulted Leila and accidentally killed her. He wouldn't be the first young person to take advantage of a vulnerable child and then panic.

'Go on,' his mother said. 'Tell her what you told me.'

Mike shifted uncomfortably in his chair and still couldn't meet Beth's gaze. 'Would you like to go somewhere private to talk?' Beth offered. 'I'll see if there's a room free.'

'No, he can tell you here,' his mother said. 'Come on, get a move on. I've got to get to work.'

Beth looked at Mike again.

'Promise you won't say it was me who told you,' he began.

'It depends on what you tell me,' Beth said gently. 'But if I can withhold your identity, I will.'

Mike shifted again. 'You need to stop harassing Kev,' he blurted.

'Kevin Bates?' Beth asked.

Mike nodded.

'I wouldn't call two visits harassment, but what's that got to do with you?'

'It wasn't him who took Leila. He had a go at Kelsey, but he didn't take her kid.'

'Do you know who did?' Beth asked.

'The bloke who lives in the flat below Kelsey. Colin, I think his name is. I don't know his surname.'

'How do you know that?' Beth asked, surprised.

'I saw Leila leave with him. So did Jason. It wasn't the first time. He bought the kid presents and sort of looked out for her. Sometimes she went to his flat if it was raining.'

Beth continued to stare at Mike, trying to gauge if he was telling the truth.

'Can you give me a description of Colin?'

Mike stared at her blankly.

'What does he look like?'

He shrugged. 'Ordinary. Middle-aged, I guess. Shortish and going bald.'

'And you actually saw Leila leave with him?'

'Yes.'

'What time was that?' Beth asked.

'Around six.'

'So why didn't you tell me this before, when Matt and I asked you?'

'You'd just arrested us for possession. We weren't going to help you. We never help the police.'

His mother gave a heart-felt sigh. 'Sorry. I do my best with him.'

Beth continued to study Mike. 'Does Kevin Bates know you're here?' she asked.

'Maybe.' He shrugged.

'Did he tell you to come?'

'Yes, but it's still the truth, honest. It wasn't Kev Bates who took Leila but that bloke Colin. She went with him, and Kev's dad is threatening to kick him out if you lot turn up again.'

'So Kevin sent you here?' Beth asked.

He nodded.

Mrs Kelly immediately saw the implications. 'You stupid boy!' she cried and clipped him over the head. 'You've dragged me all the way here to try to save that thug Bates! He's nothing but trouble! Wait till I tell your stepfather.'

'But it's true,' Mike protested. 'Kev didn't take her. Colin did.'

Angered by her son's dishonesty, Mrs Kelly stood, ready to leave.

'We'll look into what you've said,' Beth told him.

'I wouldn't bother. Sorry to have wasted your time,' Mrs Kelly said angrily. Marching to the door, she jabbed the button to release it and let them out.

Beth watched them go, then began up the stairs to her office. It was true, the police had been leaning on Kevin Bates and had paid him a number of visits lately, not only in connection with the disappearance of Leila, but breaking and entering and other recently reported offences they had reason to believe he may have been involved in. Kevin Bates was a nasty piece of work – a thug, as Mrs Kelly had said. Older than Mike and Jason, he controlled them and other kids on the estate, largely through fear. Had he killed Leila and then got Mike to lie for him by making up this story about Colin? It was certainly possible. Yet what Mike had said about Colin giving Leila presents and taking her home if it was raining had a worrying ring of familiarity about it, which left Beth feeling very uneasy. If true, it was the classic behaviour of a paedophile who'd been grooming Leila for some time.

Everyone in the office was working hard, looking at screens or going through paperwork, trying to cram in as much as possible before they went home. Beth returned to her desk.

'Well?' Matt asked, peering at her over his screen.

'It was Mike Doherty with his mother,' she replied, concentrating on the information she was reading. 'Kevin Bates sent him to tell us to get off his back because his dad is threatening to throw him out. He says Bates didn't have anything to do with Leila's disappearance and that a man called Colin who lives in the flat below Kelsey took her.' Beth paused as she moved the cursor over the page she was reading. 'I'm checking now. Colin Weaver lives in flat three-seventeen, directly below Kelsey. No previous convictions. Squeaky clean. Uniform were able to speak to him when they conducted the door-to-door and there were no concerns. A regular bloke who lives alone, out all day at work. Doesn't really know anyone in the flats and didn't see anything on the night Leila went missing.'

'And if Colin was the man in the play area and he took Leila,' Matt said, 'then surely Doris Goodman would have recognized him? Even if she didn't know him to talk to, she would have known him from sight. She knows virtually everyone on the estate and his flat is directly opposite hers.'

117

'Precisely,' Beth said. 'This will be Kevin Bates trying to get rid of us, and not very imaginatively. I think I'll pay Bates a visit on my way home and I can look in on Colin Weaver at the same time. Then we can eliminate him from our inquiries.'

'I'll come with you,' Matt said. 'I'm done here for today and you don't want to be visiting the Bates clan alone after dark.'

Beth smiled. 'That's very chivalrous of you, Matt, thank you.'

Twenty minutes later, Matt and Beth stood at the Bates's battered front door, waiting for it to be answered. A dog they knew to be a pit bull terrier barked from inside, but as yet no one had appeared. The Bates family were notorious on the estate, individually and collectively. They had the dubious reputation of having clocked up more convictions than any other family in Coleshaw. There were four siblings – three lads and a girl, all adults now. Three lived at home at present and the eldest was serving ten years for grievous bodily harm. Mr Bates boasted he'd given a whole new meaning to the term 'absent father' by being in prison for most of the time his children had been growing up. His partner had cleared off when the youngest of the children was six and they were old enough – as she saw it – to look after themselves. Various 'aunts' had moved in while Bates Senior served time, but he'd continued to rule from prison through smuggled-in phones. On his release, his idea of taking his kids on an outing was to pile into a stolen car and rob a corner shop. Kevin Bates and his siblings had never stood a chance. But was he capable of harming Leila? Undoubtedly, Beth thought.

Another blast on the doorbell and it was finally opened by Bates Senior dressed in vest and shorts as though he'd just got up.

'Late night?' Matt asked.

'None of your bleeding business.' He scratched his stubbled chin and then adjusted himself through his shorts, while leering at Beth. With a crookedly set broken nose, deep eye bags, an ugly scar running across his left cheek and a belly overhanging his shorts, he looked hard and haggard – a good fifteen years older than his forty-five years.

'Is Kevin in?' Beth asked, ignoring his leering gaze. 'We'd like to talk to him.'

'So would I. Haven't seen him for ages. What do you want him for?'

'To ask him some more questions in connection with the disappearance of Leila Smith,' Matt said.

'He's already told you lot he had nothing to do with it. He might be bad, but he's not into kiddies.'

'Do you know where we can find him?' Beth asked.

'No.'

'When he does return, tell him we would like to speak to him at the station,' Matt said. 'We'll give him twenty-four hours and then come back here with a search warrant.'

'Tell him your fucking selves,' Bates Senior said, and slammed the door.

Matt drove around the perimeter road to the block of flats where Kelsey and Colin lived.

'I wonder if Kelsey knows Colin Weaver,' Beth said, glancing up at Colin's flat window as Matt parked. 'She hasn't mentioned him.'

'Perhaps he was one of the clients in her contacts list we haven't been able to identify,' Matt suggested.

'It's possible.'

They took the stairs up to the third floor to flat 317. Matt rang Colin Weaver's doorbell. There was no answer. Beth glanced at her watch. 'Nearly seven o'clock. Perhaps he's not home from work yet. Let's go and see Kelsey and then call here again on our way out. If he's still not in, we can ask the neighbours what time he usually gets back.'

Kelsey answered her door straight away. The bruises and cuts had gone but the lines on her forehead were even deeper now from all the worry. 'Have you found her?' she asked as soon as she saw them.

'Not yet,' Beth said gently. 'But we need to talk to you.'

They followed Kelsey into the living room.

'You've had a tidy up,' Matt said, unable to hide his astonishment. The room was far neater and cleaner than he'd ever seen it before.

'I have to keep busy,' Kelsey said, wringing her hands. 'It stops me from thinking about Leila, and I'm trying to keep off the drink and drugs.'

'Well done,' Beth said, genuinely impressed, although Kelsey was clearly suffering from the effects of withdrawal. She couldn't keep still and kept twitching and scratching her arms. 'You know you can get help from a doctor?' Beth asked.

'Yeah, I know.' She smiled ruefully. 'I've got this far before.'

Beth knew that Kelsey had tried to get off the drugs and drink many times before, but it had never lasted, and one by one her children had been taken into care.

Matt positioned himself by the window as Beth sat next to Kelsey on the sofa, unusually not having to move rubbish to do so.

'Sharon's not staying with you then?' Beth asked.

'No. I can't be around her for too long. She's a bit self-righteous for my liking, and being with her reminds me of how I should be.'

Beth smiled sympathetically. 'Are you still sure you don't want a liaison officer?' Kelsey shook her head. 'All right, the offer is there if you change your mind. The reason we're here is to ask you about the man who lives in the flat immediately below you. Three-one-seven, Colin Weaver. Forty-eight, average height and build, balding. Do you and Leila know him?'

Kelsey looked thoughtful for a moment and then slowly shook her head. 'I know who you mean. I've seen him around, but I don't know him. Should I?'

'A witness said Colin used to talk to Leila in the play area and bought her presents. Did she ever mention a man buying her gifts or going to his flat?'

'No, but then I doubt she would.' Kelsey's eyes glistened with regret. 'To be honest, Leila and me hardly ever saw each other, and if she did tell me I probably wasn't listening. You don't think he has her, do you?'

'It's just another lead we're following up. We've had hundreds of them, Kelsey, and it will probably lead to nothing,' Beth said.

'Was it Doris Goodman who told you?'

'No. We're going to try to see Colin now, but we wanted to check with you first. Has he ever been a client of yours?'

'No. Never, I'm sure. Although there's some around here who are.'

'Can you give us their names, please?'

'Some of them were in the phone contacts list Sharon sent to you, and I'll need time to remember the others.'

'OK. Let us know when you do, please. It could be important.'

'Kelsey, you can see the play area from here,' Matt said, looking out of the window. 'Have you ever seen a man hanging around down there?'

'No, but when Leila was out amusing herself I was usually occupied in the other room, if you know what I mean.'

Matt nodded.

'OK, thank you,' Beth said. 'That's all for now. We'll keep you informed of any new developments. And please let us have those other contacts as soon as you remember.'

'I will.'

Beth stood to go and Matt moved away from the window.

'Do you think she's still alive?' Kelsey asked Beth anxiously.

'Until there is any evidence to the contrary, Leila is a missing person,' Beth said tactfully. 'We're doing all we can to find her.'

'Thank you.'

Kelsey went with them to the front door. 'Peter, our social worker, was here today,' she said as Matt opened the door. 'He's taken out a court order, so when Leila is found she'll go straight into care.'

'That was sensitive of him,' Matt said sarcastically. 'You didn't need to hear that right now.'

'Well, it's his job, I guess,' Kelsey said with a resigned shrug. 'If parents can't look after their kids then social services has to.'

'I do feel sorry for her,' Beth sighed as she and Matt made their way down to the floor below. 'She's trying to get clean, but what has she got left to aim for?'

'Strange that her sister appears to be so different,' Matt said.

'There is a back story, but I don't know the details.'

They arrived outside 317, Colin Weaver's flat, and Matt pressed the bell, then knocked on the door. They waited, but there was still no reply or any sound coming from inside to suggest someone was in.

'It's seven-thirty,' Beth said, glancing at her watch. 'Let's speak to his immediate neighbours and then call it a day. You try the neighbour that side and I'll take this.'

Matt knocked on the door of flat 315 and it was immediately opened by a teenage boy on his way out. 'Detective

Constable Matt Davis,' he said, showing his ID. 'Do you know the guy who lives next door at three-one-seven?'

'No. My mum might, but she's not back until ten.'

'And there's no one else in your flat who might be able to help?'

'No. Just me and Mum.'

'OK, thanks.'

The lad jogged off as Matt joined Beth outside flat 319. On the second ring, a woman opened the door.

'Sorry to trouble you. I'm Detective Constable Beth Mayes,' she said, flashing her ID. 'This is my colleague Matt Davis. 'Do you know the man who lives in the flat next door – Mr Colin Weaver?'

'A little. Why?'

'He hasn't done anything wrong,' Beth said quickly. 'But we'd like to talk to him. What time does he usually get back from work?'

'Around five-thirty, but he hasn't been in the flat for some time. At least, I haven't seen or heard him. Perhaps he's away on holiday.'

'When was the last time he was home, do you know?' Beth asked.

The woman paused to think. 'It must be over a week now. He's a bit of loner and I only really see him to say hello on our way in and out.'

'I don't suppose you know where he works?' Beth tried.

'Yes, as a matter of fact, I do. It's the same firm where my brother works. Sparks Electronics in Coleshaw – he's a clerk in the office.'

'Thank you, that's most helpful.'

TWENTY-TWO

'There's a Mr Kevin Bates in reception, asking for you or Matt,' the desk duty officer said as Beth answered the phone. 'It's in connection with Leila Smith.'

'Really?' Beth's pulse immediately stepped up a few beats. 'Thank you, I'll be right down.'

Beth stood. Slipping on her jacket, she crossed the office, then hurried down the stairs. Matt was out following up a new lead, but they'd both fully expected to have to issue an arrest warrant before they saw Kevin Bates again. Yet here he was, and it was only 10 a.m. Far too early for any of the Bates family to be out unless it was crucial to their well-being and advanced their own interests. That Kevin was here at all, and the morning after they'd spoken to Mr Bates Senior, suggested it could be highly significant and possibly the breakthrough they'd been waiting for. Was it possible that Kevin, pressurized by his father, had come here with valuable information about the disappearance of Leila Smith? Or even to confess?

Beth keyed in the code to release the security door that led into reception. Straight away she saw Kevin Bates slouched in a chair in the waiting area, legs spread wide open. He saw her and stood – not out of any respect, but so he could tower over her and have the advantage.

'Good morning, Kevin,' Beth said, unfazed. 'Thank you for coming in so promptly.' In the police station, surrounded by CCTV, she didn't feel threatened, regardless of how much he glared menacingly at her.

'What do you want with me?' he snarled, his scarred face a younger version of his father's. 'You're harassing me and my family. We're all pissed off with you. I didn't have anything to do with that kid going missing, so get off my back or else.'

'Or else what?' Beth held his gaze as the duty officer looked over from the counter, checking everything was OK. 'It wasn't our intention to make you feel harassed,' Beth continued evenly. 'You were one of the last people to see Leila before she vanished. I have a witness who says you assaulted Kelsey and made suggestive sexual remarks about her daughter.'

She saw his jaw clench, causing a vein to stand out in his neck as he fought to keep control. 'Kelsey had a go at me first. She deserved it! But I haven't touched her kid. She keeps away from me.'

'Sensible child,' Beth said. 'But you were there on the evening Leila disappeared.'

'I might have been.'

'You were. Come on, Kevin, I'm very busy. Tell me what you came to say or go home and we can do this there.'

The vein in his neck pulsed. 'I saw the kid leave with a bloke, Colin. He lives in the same block as Kelsey.'

'You actually saw them leave together?'

'Yes. Ask Mike and Jason if you don't believe me. I had nothing to do with the kid going missing.'

'I have spoken to Mike and I'm struggling to believe what you're telling me. Mr Weaver has no previous convictions.

And if what you're saying is true, why didn't you tell me before?'

'Like I'm going to help you lot unless I have to. But this has got serious.'

'A missing child is always serious, Kevin.' Beth looked at him carefully. 'What I think happened is that you – or possibly all three of you – were responsible for Leila disappearing and have concocted this story about Colin. I think maybe you panicked and didn't intend to kill her.'

'Bullshit!' he spat angrily. The duty officer looked over again. 'Think what you like, but it wasn't me. You don't have a shred of evidence, so keep away from me and my family if you know what's good for you.'

'I hope that wasn't a threat,' Beth said in the same calm manner. His face tightened as he struggled to keep control. 'Was that all you wanted to tell me?' she asked. She could see from his expression that it was.

'You'll be sorry,' he said and turned to let himself out. The door swung shut behind him.

That was a strange meeting, Beth thought, as she went up to the office. Kevin Bates had bothered to come in, and early, but had nothing new to add. She supposed Mr Bates Senior had put pressure on him so they wouldn't return with a search warrant. But it was a wonder Kevin hadn't thought up a better alibi for the night Leila went missing, one that relied on more credible witnesses than Mike Doherty and Jason O'Leary. Unless of course they were telling the truth and Colin Weaver had taken Leila.

Beth picked up the desk phone and drew her notepad towards her, where she'd written the number for Sparks Electronics. She'd been about to phone the company when the duty officer had called to say Kevin Bates was in reception. Sparks Electronics was a well-established firm on the industrial estate, manufacturing electrical items and employing approximately forty staff. Beth listened to the recorded message telling her the number to press for each department – one for sales, two for billing and so forth. She pressed five for general enquiries.

'I'd like to speak to the head of Human Resources,' she said. 'It's Detective Constable Beth Mayes calling from Coleshaw Police Station.'

'That will be Mrs Conway. Can I tell her what it's in connection with?'

'A member of your staff,' Beth said. 'Sorry, it's confidential.'

'I'll put you through.'

Beth listened to a few seconds of hold music – 'The Blue Danube' – then a clipped but slightly hesitant voice said, 'Abby Conway speaking.'

'DC Beth Mayes, Coleshaw Police Station. I believe Colin Weaver is an employee of yours?'

'Was. He left without any notice nearly two weeks ago.'

'Really?' Beth picked up her pen.

'He was in one day and didn't show the next. We tried phoning and emailing him, and we were going to call the police when we received his letter of resignation in the post.'

'I see.'

'Why? Is there something wrong?' Abby Conway asked.

'I'm not sure. When was the last time Mr Weaver was at work?'

'Fourteenth of November. He didn't show on the fifteenth and his letter of resignation arrived a few days later.'

'Did his letter give a reason for him leaving?' Beth asked, making a note.

'No. It was very short and formal. It just said, "Please accept this as my resignation."'

'I don't suppose you know where he is now?'

'I don't know where he's working now. We haven't received a request for a reference. Do you want his home address?'

'I have it, thank you. It seems he hasn't been at home for a while.'

'Oh dear. I hope he's all right. He was a good worker, but he kept himself very much to himself. He'd didn't socialize with his colleagues outside of work, but even so, it was a shock when he suddenly left.'

'How long had he been working for your company?'

'Seventeen years. Hardly missed a day. It was completely out of character, him leaving so abruptly. I replied to his home address accepting his notice and wishing him well for the future.'

'I don't suppose you noticed the postmark on the envelope his letter came in?'

'No, sorry, I didn't. The letter is on file, though. Would you like a copy?'

'Yes, please.'

Beth thanked Abby Conway for her time and replaced the handset. She studied the notes she'd made, deep in thought, then swivelled her chair round to see who was in the office. She needed permission – someone of a more senior rank – to authorize a search warrant, but Detective Sergeant Bert Scrivener wasn't around. Grabbing her jacket, Beth crossed the office and went up a floor in search of DCI Aileen Peters. The door to her office was open but Beth knocked anyway.

'Come in. Good morning, Beth.'

'Good morning, ma'am. I now have three witnesses – Mike Doherty, Jason O'Leary and Kevin Bates – who say they saw Leila Smith leave with a man we've identified as Colin Weaver on the night she went missing.' The DCI rolled her eyes. 'I know,' Beth said. 'They're not the most reliable of witnesses, but Matt and I called at Colin Weaver's flat yesterday evening and couldn't get a reply. A neighbour said she hadn't seen him for over a week. I've just spoken to HR at Sparks Electronics where Colin worked for seventeen years and he suddenly left without any notice, two days after Leila went missing. Then a formal letter of resignation arrived a couple of days later, not giving any explanation. The head of HR said it was completely out of character. I'd like permission to enter his flat.'

It only took DCI Aileen Peters a moment to agree. 'That would seem a sensible next step. Take someone with you with an enforcer in case you need to break in.'

'Thank you, ma'am.'

Half an hour later Beth parked outside the block of flats where Colin and Kelsey lived, and waited for the patrol car to arrive. They were bringing the enforcer to open Colin's front door if necessary. Beth wasn't sure what she was expecting to find inside the flat. The worst-case scenario – the one she was dreading – would be to find Leila's dead body, which was certainly possible. Colin's sudden disappearance from work and home seemed to bear all the hallmarks of suicide. Yet Doris Goodman hadn't identified the man she'd seen as Colin and indeed was now unclear if Leila had left the play area with a man at all. And as DCI Peters had indicated, you couldn't get more unreliable and dubious witnesses than Bates, O'Leary and Doherty, so there was still a good chance they had concocted the story about Leila going off with Colin to cover their own backs.

As Beth continued to stare through the windscreen, she saw the patrol car sweep into the road. With an acknowledging flash of its headlights, the car drew up and parked just in front of her. She got out and said hello to the officer who'd been driving – Ishaan Patel, who she knew. He introduced Lisa, the trainee he had with him, then took the enforcer from the boot.

'Are we expecting to find a body?' Lisa asked Beth.

'It's possible.'

'It would be my first.'

Beth nodded sympathetically and prayed it wasn't Leila Smith's. It was upsetting enough when you discovered your first decomposing corpse, without the added trauma of it being a child.

Beth led the way into the block of flats, up the stairs to the third floor and to Colin Weaver's flat. She pressed the bell and banged on the door. 'Colin. Are you in there? It's the police.'

There was no reply.

She stood aside and Ishaan raised the metal enforcer and aimed it at the door. It burst open on the second strike. 'Colin? Are you in here?' he called, going in first.

Silence. But thankfully, Beth noted, there was no putrid smell of decomposing flesh. It would have hit them the moment the door opened if there'd been a body in here. The flat was cold and smelt musty from being shut up, but that was all.

Beth made a preliminary search of the flat, going in and out of the rooms with Lisa following just behind, as Ishaan returned the enforcer to the car. Two bedrooms, a bathroom and a lounge with a small kitchen leading off it. It was the same layout as many of the other flats here, although Colin Weaver's was much neater than most Beth had seen. Sparsely furnished with dated furniture, it was functional rather than homely, and didn't contain the usual clutter of everyday living. It was a single person's flat, and bland with all the walls painted off-white. There was no sign of a woman's presence or of a child having been here. A grey two-seater sofa stood at one end of the living room with a reading lamp on a stalk angled over it. A large framed mock-antique world map was on one wall, with a bookcase below it. To the right stood a modest television and sound system. Beth's gaze travelled to the small wooden coffee table next to the sofa. Going over, she picked up the sheet of folded paper that lay on top and opened it. Her eyes skimmed the handwritten lines and then she read the words out loud.

To whom it may concern,

By the time you find this I will be long gone. I've had enough of my life. Please inform Belsize Nursing Home. My mother is a patient there. She won't understand I'm dead, but the staff need to know.

Colin Weaver

'That's so sad,' Lisa said.

'Yes, it is,' Beth agreed. But not as sad as finding the body of a child, she thought.

Ishaan returned briefly to say he and Lisa were needed elsewhere. 'Are you OK here now?'

'Yes. Thanks for your help,' Beth replied. She was in the kitchen now, checking the cupboards. 'Good luck in your job, Lisa.'

'Thank you.'

Beth heard them close the broken front door behind them. She would need to phone the locksmith to get the flat secured before she left. Lisa had clearly been relieved not to find a dead body in here, as had Beth, but Colin's suicide note had effectively brought an end to one of their main lines of inquiry. On the face of it, the reason he'd disappeared was because he'd gone somewhere and committed suicide. There was no evidence to suggest that any contact he may have had with Leila was anything other than altruistic – giving a neglected child gifts and shelter in the rain. If, of course, he'd been in the play area at all, which was still not certain.

Except, Beth thought.

She returned to the living room and reread the note. It was a coincidence that Colin had decided to commit suicide around the same time Leila had gone missing. Was it possible he *had* taken her, abused and killed her, and then committed suicide? In which case his flat would be a crime scene with valuable DNA evidence. Returning the note to the table, Beth took out her phone and called DCI Aileen Peters.

TWENTY-THREE

'I want Buttons,' Leila said, rubbing her eyes as if she were about to cry again.

'I know, you said!' Colin snapped, irritated. 'But it's gone, for good, so amuse yourself. You're getting on my nerves again.'

He was trying to do a crossword in the book of puzzles he'd brought with him, but it was proving virtually impossible to concentrate with the child whinging and whining.

'I want to watch another film, but there's no battery left,' Leila grumbled.

'And whose fault is that?' Colin asked, glancing up, annoyed.

She pouted.

'If you watch films all day, of course the battery on my laptop will run down quickly. You need to ration yourself.'

'What does ration mean?'

'Limit the time you use it, like I do with my phone.' Although in truth he didn't have much choice but to limit his phone usage as there was no bloody signal anywhere in the cottage. It was a mile or so up the lane before any signal reached his phone.

He returned to his crossword and there was a few moments' silence before Leila said again in that infuriating voice, 'I want Buttons. I want to go home.'

'Impossible,' he snapped. 'Your mother doesn't want you and I can understand why.'

He tried to ignore her, but it was difficult, and the longer it went on the more it grated. They'd been here two weeks now and it would be at least another two weeks before the fervour surrounding Leila's disappearance had died down enough to make it safe for them to leave. Only then would he be able to start his new life. He felt like a prisoner in a cell, notching up the days till his release, or a castaway on a desert island. It was Wednesday, and he didn't want to return to the shopping centre until Saturday when it would be busy. There'd been another appeal in the media with a picture of Leila and her teddy bear, so he was even more wary now of taking her out. The other towns were further away and much smaller. They were more likely to stand out there and be noticed. Even though her hair was short now and she didn't have the bear, he dared not risk it. Also, there might not be a convenient place to recharge his laptop and phone. Better to wait and go to the shopping centre on Saturday when he knew for certain it would be full of families.

He glanced at his watch. One o'clock. He had the rest of today and then all of Thursday and Friday before they could have another outing. Nearly three days with the kid bleating, going on and on. He wasn't sure he could stand it. He was used to peace and quiet and his own space at home. Then he had an idea.

'You used to spend a lot of time alone in your flat when your mother was out, didn't you?' he asked her.

Leila nodded.

'If I leave you here and go to the shopping centre to

134

recharge the laptop so you can watch more films, will you promise to be good?'

'I promise,' she said enthusiastically. 'Will you try to find Buttons?'

'Yes.' Although of course he wouldn't. The bin in the shopping centre where he'd dumped the bear would have been emptied ages ago and the rubbish incinerated. 'Remember, you mustn't stand near the windows,' he said, setting aside his puzzle book. 'If anyone should come to the door, which is highly unlikely, you hide and stay quiet.' In the two weeks they'd been here they hadn't had any callers, although a couple of intrepid hikers had passed along the lane.

'Will you bring me back some sweets and a McDonald's?' Leila asked.

'Yes, if you promise to be good and do as you're told.'

'I will.'

He managed a small smile, more for his own benefit than hers, pleased with himself for having hit upon this idea. He stood and, spurred on by the promise of time alone and a decent cup of coffee, began gathering together what he needed to take with him. Laptop, phone, chargers, wallet, keys, shopping list – they needed more groceries. He put on his coat and shoes as Leila watched him. He felt he might be getting the hang of this parenting lark – you bribed the child into doing what you wanted with the promise of sweets, films and McDonald's. It was a lesson to be remembered for the future, he thought.

With a final warning to Leila not to touch anything and to stay out of sight, Colin left the cottage, locking the door behind him. It was as dingy outside the cottage as it was inside. Here, on the edge of the moors, one murky day seemed to follow another, and at this time of year the sky never got properly light. They were going through batteries to power the lamp very quickly, so they were on his shopping list.

As he thought might happen, his car didn't like the damp weather either and the engine took a while to start before finally spluttering into life. Then he was off, bumping along Fern Lane, which eventually joined the main road that would take him into Marsborough.

Try to concentrate on the positives, Colin told himself as he drove. A whole afternoon all to himself. It was a wonder he hadn't thought of leaving her alone sooner. She was used to it at her mother's and would probably enjoy the time away from him as much as he was going to enjoy being away from her. He could tell she didn't like him anymore, but that didn't matter. Now he'd had to look after her, he'd changed his views on parenting and believed children should be seen and not heard – and ideally not even seen. The Victorians had the right idea. Nanny raised the children and just brought them to their parents to say goodnight. If this afternoon was a success – and there was no reason why it shouldn't – he'd go to the shopping centre alone tomorrow and every afternoon until they could leave that awful cottage for good.

An hour later, having bought the provisions they needed and sweets for Leila, Colin sat at a table in the shopping centre with a coffee and slice of sponge cake, checking his emails as his laptop and phone charged. There was nothing of interest or concern in his inbox. Apart from a reminder about a standing order, the rest was junk mail, which rather proved to him how drab and unimportant his life had been. Until now. He still couldn't believe how easily the plan to change his life forever had fallen into place. The future beckoned and life would be good.

Having dealt with his inbox, Colin clicked the icon to access the Internet and began looking for any further updates on missing Leila Smith. He was pleased to find the media interest was finally waning. Since the last missing person's appeal, the only new mention he could find was very short. *Police are growing increasingly concerned for missing schoolgirl Leila Smith, who disappeared ... etc. If anyone has any information, phone the number below or contact your local police station.* Clearly the active search was being scaled down and he assumed that at some point it would stop.

Suddenly he was aware of someone standing at his shoulder – far too close for comfort. He instinctively turned and looked up, straight into the face of a woman, not passing by but waiting to speak to him.

'Yes?' he asked cautiously, closing the lid on his laptop. She seemed slightly familiar. 'Can I help you?'

'Sorry to trouble you but I've been sitting over there watching you. I've just realized who you are.' Panic gripped him and his instinct was to run. Stay calm, he told himself, and his stomach clenched. 'Did your little girl find her teddy bear?' she asked.

Colin stared at her. A buzzing sound filled his ears as he struggled to make sense of what she was saying.

'You probably don't remember me, but a while back I spoke to you as you were leaving the shopping centre with your daughter. She was very upset because she'd lost her teddy bear. I wondered if she'd found it.'

'Oh,' Colin said, finally understanding. 'That was you. Yes, of course.'

'Did she find her bear?'

'She did,' he replied, trying to keep his voice even and silence his racing heart.

'Good, I am pleased.' The woman smiled. 'I remember she was so upset.'

'Yes, she was,' Colin said. But the woman didn't immediately move away and seemed to want to talk.

'Nice here, isn't it?' she said. 'Especially with the Christmas decorations. I come here two or three times a week with my children and meet other mums and dads with pre-school children.'

Colin nodded stiffly.

'OK, sorry to have disturbed you,' she said, finally realizing he didn't want to talk. 'I'll leave you in peace now. I am pleased she found her bear.'

'Thank you,' Colin managed to say.

The woman turned and walked away. He waited a few seconds and then tentatively glanced in the direction she'd gone. She was sitting with two other women at a table not far away, facing him. All three were looking at him and talking. He'd have to leave. The battery on his laptop was only half charged but he dared not stay now. There was a chance she'd seen one of the appeals on television. Supposing she eventually made the connection or one of her friends did?

Trying to calm himself, Colin unplugged the chargers and dropped them, his laptop and phone into his briefcase, forcing himself not to appear too hurried. He stood, slipped on his coat and then, keeping his gaze away from the table where the women were, made his way out of the café area the long way round, so he didn't have to pass their table.

Bloody nosy cow, he silently fumed as he headed towards the exit. He'd have to find somewhere else to go now. She said she came here two or three times a week, so he'd be sure to bump into her again. And just when it was working out so well! But he consoled himself that at least this had happened when he'd been alone. If Leila had been with him, she could have so easily given them away.

It was now three o'clock as he left the shopping centre and made his way to the car. Since he'd been inside, the mist had thickened into fog. He wasn't going to drive around in this trying to find another coffee shop with charging points and

138

Wi-Fi. He'd come back tomorrow, when hopefully the weather had improved and he could see more than a few yards.

Getting into his car, he turned the ignition key and on the second go the engine spluttered into life. He pulled away, aware that not even the CCTV cameras could pick up detail in this fog. As he drove, he found the lights of the town helped with visibility for the first mile or so. But as soon as he left the town and the streetlamps, houses and shops became fewer, it was increasingly difficult to see the road ahead. For a while he was able to follow the red tail lights of the car in front, but five miles on, as the road began winding its way across the moor, the fog thickened further still and then the car in front turned off.

Visibility was now down to nil. Alone on an unfamiliar road and surrounded by a wall of fog, Colin slowed down to twenty miles per hour, then fifteen, but even that seemed too fast when he couldn't see a damn thing. He was driving blind and it was frightening. For the first time in his life Colin wished he had a sat nav. He'd always been a map and sense-of-direction type of person, but now he'd have happily accepted a sat nav. He didn't know where the hell he was or how far he had to go.

He glanced at the mileage and guessed he had about six miles before he needed to turn into Fern Lane, but it really was a guess. The fog continued, blanketing the road and fields either side of him, then suddenly a car's headlights appeared coming towards him. He dropped down to second gear and they crawled past each other. He saw the outline of the driver in the other car, and then he was alone again. He tried the car's headlights on full beam, but the light reflected back off the fog, decreasing rather than increasing visibility. Hunched forward over the steering wheel, Colin peered through the windscreen, hoping something would seem familiar before long.

Twenty minutes later, he knew he must have missed the turning to Fern Lane. Angry with himself, he drew to a halt, checked there were no other headlights coming in either direction and then began a three-point turn. It was a nightmare, not being able to see and trying to turn the car in a narrow lane, but then he was heading back in the direction he'd come.

He flicked on the windscreen wipers to try to clear the screen, but they made little difference. He was now travelling at ten miles per hour. If he'd known the fog was going to be this bad, he would have booked into a bed and breakfast in Marsborough for the night. His heart leapt at the thought of a hot shower and a comfortable bed in a warm room instead of sleeping on the sofa in a damp cottage. Leila was locked in the cottage and would have been fine spending the night alone. She'd done it plenty of times when she'd lived with her mother.

Abruptly, out of nowhere, the small sign for Fern Lane appeared. Colin sighed with relief. Turning left, he began bumping along the unmade single-track lane. Visibility had been bad on the road, but now it was even worse. With no road markings, the lane was indistinguishable from the fields and heathland either side. He could so easily end up in a ditch where he might be trapped in his car, undiscovered for days, even weeks. He shuddered at the thought. The two miles to the cottage seemed endless and nothing was familiar in this fog – he almost drove past it. Set back from the track, the stone cottage had blended into the fog and only the vaguest outline was visible, an eerie darker shade of mist. He pulled onto the hard standing at the front and cut the engine. Thank goodness.

The cottage was in darkness, as it should be. The battery-powered lamp didn't show through the curtains at the front. He'd checked. Collecting the carrier bag containing

140

the groceries and his briefcase from the passenger seat, Colin climbed out. It was only then he remembered that he was supposed to have bought Leila a McDonald's. Too bad. He'd had other things on his mind and had had to leave quickly because of that woman and her friends. He'd remembered the sweets, so Leila should be grateful, although he doubted she would be. Grateful wasn't a term she was familiar with.

Colin took the key from his trouser pocket and unlocked the front door. It was very quiet inside, not a sound, and also still dark.

'Leila?'

The battery-powered lamp was hanging on its hook by the door, where it was left when not in use. Why wasn't the child using it? She knew how to switch it on. Leaving his carrier bag and briefcase in the lobby, Colin unhooked the lamp and turned it on. 'Leila!' he called as the dim light fell across the living room. The room was empty.

'Leila! Where are you?'

Holding the lamp high, he crossed the living room and went into the kitchen. She wasn't in there either. He checked her bedroom and the bathroom – the only rooms where she could be.

'Leila! Where the hell are you, child?'

There was no reply.

He stood in the living room and looked around, unable to make sense of what he was seeing and half expecting Leila to appear. She couldn't have just vanished, and the front door had been locked. Then he moved swiftly to the second bedroom. They hadn't been in it since they'd arrived because of the leaking roof. As he threw open the door, fog greeted him. Fuck! The small casement window, stuck shut from years of paint, was now wide open. The kitchen knife she'd used for cutting through the layers of paint lay on the floor. 'Leila!' he shouted, going to the window. 'Leila! Come back here now!'

Thick, dark silence.

Panic-stricken, he returned to the living room and saw that Leila's coat and shoes had gone from where they were kept. How could he have been so stupid! He should have known she couldn't be trusted. She was feisty and streetwise, not like the average kid her age. Of course she'd find a way to escape. The child – his passport to the future – had gone and he needed to get her back. Still holding the lamp, he rushed out of the cottage to look for her.

TWENTY-FOUR

'Leila!' Colin shouted into the fog. He listened for any sound suggesting she might be close by. Nothing. Where the hell was she? Surely she couldn't have gone very far in this? He hadn't passed her on the lane when he'd driven down it, but then the fog was so thick she would have had to be directly in front of the car's headlights for him to have seen her. 'Leila!' he shouted again as the freezing fog swirled around him.

His anger and frustration increased with every second. Just wait until he found her! She'd be sorry. A normal kid would never have run off in this weather; they'd have been too scared. But Leila – neglected by her mother – would have had to deal with far worse situations than fog. Whatever had he been thinking of! Just for a decent coffee and some time alone. He was as angry with himself as he was with her.

Holding the lamp high for maximum effect, Colin continued along the lane, pausing every so often to call her name and listen for any sound that might be her.

'Leila! I know you're out here somewhere. If you don't come back right now, you'll be sorry. I'll—'

Then he thought it might be better to take a softer

approach. 'Leila, I've bought you the sweets you wanted. You're not in any trouble, so come back now. Please.'

Still nothing. The fog was freezing. His face and hands were growing numb.

'Leila! Leila!' he shouted again, desperation in his voice.

But the only sound that came back was the crunch of his shoes on the rough surface of the lane. Even the wildlife seemed to have taken cover on a night like this.

'Leila! Get the fuck here now!'

Surely she couldn't have got this far, he thought, pausing again, unless of course she'd left straight after him when there'd just been a light mist. How long would it have taken her to force the window? Maybe not that long. It was two miles to the end of Fern Lane and then nearly another mile into the village, assuming she'd gone in the right direction. If she hadn't then she'd be lost on the moor, because there was nothing in the other direction but marshland. As far as he knew she didn't have any money with her, which was a plus. But supposing she had made it into the village and had then stopped someone and asked for help? His stomach contracted with fear. If she'd told someone everything then the police were very likely out looking for him now. He stopped dead in his tracks, unable to think. What the hell was he going to do?

With trembling hands, he took his phone from his coat pocket. The screen illuminated and showed he had half a bar of signal strength. Not enough to make a call. He continued along the lane with his phone in his hand, cold, angry and dreading the consequences of his negligence. Finally the signal strength rose to two bars – enough to make a call.

'Leila!' he shouted one more time.

He waited a second for a reply and then pressed Doris Goodman's number. She'd be annoyed he was phoning when she'd explicitly told him not to, but this was an emergency and she was the only person who would know what to do.

He prayed Leila hadn't already told someone, or the police could already be on their way to arrest him. How he yearned for his flat and the humdrum life he'd left behind. He would have swapped back in an instant, regardless of the rewards he'd been promised.

The phone rang, but Doris Goodman didn't answer. Colin suspected it was because she'd seen his number appear on the display. He waited until the call went through to voice-mail, didn't leave a message, cut the call and tried again. On the third attempt she answered.

'I told you not to phone me under any circumstances!' she said, annoyed.

'I know, but I'm in trouble and I don't know what to do.' His teeth were chattering so much from cold and worry he could hardly get the words out.

'What sort of trouble?' she asked.

'I don't know where Leila is.'

'How can you not know where she is? She's supposed to be with you at my cottage.'

'She was, but I had to go out to buy things and her whining was driving me mad. I only left her for a few hours and when I got back she'd escaped through a window.'

'Colin! You were told not to let her out of your sight. You'd better find her damn quickly. It shouldn't be difficult. There's nowhere for her to go there and she doesn't know anyone.'

'You don't understand. It's not that easy. I'm looking for her now, but it's thick fog here. I can't see a fucking thing.'

'Where are you?'

'Fern Lane, about halfway along, but it's hopeless in the fog. I don't know what to do.' He knew he sounded pathetic, but he was past caring.

'You keep looking for her until you find her. That's what you do. I doubt she's got far in the fog. When was the last time you saw her?'

145

'Around one o'clock, when I left the cottage. I told her to keep away from the windows and not to go outside.'

'It's four-thirty now! I can't believe you were so stupid to have left her alone.'

'Neither can I,' Colin admitted miserably.

'When did you discover she was missing?'

'About half an hour ago.'

'And you've thoroughly searched the cottage? She's not hiding in there?'

'No,' he said wearily.

'How long has the fog been down?'

'I don't know. It was only misty when I left, and then when I came out of the shopping centre in Marsborough, around three o'clock, it was thick fog.'

Doris paused. 'So if Leila left straight after you she might have had enough time to walk to the village. You've got to admire her pluck. I remember being scared stiff of the fog there when I was a child.'

Colin grunted; he wasn't impressed at all.

'I doubt she's got any further than the village,' Doris said. 'There's only one bus an hour, and when the fog comes down the service stops completely until it clears. My guess is she's either walking to the village or somewhere in it. Go there now.'

'But supposing she's not there?'

Colin heard her sigh. 'You could ask Maggie who runs the village store if she's seen a young girl. She doesn't miss much. But only ask her as a last resort. And think carefully about what you can say to explain a missing child that won't raise suspicion.'

'I've had enough of all this,' Colin moaned, staring into the swirling fog. 'I want to go home. Leila can take care of herself.'

'Don't be ridiculous! She's eight years old. And there's no

146

going back for you now. The police were at your flat yesterday. I saw them from my window. After they'd gone, I went over to have a look. There's a padlock on your front door with a police notice and a number to phone if anyone needs to get in.'

Colin let out a small cry of distress, but of course his work would have alerted the police by now. It was over two weeks since he'd gone missing. Doris was right: there was no going back, and that had been what he wanted. But whether he continued to look for Leila or not was a different matter.

'Pull yourself together and find Leila,' Doris said firmly. 'She can't be far. Take her back to the cottage and don't let her out of your sight again.'

'Supposing I can't find her?'

'You have to, or I'll tell the police all I know. They've been here again asking questions.'

'You wouldn't.'

'I might not have a choice if you don't find her.'

Furious and gripped by panic, he cut the call. A noise, a rustle, came from his right. He spun round. 'Leila?' He held out the lamp in the direction the noise had come from but couldn't see beyond the mist-laden bracken.

'Leila?' he asked again. He moved the lamp so it illuminated a different part of the heathland. He had the feeling someone or something was watching him, ready to pounce or playing a waiting game. He shivered uncontrollably. The area abounded with tales of lost travellers dying on the moor and their ghosts walking at night. He kept very still, senses alert, pure fear creeping up his spine. Get a grip, he told himself. 'Leila? Is that you?' he whispered.

Suddenly he started. A pair of eyes glowed orange from the bracken. Not human; they were slanted and too far apart. Frozen to the spot, Colin stared back, trembling, his hand knuckle-white from clasping the lamp. Then another movement. His heart lurched. A fox leapt out, tore past him and disappeared into the fog. His heart pounded and he gasped for breath. Not Leila, not this time. But he'd have to keep looking, and when he found her she'd be sorry for all the trouble she'd caused him. Very sorry indeed.

TWENTY-FIVE

Sharon looked at her sister sitting beside her on the sofa, shivering and wiping tears from her eyes. Without the props of alcohol and drugs, she was in a worse state than she had been in before. Why Kelsey had decided to get clean now, with all the worry and stress she was under and when she had nothing left to lose, Sharon had no idea. It didn't make sense. Kelsey had had countless opportunities in the past to stop her substance misuse and get her life back and look after her kids, but she'd failed. Now, when she was at rock bottom, she seemed to be managing it, by herself and despite the awful side effects of withdrawing. It annoyed Sharon.

She'd witnessed Kelsey wreck not only her own life, but the lives of her children too. Piece by piece, year after year. Kelsey always phoned her for help in times of need. It was as if Kelsey had been proving to her just how much damage their stepfather had done to her, even though Sharon didn't need any more proof. She knew the sacrifices her sister had made in order to protect her and had lived with the guilt ever since. She probably should be grateful, but she wasn't. She resented what Kelsey had done for her, or rather, resented that she'd told her.

If she'd never found out the truth, her life might have been very different too. Maybe she'd even have a loving partner and family of her own. Knowing had put a stop to that. She'd never let a man get close, because she didn't trust any of them. How could you be sure what you were getting? Men didn't come with a health warning: with 'paedophile' stamped on their foreheads. Even if they did, Sharon doubted their mother would have taken notice of it. No, she would have been like a dedicated smoker, convinced that the ill effects didn't apply to her. Kelsey had told their mother what their stepfather was doing and she had called her a liar, then sent her to apologize to the bastard, which had in effect given him permission to continue. Both their mother and stepfather were dead now, but their legacy continued.

'I saw Peter Harris this morning,' Sharon said, breaking out of her thoughts.

'Why?' Kelsey asked, surprised.

'I needed to talk to him about what will happen when Leila is found.'

'*If* she's found,' Kelsey said, fresh tears forming.

'I'm sure she will be,' Sharon reassured her.

'I wish I had your confidence. I know the police think she is dead.'

Taking a deep breath, Sharon chose her next words very carefully. 'Kelsey, what's your understanding of what will happen to Leila when she's found?'

'*If* she's found,' Kelsey corrected again. 'You don't have to worry about that. Peter's already told me they have a care order, so Leila will go straight to a foster carer.' Her tears spilled over and her hands shook.

'There is another way,' Sharon said.

'What are you talking about?'

'Leila could come to live with me. I know when I've

offered this before you've always refused and said you were going to make good so you could look after her. Clearly that's not an option now, so wouldn't it be better if Leila lived with me, rather than go to a foster carer she doesn't know?'

Kelsey thought for a moment. 'When you put it like that it does make sense. What did Peter say?'

'He agreed. He said that generally the social services prefer children to live with a relative if they can't be looked after by their own parents. He couldn't see a problem, as long as you didn't raise any objection.'

'Sounds like you two had a good chat,' Kelsey said suspiciously.

'Yes, we did, but only because we want what's best for you and Leila.'

'You're talking about her as if you know she's still alive,' Kelsey said, suddenly looking at her sister.

'I'm hopeful. We have to stay positive. Well, what do you say? Surely it's better if Leila lives with me rather than a complete stranger?'

'I guess, but for how long?'

'Probably until she's an adult.'

'But you don't really like kids,' Kelsey said. 'I mean, you never had any of your own.'

How little her sister knew of her and what she'd been through. 'I might have, given the opportunity.'

'I'd be able to see her whenever I wanted?' Kelsey asked.

'Yes. The exact contact arrangements would be set by the social services, but I don't see why not. Peter said contact would probably need to be supervised, but I can do that.'

Kelsey held her sister's gaze. 'You've gone into this in a lot of depth, even though Leila hasn't been found, and might never be.'

'It makes sense to plan ahead, doesn't it?'

'I guess.'

'So you agree?'

'Yes, assuming she's found alive. Which I doubt she will be.'

TWENTY-SIX

Beth picked up her desk phone, ready to key in the number for Belsize Nursing Home. It was always difficult, informing the next of kin that a loved one was missing and a suicide note had been found so they should expect the worse. Usually an officer went to see the next of kin in person, but in this case it was different. Colin Weaver was still a suspect in the disappearance of Leila Smith and his mother was in Belsize Nursing Home, which specialized in the care of dementia patients. Beth felt it was appropriate to speak to the person in charge of the home first, because quite possibly Mrs Weaver's dementia would mean she didn't understand what she was being told.

The call was answered by a woman who simply said, 'Belsize Nursing Home.' Beth asked to speak to the manager.

A minute later the care-home manager came on the line. 'Margaret Evans speaking.'

Beth introduced herself and said, 'Thank you for making the time to speak to me. I understand Mrs Jean Weaver is a patient of yours?'

'Yes, that's correct.'

'I'm afraid I have some bad news. Her son, Colin, is missing – possible suicide, although his body hasn't been found yet.'

'Oh dear, that's dreadful,' the woman gasped, clearly shocked. 'I am sorry. Whatever drove him to that, I wonder? But it explains why our last payment was refused by his bank.'

'Payment for Mrs Weaver's care?' Beth asked.

'Yes, part of the cost of Mrs Weaver's care was being met by her son. The payments were taken by Direct Debit from his bank each month, but the last one was refused – the reason given was insufficient funds.'

'I see,' Beth said. 'Did Mr Weaver visit his mother often?'

'About every four weeks, usually on a Sunday.'

'How would you describe him? Did he talk to you or the other staff?'

'No, he hardly said a word to any of us. He sat with his mother for an hour and then left.'

'So did you feel his visits were more out of a sense of duty than a close bond?' Beth asked. It wasn't really pertinent to the inquiry, but Beth was trying to build a clearer picture of Colin Weaver.

'I would say so. I don't think he and his mother were very close.'

'Did Mrs Weaver recognize her son?'

'Difficult to say, but I doubt it. Certainly not in the last year. Like many here, she's lost the power of speech and is very confused. But she enjoyed the chocolates he brought her.'

'So she's unlikely to know where Mr Weaver might be?'

'I'm sure she wouldn't be of any help at all.'

'Does anyone else visit her?'

'No. As far as I'm aware there are no other living relatives.' Which was the conclusion Beth had drawn from her own research. 'A friend of Mrs Weaver used to visit occasionally, but she died earlier this year.'

'How long has Mrs Weaver been a patient with you?' Beth asked.

'Just over five years.'

'Will she understand her son is missing?'

'Doubtful. But I'll tell her.'

'Thank you. I'll let you know when we have any more news.'

'That would be helpful. If Mr Weaver is dead, we'll need to amend our records accordingly.'

'What will happen now the care-home fees aren't being paid in full?' Beth asked, concerned.

'Don't worry, Mrs Weaver won't be thrown out on the streets. When there's a change in circumstance we can apply for additional state funding.'

'Good. Thank you for your time.'

'You're welcome. I'll go and see Mrs Weaver now.'

Beth replaced the handset and opened the ring-bound folder containing Colin Weaver's bank statements that she'd taken from his flat. It wasn't a surprise that the payment for Mrs Weaver's care hadn't been met. According to her son's last bank statement, his current account was down to £2.48. Beth had had an initial look through the statements when she'd first found them, but now she was going through in more depth. They went back seven years. Colin had a current account with a high-street bank and a savings account running alongside it. Each month his modest salary was paid into his current account and the day after he transferred £500 online into his savings account. He'd been doing this for six years and his savings had grown to £38,942 with interest. Beth saw the monthly Direct Debit that went out to Belsize Nursing Home, and standing orders for utilities, insurance and a mobile phone contract. She'd asked forensics for his call data and, if possible, the time and location his phone was last used, but she was still waiting to hear from them.

Beth noted the small sums of cash – £50, £75, £30 – that had regularly left his current account, presumably for day-to-day living expenses. He appeared to live quite frugally – no sign of expensive holidays or flash cars. But then abruptly in April this year he'd begun withdrawing large sums in cash from his savings account: £5,000, £3,000, £7,000, £2,600. These amounts weren't large enough to raise the bank's suspicions about money laundering, but clearly they were far more than his meagre lifestyle seemed to merit. Over the previous six months he'd drained his savings account to zero – the last withdrawal of £560 had been made three weeks ago.

Beth stared at the page, trying to work out what it meant. Where had all that money gone? There was no evidence of any other savings accounts among his paperwork. Was he a gambler who'd lost the lot? It was possible. Gambling addiction was becoming a real social problem. Or was it possible Colin Weaver was being blackmailed? An outwardly respectable guy, perhaps he had something sordid in his past that the police weren't aware of but someone else was? Yet how could this be linked to the disappearance of Leila Smith? If indeed there was a link. The money had been taken out long before she'd gone missing.

Beth's desk phone rang. She picked it up and listened for some minutes to what John Herald from forensics was telling her, her expression growing increasingly incredulous.

'Thank you very much indeed,' she said as the call ended.

Matt was looking at her expectantly.

'That was John in forensics,' she said, slipping on her jacket as she stood. 'Colin Weaver's phone has been traced to a rural location a hundred miles from here, about fifteen miles south-west of Marsborough. It was active yesterday evening.'

'So he hasn't committed suicide!' Matt said. 'Unless someone else is using his phone.'

'Exactly. There's more. Leila's DNA has been found all over Weaver's flat – which would be expected if she went there to shelter from the rain as has been claimed. However, there was a particularly high concentration in the second bedroom, especially on the bed, despite the room being thoroughly cleaned and the bed stripped. They also found traces of Leila's urine on the bedroom floor and there were signs that a bolt had recently been fitted to the outside of the second bedroom door and then removed. Someone, presumably Weaver, had tried to fill in the screw holes, though not very successfully.'

Matt gave a low whistle. 'So Weaver *did* take Leila and kept her locked in that bedroom?'

'It would seem so. I'll update the DCI and hopefully Weaver is still where he was when he made that call.'

TWENTY-SEVEN

Colin sat on the sofa in the damp, cold cottage, the bag of money held firmly on his lap. He was seething with anger. The little cow had taken nearly two thousand pounds of his life's savings before she'd run off. He supposed he should be grateful she hadn't taken the lot! He wouldn't be letting the bag out of his sight again, for sure.

He'd discovered the money was missing when he'd returned from looking for Leila the night before. He'd walked all the way into the village in the freezing fog but had stopped short of asking the woman who owned the store if she'd seen a child, as Doris had suggested. She was about to lock up and he couldn't think what to say that wouldn't sound suspicious. And if he was honest, he'd reached the point where he didn't really want the kid back anyway. She was more trouble than she was worth, and he'd convinced himself that their plan would work just as well without her, if not better.

Even so, he had a nagging feeling Leila might return to the cottage of her own accord, because where else could she go? She had his money, yes, but a kid her age could hardly book into a hotel or buy a train, bus or plane ticket. As Doris had said, she didn't know anyone in the area. This was the one place she knew. The chances were she was already on her way back, and he really didn't need that. She was a thief, a liar and a pain in the arse, just like her mother. Without her, life would become much simpler and he would be free to start his new life straight away, rather than having to wait.

With renewed optimism and confidence, Colin picked up his phone to make the call he wasn't supposed to make for another two weeks – to say he was on his way to the airport. Then he remembered there wasn't a signal in the cottage. No worries. The fog had lifted so he'd drive up the lane, make the call, return, pack his things and leave. If Leila came back in the interim, he'd deal with her. If she returned later, she'd find him gone. If she had turned right instead of left when she'd left the cottage in the fog she had probably stumbled into one of the bogs and would never be seen again, which also suited him fine.

Slipping on his coat, Colin tucked the carrier bag of money under his arm and stepped outside. At midday the wintry sun was trying to make an appearance, although precious little of it filtered in through the small, low windows in the cottage. However, all that gloom and doom would soon be a thing of the past, he told himself. Free of Leila and with his plans in place, his life was about to get a whole lot better.

Colin walked around the back of his car and was about to open the driver's door when he heard a noise. Before he had time to turn to see what it was, strong hands grabbed him from behind and forced him face down onto the bonnet of his car.

'Police! Stay where you are.'

'What the—!' he cried, his bag of money falling to the ground.

'Colin Weaver?'

'Yes, but I haven't done anything wrong.'

He was spread-eagled against the car, one police officer holding him in place as another began to search him, patting him down. The officer removed his phone and wallet.

Head sideways on the cold, hard metal, Colin could see another officer pick up his carrier bag and look inside. 'That's a lot of money,' he said.

'It's mine.'

He heard another officer inside the cottage, calling out, 'Leila! Leila Smith, are you here?'

'She's not,' Colin said.

'Where is she?' the officer to his right asked.

'I don't know. Really, I don't.'

He was suddenly straightened, pulled upright, with an officer either side gripping his arms. A female officer appeared in the doorway of the cottage. 'She's not in here, but a child has definitely been living here.'

'Where is she?' the officer on his right asked again, gripping his arm painfully tight.

'I don't know! She's run away. You're hurting my arm.'

In an instant, his hands were in front of him and cuffs were being snapped around his wrists. Then he was read his rights. 'You are under arrest on suspicion of the abduction of Leila Smith. You do not have to say anything, but it may harm your defence . . .'

'You don't understand,' he cried. 'You've got it all wrong. Where are you taking me?'

'To Coleshaw Police Station to be questioned about the abduction of Leila Smith.'

'But I didn't do it. Honestly.'

'So who was the child in the cottage?' an officer asked.

'Leila,' he admitted quietly. 'But it isn't what you think.'

*

160

A hundred miles away at Coleshaw Police Station, a small cry of relief went up as DS Bert Scrivener announced to Beth, Matt and the rest of the team that Colin Weaver had been arrested and was now on his way back to the station. The bad news, he added, was that although Weaver had admitted Leila had been in the cottage, he wasn't saying where she was now. Worse, what looked like human hair – thought to be Leila's – had been found in a bin in the cottage.

'Forensics will be at Heath Cottage shortly,' DS Scrivener finished. 'Now back to work, please. We need to find Leila Smith. And can someone find out who owns Heath Cottage?'

'Already working on it, sir,' Beth replied.

The open-plan office fell silent as everyone returned to their screens. Beth was searching the Land Registry for the owner of Heath Cottage, Fern Lane, with a Marsborough postcode. She tapped her keyboard, scrolled through the pages and then stopped and stared in disbelief.

'Sir,' she called to the DS. 'Heath Cottage is owned by Mrs Doris Goodman. She's an elderly widow who lives on the Hawthorn Estate, not far from Colin Weaver.'

'Yes, I know who Mrs Goodman is,' DS Scrivener said impatiently, coming over and looking at Beth's screen. 'This can't be a coincidence, can it?'

'I don't know, sir,' Beth said. 'Matt and I have spoken to Mrs Goodman twice since Leila went missing. She told us – as she told Kelsey Smith – that she'd seen Leila go off with a man, but she couldn't give a description of him. Later she admitted she hadn't actually seen Leila go with him, she just assumed that was the case. She hasn't been able to tell us any more.'

'According to the Land Registry records,' DS Scrivener said, pointing to Beth's computer screen, 'Mrs Goodman has owned the property for over twenty years. I want you and Matt to go to see her now. Find out all she knows about

Weaver and why he might be in her cottage. Bring her in for questioning if necessary, but go easy; she's been useful to us in the past. There could be a completely rational explanation for this – although I can't for the life of me think of one right now.'

'God, I hope we didn't miss something obvious when we interviewed Mrs Goodman,' Matt said as he and Beth got into the car.

'I was thinking the same thing,' Beth said, worried. 'But what?' She started the car and pulled away.

Matt shook his head. 'No idea. But I remember saying to you at the time I thought Doris Goodman could be losing her touch. She was able to see the emblem on Leila's school bag and that she was smiling at the guy she was talking to, but she couldn't give a description of him beyond average height and build.'

'But what motive could she possibly have for covering up for Colin Weaver?' Beth asked.

'I can't imagine. It doesn't make any sense!'

Ten minutes later, Beth parked the car outside Mrs Goodman's home. They were half expecting her to appear at her door as she often did, but apparently she hadn't seen them arrive. Matt pressed the doorbell once, twice, three times, before she appeared. 'Oh, hello,' she said, seemingly surprised.

'Can we come in?' Beth asked formally. 'We need to talk to you.'

'I'm afraid I was about to go out.'

'It's important,' Matt said. 'Urgent, in fact.'

Mrs Goodman looked from one to the other, then said, 'All right, you'd better come in.' She stood aside to let them pass, closed the front door, and followed them into her living room. Matt sat in the chair by the window and Beth took the armchair at a right angle to Mrs Goodman. Go easy, the DS had said, but they needed to get to the truth.

'Mrs Goodman, how well do you know Colin Weaver?' Beth asked.

'A little. He lives in one of those flats opposite.' She nodded towards the window.

'So you would recognize him if you saw him?'

'Yes.'

'Did you see him the night Leila Smith went missing?'

She paused to think. 'Not as far as I can remember.'

'You told Kelsey Smith and us that you saw Leila talking to a man in the play area the night she disappeared. You described him as average height and build. Could it have been Colin Weaver?'

She paused again and looked thoughtful. 'It's possible, I suppose, but I couldn't be sure. It was very dark and I was looking from my window. I didn't go outside.'

Beth held her gaze as Matt began taking notes. 'Have you seen Mr Weaver since that night?' Beth asked.

'No. Why?'

Beth ignored the question and continued. 'Mrs Goodman, do you own another property apart from this one?'

'As a matter of fact, I do. A very old, dilapidated cottage on the moors near Marsborough. It's been in my family for generations and I haven't the heart to sell it.'

'Do you stay there?'

'Very occasionally in summer.'

'When was the last time you used it?'

She thought for a moment. 'June, last year, I believe, but I couldn't be sure. Why? Is it important?'

Again, Beth ignored the question. 'Mrs Goodman, do you let other people stay in your cottage?'

'Sometimes, yes.'

'Have you ever let Colin Weaver stay there?'

Another pause. 'Yes.'

'When?'

'Recently. He's probably still there now if he's not in his flat.'

Beth threw Matt a glance. 'So you're aware he's been staying there?'

'Yes.'

'Did he have a key?'

'No, I told him where to find it. I leave the key under some stones at the front of the cottage. You don't get the crime there you do here. And there's nothing of value in the cottage to steal.' She gave a small resigned smile.

'Was this Mr Weaver's first visit to the cottage?'

'Yes.'

'How long has he been there?'

'A couple of weeks, I think. Maybe a bit longer. He wanted to get away, use it as a retreat, what with his mother being ill.'

'Have you been to see him while he's been there?'

'Goodness me, no. The place is freezing in winter and he wanted to be alone. Why would I go?'

'Was anyone else staying with Mr Weaver at the cottage?' Beth asked.

'I don't think so. If they were, I didn't know about it.'

'How long did he intend to stay at the cottage?' Beth continued.

'I've no idea. That was up to him.'

'Has he contacted you while he's been there?'

'Yes, once. He phoned to complain about the cottage being cold, but I'd warned him what it would be like before he went.'

'When did he phone you?' Beth asked.

'Yesterday evening.'

'Really? Are you sure?' Beth asked.

Doris nodded.

Matt looked at her carefully. 'It took Mr Weaver rather a long time to realize the cottage was cold when he'd been living there for two weeks,' he said. 'It's a wonder he hadn't contacted you before if there was a problem.'

'Not really,' Doris replied. 'There's no mobile signal or Wi-Fi in the cottage. You have to walk over a mile down the lane to get a signal. And from what he said his car has been playing up and the weather was bad.'

'What else did he say?' Beth asked as Matt wrote.

'Nothing, really. It was just a short call. I mean, if he didn't like the cottage, he could always go home.'

'How did Colin Weaver know you owned the cottage?' Beth asked.

'It's general knowledge around here. Others have stayed there, but in summer. Why? Am I in trouble? I don't charge for the cottage, so I don't have to declare it on my income tax, do I?'

'No, you're not in any trouble,' Beth said.

'Well, that's a relief.' Mrs Goodman clasped a hand to her chest.

Beth looked at Matt to see if he had any questions, but he shook his head. 'Thank you for your time, Mrs Goodman.'

'Is there any news about Leila Smith?' she asked as they stood. 'I've been so worried about her.'

'Not yet, unfortunately. But we're still actively searching for her.'

'I do hope you find the poor child soon. Kelsey Smith has a lot to answer for.'

'I think she knows that,' Matt replied.

TWENTY-EIGHT

'What do you think of her story?' Matt asked Beth as they left Mrs Goodman's. 'I get the feeling she knows Colin Weaver better than she's letting on.'

'I agree,' Beth said. 'She was aware his mother was in a nursing home, but I suppose she could have got that from someone else on the estate. There's nothing to suggest she knew Weaver had Leila with him at her cottage, but why would he risk phoning her when he was supposed to be dead?'

'Perhaps he was getting tired of the pretence once reality kicked in,' said Matt. 'Or perhaps he panicked and wanted to incriminate her.'

'Maybe,' Beth replied. 'His call data should confirm just how much contact they had.'

'What the—!' Matt exclaimed as they arrived at the car. A large bright-red penis had been spray-painted on the bonnet.

'It's only just happened, the paint's still wet,' Beth said, looking around.

There was no one in sight but Matt set off at a jog up the road, while Beth took a roll of paper towels they kept in the boot for mopping up spillages and began rubbing off the paint.

Five minutes later Matt returned, out of breath, but without having found the culprits. All that remained of the graffiti on the car were some smudges of red paint that would have to be dealt with by the garage.

'Let's drive for a bit and see if we can spot them,' Matt said, still annoyed, and jumped into the driver's seat. Beth got into the passenger seat.

As Matt drove around the ring road on the estate they looked for anyone acting suspiciously. Beth's phone rang and she switched it to speaker. It was DS Scrivener.

'We've just left Mrs Goodman's,' she said.

'Update me when you get back to the station. Are you still on the Hawthorn Estate?'

'Yes, sir.'

'Can you visit Kelsey and tell her we've arrested Colin Weaver? She has a right to know.'

'Will do, sir.'

Matt completed the circuit and, having to accept he wouldn't be catching whoever had graffitied the car today, drove to the block of flats where Kelsey lived.

'Any news?' Kelsey asked anxiously as soon as she opened her front door.

'We haven't found Leila,' Beth said straight away. 'But there has been a development.'

'What? You haven't come to tell me she's dead!' Her desperation was obvious.

'No. Let's go in and sit down.' Beth touched her arm.

The living room was as clean and tidy as it had been on their last visit, and Beth thought Kelsey seemed to be suffering less from the effects of drug and alcohol withdrawal. 'How are you doing?' she asked her gently, sitting beside her on the sofa. Matt took up his usual position by the window.

'Not so bad. I'm still clean.'

'Well done,' Beth said.

'My sister thinks it's a waste of time being clean now. She doesn't say it, but it's written all over her face. She believes I'm a lost cause. I know it's unlikely I'll get Leila back, but I need to try, just in case she's still alive.' Tears filled her eyes.

'You're doing very well,' Beth said, lightly rubbing her arm. She waited as Kelsey wiped her eyes before continuing with what she had to say. 'Kelsey, the man who lives in the flat below you, Colin Weaver, was arrested this morning on suspicion of the abduction of Leila.'

Kelsey stared at them with a mixture of astonishment and fear.

'There is no evidence to say Leila is dead, but her DNA was found in his flat,' Beth said.

'What, the flat below me?' Kelsey asked, horrified.

'Yes. But Weaver was arrested in another part of the country, a hundred miles from here. He'd been staying in a remote cottage. Leila wasn't with him when he was arrested, but we're certain she's been living there.'

'Where is she then?' Kelsey cried in desperation. 'What's the bastard done with her?' Her face crumpled and tears fell.

'We don't know yet,' Beth said gently. 'But we will find out. Mr Weaver is being brought back to Coleshaw now for questioning.'

'Has he said if Leila's still alive?' Kelsey asked in anguish.

'He's not saying much at present,' Beth said. 'But we thought you should be aware of this new development. We'll be putting out a fresh appeal for information tomorrow.'

'How long was she in his flat for?' Kelsey asked, wiping her eyes and clearly struggling to take it all in.

'We don't know for certain, but we think a couple of days. Then he moved her to the cottage. We're looking at CCTV cameras along the route he would have taken.'

Kelsey straightened and looked from one to the other. 'So I was right about hearing a man's voice in my flat the night Leila went missing.'

'What makes you say that?' Beth asked.

'I told you I thought I heard Leila laugh and a man's voice that sounded familiar close by. It was Weaver's voice. I put it down to hallucinating from all the drugs and drink I'd had that night. But I'm right. It was him. They were in my flat. Leila must have come back for Buttons, and he was with her.' Her voice trembled.

'How would you recognize his voice?' Beth asked. 'Did you ever talk to him?'

'A little, when Leila and I first moved in. And he used to open his window and shout at the kids in the play area if they were causing trouble. Doris Goodman does it too. I've heard his voice plenty of times, but I didn't make the connection until now. Have you found Buttons?'

'No. The bear wasn't in Weaver's flat and as far as we know it hasn't been found in or around the cottage. Forensics are doing a more thorough search now.'

'That gives me some hope Leila is still alive,' Kelsey said quietly. 'She's inseparable from Buttons.'

Beth gave a small nod, although she couldn't share Kelsey's optimism.

'Has Weaver done this sort of thing before?' Kelsey asked, her face creasing with pain. 'Taken kiddies.'

'Not as far as we know. He wasn't on the sex offenders' register,' Beth replied.

Kelsey grimaced. 'But he might have done things and not been caught?'

'It's possible,' Beth had to agree.

Kelsey took another tissue from the box and wiped her eyes.

'We're doing all we can to find Leila,' Matt said. 'And if Weaver has harmed her, he'll pay for it.'

Beth waited while Kelsey tried to compose herself before asking, 'Did you know Doris Goodman owned a cottage that she lets people use?'

Kelsey shook her head. 'She wouldn't tell me about something like that. I only spoke to her when I couldn't find Leila. She always gave me a lot of grief for being a crap parent. Was it her place then, where Colin Weaver took Leila?'

'Yes,' Beth said. 'But there's nothing to suggest Mrs Goodman knew Colin had taken Leila there.'

Kelsey looked at them in disbelief. 'So the old cow knows everyone's business but her own!'

'We'll keep you informed,' Beth said. 'Are you still sure you wouldn't like a liaison officer?'

'Yeah. I've got this far. Just find Leila for me, will you?'

TWENTY-NINE

'Good, you're back,' DS Scrivener said as Matt and Beth returned to the office. 'Just in time to join the team brief. Weaver's arrived. We're waiting for his solicitor. Perhaps you'd like to share with us what Mrs Goodman had to say.'

'Of course,' Matt said, stepping forward and addressing the team. 'She admitted she owns Heath Cottage and she knew Colin Weaver was staying there. It seems she lets people stay there, like a retreat. But she says as far as she was aware, Weaver was there alone. Apparently he phoned her last night complaining about it being cold. We also updated Kelsey Smith. She's very upset, obviously, but she's now convinced she heard Weaver and Leila in her flat the night Leila went missing. She thinks they were getting Leila's teddy bear.'

'Thank you,' DS Scrivener said. 'I'm not surprised Weaver phoned Mrs Goodman complaining about the cold,' he resumed, addressing the team. 'Local forensics phoned in with some preliminary findings. The place is falling down, the roof leaks and there's no proper heating, lighting or cooking. Indications are that Leila spent a lot of time in the only bedroom that was habitable. She carved her name on the wooden bedhead in various places. It appears Weaver slept on the sofa. He'd been warming food on a camping stove and had visited Marsborough at least once to buy provisions. Forensics found a receipt from a supermarket there. A local officer is going to talk to the staff at the supermarket to see if anyone remembers him. An updated missing person's appeal for information will be going out this evening, focusing on that area. If Weaver took Leila with him shopping, it might jog someone's memory.

'A stain that is almost certainly blood was found in the kitchen, but at present we don't know if it's Leila's,' DS Scrivener continued. 'There is no sign of recent digging in the garden, but the cottage is on the edge of the moors and surrounded by marshland, so there are plenty of places to bury a body. Sniffer dogs are being deployed there shortly. A quick look at Weaver's laptop showed he'd downloaded a number of children's films, but so far no porn has been found. Digital forensics are going through it more thoroughly now. I'll let you two interview Weaver when his solicitor arrives,' he said to Beth and Matt. 'Make it good. We need to find Leila. And ask him about the money he had on him. When he was arrested he was carrying a bag containing just under forty thousand pounds in cash.'

'That fits, sir,' Beth said, also addressing the team. 'Weaver's bank statements show he's been withdrawing large sums of cash regularly over the last six months. He ran his savings account to zero. It's possible he'd been planning Leila's abduction for some time.'

DS Scrivener nodded. 'Good work, everyone. Now let's find Leila.'

An hour later, Beth and Matt entered Interview Room 2. Colin Weaver and his solicitor were already there, sitting on one side of the table. 'Good afternoon,' Beth said. 'I'm Detective Constable Beth Mayes and this is my colleague DC Matt Davis.'

'Deborah Harold, representing Mr Weaver,' his solicitor said.

Weaver was smaller than Beth had anticipated. She'd seen photographs of him, but sitting down, shoulders hunched forward, he looked insignificant and feeble. There was none of the arrogance or bravado that some suspects showed when about to be questioned.

Beth sat opposite Weaver and Matt next to her.

'Colin Weaver,' Beth started the formalities. 'This interview is being monitored and recorded and may be given in evidence if your case is brought to trial. We are in an interview room at Coleshaw Police Station. I am Detective Constable Beth Mayes and the other police officer present is Detective Constable Mathew Davis.' She stated the date and time and then asked Colin Weaver to give his full name and date of birth.

'Colin James Weaver,' he said, his voice slight. 'My date of birth is the third of November 1970.'

'Also present is Ms Deborah Harold, Colin Weaver's solicitor,' Beth continued for the sake of the recording. 'Do you agree that there are no other persons present?'

'Yes,' Colin said in the same small voice.

'Colin,' Beth said, leaning in slightly. His solicitor prepared to take notes. 'Before we talk about the abduction of Leila, can you please tell us where she is? We are all very worried about her and Leila's mother is heartbroken. We need to find her quickly.'

Colin stared at her, tense and anxious. 'I don't know where Leila is. Honestly. This is all her mother's fault.'

'What makes you say that?' Beth asked, surprised, as was his solicitor, who was looking at him.

'If she'd taken proper care of her daughter, none of this would have happened.'

'Can you explain, please?' Beth said.

173

Colin thought for a moment and then shook his head.

'Whatever you think about Mrs Smith's parenting,' Beth said, 'she is desperate for news of her daughter. If you cooperate and tell us where Leila is, it will help your defence in court.'

'I don't know where she is,' Colin replied, his voice rising.

'You were the last person to see her,' Beth continued evenly. 'We need to find her quickly. It's not a murder charge yet.'

'Murder? I didn't murder her!' Weaver cried. 'I'm telling you, I don't know where she is!'

'You must have some idea,' Matt said. 'You kept her hostage, first at your flat, and then at Heath Cottage. Where is she now?'

'I don't know!' he cried again.

His solicitor looked up. 'My client has told you he doesn't know where the child is, so can we move on?'

Beth nodded. 'Colin, if you change your mind at any time during this interview then please tell us where Leila is.'

He shook his head, but Beth wasn't unduly disappointed by the way the interview had opened. They'd all been expecting a no-comment interview, which was doubtless what Weaver's solicitor would have advised him to do – not to admit to anything. It was heartening he had engaged even this much. Beth was hopeful it wouldn't be too difficult to lead him into a confession and for him to tell them where Leila was – dead or alive.

'Where were you on the evening of Tuesday, the thirteenth of November?' Beth asked.

'In my flat,' Colin said.

'Which overlooks the children's play area on the Hawthorn Estate.'

'Yes.'

'You often watched Leila and other children playing there, didn't you? Sometimes you told them off.'

'If you say so.'

'But Leila stood out from the others. She was there every evening after school and stayed much later than the other children, even after dark. You began going down there when she was alone, talking to her, giving her presents and forging a relationship with her.' Beth paused and looked at him.

'So what if I did?'

'Leila was a highly vulnerable child, not very popular at school and crying out to be liked and to have someone take an interest in her. You offered her what she needed, gradually gaining her trust, grooming her for what you had in mind.'

'I didn't groom her!'

'Then, on the evening of Tuesday, the thirteenth of November,' Beth continued, 'you waited until she was alone, then went down and talked to her for a while before taking her to your flat. Whatever you told her made her feel comfortable going with you. Then what happened, Colin? Did she fight off your advances?'

'I'm not a paedophile,' he shouted, his face creasing and his bottom lip trembling.

'What else would you call a person who grooms a child and lures them back to their flat?' Matt asked.

Colin shook his head. 'I was trying to help her.'

'How?' Beth asked.

Weaver stared at the table, then said, 'No comment.'

Beth took a breath and glanced at the notes in the folder in front of her before continuing. 'At some point that evening Leila must have known she wasn't going home and wanted her favourite teddy bear, Buttons. I'm guessing she must have been pretty insistent, because you took the chance of going into her flat while her mother slept.' Beth paused for Colin's reaction, but he just shrugged.

'Leila might have thought it was a bit of game at this point,' Beth continued, 'because her mother heard her laugh.

175

Kelsey also heard your voice, Colin. She recognized it from when you spoke to her when she first moved into her flat, and from hearing you shouting at the children from your window.' Beth stopped. Colin was shaking his head. 'Do you want to say something?'

Colin stared at her, and then said, 'No.'

'Later that same night,' Beth said, 'Leila must have realized it wasn't a game any longer, probably when you began abusing her.'

'I didn't abuse her!'

'From then on you held her captive, locking her in the bedroom in your flat, at your mercy to abuse whenever you wanted. I can't begin to imagine what that poor child went through.'

'No! It wasn't like that!' Colin cried, his face reddening.

'What was it like then?' Matt asked, leaning in.

'Please give my client a moment to compose himself,' his solicitor said. Then to Colin, 'Would you like to take a break?'

'No. Let's get this over with. It's ridiculous.' He sniffed, pulled a crumpled tissue from his pocket and blew his nose.

Beth moved the plastic cup of water closer to him and continued. 'In line with your plan, you went to work the following morning – Wednesday, the fourteenth of November – as if nothing had happened, locking Leila in the bedroom before you left. That night you moved Leila in your car to Heath Cottage, Fern Lane, which, as you know, is owned by Doris Goodman, having previously told her you were going there alone.' Colin made as if to say something but then decided otherwise.

'CCTV on all major roads along the route you are likely to have taken is being examined now for sightings of your car,' Beth said. 'We have found Leila's DNA all over your flat and we're expecting to find it in your car and the cottage too.

A large amount of human hair, almost certainly Leila's, has been found in a bin at Heath Cottage. The evidence against you, Colin, is overwhelming. If you tell us where Leila is, it will help your defence.'

Dropping his head into his hands, Colin cried out in anguish. 'It wasn't meant to be like this.'

'How was it meant to be?' Beth persisted, keeping up the pressure. 'What went wrong, Colin? You spent six months planning Leila's abduction, so what happened?'

'You don't have to answer their questions,' his solicitor reminded him.

He shook his head in despair.

'When you were arrested,' Beth continued, 'you had your life savings and your passport with you, but there was no sign of Leila. Where is she? I believe you sexually abused her, then killed her and buried her body on the moors. You were about to flee the country when you were apprehended.'

'No. I didn't kill or abuse her. I'm not like that,' he said, visibly shaking.

'What are you like, Colin? Tell us,' Matt said. 'Tell us what happened and perhaps we can understand.'

Weaver raised his head, looked helplessly around the room and brought his gaze back to Beth. 'I can't tell you what happened, but I can tell you I didn't take Leila because of that.'

'Because of what?' Beth asked.

'Because I was going to abuse her,' he said desperately.

'Where is she, Colin?' Beth asked again. 'I can see from your face this is weighing heavily on your conscience, so tell me what happened.'

He shook his head.

'Was she the first child you abused?'

'I didn't abuse her!' he shouted. 'I don't know where she is. I'm not a paedophile. I did it for love. She liked me.'

The room fell silent, then Matt, unable to hide his contempt, said, 'That's what every paedophile says. That the child likes it, they enjoy it. I loved her and she loved me. Leila was eight years old, you sick bastard! She would have hated you.'

'That's enough,' Ms Harold said sharply. 'My client is entitled to be treated with respect.' Then, turning to Colin, 'I suggest we take a break now.'

He nodded.

'Is ten minutes all right?' Beth asked.

'Yes, and please have a word with your colleague before you return. I won't have my client spoken to like that. Any more verbal attacks on him and I'll terminate the interview and make a formal complaint.'

THIRTY

'Sorry,' Matt said to Beth as soon as they were outside the interview room.

'You need to keep a lid on your feelings,' Beth replied. 'You'll get us reported, and Weaver isn't the type to respond to anger or threats. He looks like a scared rabbit.'

'Because he's been caught!' Matt said contemptuously. 'He really believes he's done nothing wrong.'

'I know, but we'll get there. Just be patient.'

DS Scrivener looked up as they entered the incident room. He'd been monitoring the interview live on screen. Following procedure, he'd switched it off while the client and solicitor were alone. He looked pointedly at Matt.

'I know,' Matt said. 'Sorry. It won't happen again.'

'It better not. Remember your training – an anxious interviewee is less likely to confess than one who is relaxed. And our approach should always be one of respect.'

'Yes, sir. I'll remember.'

'While you've been interviewing Weaver, we've had some encouraging results from the CCTV,' DS Scrivener said. 'Weaver's car was recorded on the High Road leaving Coleshaw, heading north at one-fifteen in the morning on

Thursday, the fifteenth of November. That's two days after Leila vanished. The image is clear. He can be seen in the driver's seat and Leila is in the back. Her eyes are closed, so she was either asleep, drugged or already dead. You can't tell from the picture. The top of what could be her teddy bear is just visible. There's still a lot of footage to go through, but Weaver seems to have followed the main route north, which is helpful. The moorland around the cottage is being searched now, but so far nothing.'

'I think I'm going to try a slightly different approach. Go back in time and ask him about his childhood and mother,' Beth said. 'He visited her every month in the care home, but according to the manager it was more likely out of a sense of duty than love.'

'Yes, worth a try,' DS Scrivener agreed.

Matt and Beth returned to the interview room ten minutes after they'd left. Colin looked just as anxious as he had before the break. Beth began with the formalities: 'The interview is continuing at three-forty-five p.m. Colin Weaver, you understand you are still under caution?'

'Yes.'

Lowering her voice so it was non-threatening, Beth said, 'I'd like us to start by talking a bit about your childhood. Your mother—' But before she got any further, his solicitor interrupted.

'My client is very concerned that you believe him to be a paedophile, so against my advice he wishes to tell you his version of events.'

'Oh, OK,' Beth said, surprised. She and Matt both looked at Colin Weaver as he fiddled with the cuff on his sleeve. His solicitor sat rather stiffly and prepared to take notes, as did Matt.

Weaver cleared his throat and then looked at Beth. 'It's true, I used to talk to Leila – building a relationship, as you call it – but not because I intended to abuse her; that is abhorrent to me. It was because I felt sorry for her. Her mother didn't care about her and the social services weren't doing anything. I knew it was only a matter of time before something bad happened to her, left alone on the estate late at night. I probably wouldn't have done anything except talk to her, but someone I know who also knows Leila approached me with a plan for taking her and keeping her safe.'

'Who?' Beth asked.

'Let me continue, please.'

Beth nodded.

'Leila knew her mother was rubbish and was happy to come with me that night, but when she realized she'd have to do as she was told she began playing up and wanted to go home. She was used to running wild and doing what she wanted, and she didn't like my discipline.' Beth forced herself to say nothing and stay calm at Weaver's admission that he'd taken and then disciplined the child.

'Obviously I couldn't let Leila go home,' Weaver continued. 'She was sure to tell someone where she'd been, however much she promised not to. I hadn't intended to take her to the cottage until much later, but she kept shouting, and your officers were all over the estate. I knew that before long someone would report hearing a child in my flat. So I took her to Heath Cottage, where I looked after her in very difficult circumstances. The place is a dump – cold and damp and without any electricity – but we were only staying there for a few weeks. I made her meals on a camping stove, boiled water so she could wash, allowed her to watch films on my laptop, but she was rude and ungrateful. I cut her hair so I could take her out and she wouldn't be recognized. That's the hair you found in the bin. Yes, I had to smack her sometimes because she was a very unruly child, but I didn't sexually abuse her.'

He stopped. A myriad of questions hung in the air. 'So

181

where is Leila now?' Beth asked – the most important question of all.

'I don't know. I left her in the cottage on Wednesday while I went into town. When I got back, she had climbed out of a window that I thought couldn't be opened. There was a thick fog – you can check the weather report. I spent ages looking for her, but she was nowhere to be found.' His fists were clenched and anger showed on his face. Beth guessed that this had been the point when he'd killed her. His solicitor was still writing.

'Then you phoned Doris Goodman. Why?' Beth asked.

'No comment.'

'So who is the other person who knew you had Leila?' Beth persisted.

'I'm afraid I can't tell you yet,' Weaver replied. 'Once she knows I've been arrested, I'm sure she'll contact you and confirm what I'm saying.'

'Really?' Matt asked sceptically.

'Yes, really.' He then responded to all Beth and Matt's other questions with 'No comment'.

THIRTY-ONE

'I could kick myself,' Beth said, disappointed, as she and Matt made their way back to the incident room. 'It was looking so promising at the start and then all that nonsense about it was a friend who made him do it! He must think we're stupid.'

'He scores nought out of ten for imagination,' Matt said. The interview over, Colin Weaver had been returned to his cell and his solicitor had left. 'I don't think we could have handled the questioning any differently, though. Perhaps he'll reflect on it overnight and have a change of heart by morning.'

'Let's hope so,' Beth said. 'We can hold him for another eighteen hours without charging him, but we will have to apply for an extension.'

'We must be nearing the point where we have enough evidence to charge him without a body,' Matt said reflectively.

DS Scrivener looked up and nodded sympathetically as they entered the incident room but didn't say anything. He'd watched the interview on screen so knew the outcome.

Beth returned to her desk as Matt went to consult with a colleague. Although it was nearly 7 p.m., many of the team were still working. The updated missing person's appeal had gone out with the six o'clock news and the phone lines were busy as members of the public called in with possible new sightings of Leila. As usual it was a matter of prioritizing promising leads and discounting the impossible or fanciful. If they could plot Leila's last movements, it would make finding her or her body more likely.

Beth looked at her computer screen and set about going through the list of callers who'd phoned in response to the new missing person's appeal. Beside each name was the time they'd called, their contact information and a brief summary of the possible sighting of Leila. Many of the callers were from the Marsborough area, which wasn't surprising as the town had been mentioned in the appeal.

Those callers who had described Leila as having long hair were being discounted as they now knew Weaver had cut her hair short before taking her out of the cottage. Most of the calls marked as significant mentioned that the girl was carrying a teddy bear, so Beth began phoning those to ascertain more details – as others were doing. It took time, but in each case she established that the child seen carrying a bear couldn't possibly have been Leila. Finishing one call, Beth made a note and moved on to the next.

Suddenly DS Scrivener stood and called for everyone's attention. The room fell silent as they turned towards him. This would be news of a significant development. Good or bad?

'An employee of Marsborough Refuse Collection Service has phoned in. He spotted a teddy bear similar to the one Leila had with her when she went missing. It was collected from a bin in Marsborough shopping centre when they cleaned it on the night of Saturday, the seventeenth of November. That's four days after she went missing. It was disposed of with the other rubbish, but the CCTV for that day has been requested. Thank you for your attention.'

'Four days,' Matt said grimly to Beth over their computer

screens. 'So she was dead by then if he was disposing of her possessions.'

'The poor child,' Beth said. 'She didn't stand a chance.'

All the team knew this new information was a huge blow to the possibility of finding Leila alive, and Kelsey would need to be told at some point. However, evidence still needed to be collected to charge Weaver with murder and make sure the charge stuck.

Beth keyed in the number for the next caller on the list, introduced herself and said she was following up on the sighting she'd reported of Leila Smith. 'It's OK,' the woman said straight away, 'I made a mistake. The child I thought could be Leila lives in the next road to me with her brothers and sisters. That's why she looked familiar.'

Beth thanked her, made a note on the system and then phoned the next caller. 'Mrs Julie Branston?'

'Speaking.'

'This is Detective Constable Beth Mayes from Coleshaw Police Station.'

'Just a moment,' she said. Beth heard a door close, then Julie Branston came back on the phone. 'Sorry, I didn't want to disturb my little one. She's only just gone off to sleep.'

'I'm following up on your call earlier regarding Leila Smith,' Beth said.

'Yes, I'm sure I saw Leila with a man I assumed to be her father in Marsborough shopping centre.'

'When?'

'On Saturday, the seventeenth of November. She looked like the girl in the photo. She was very upset – shouting and crying. I was worried – I mean, you hear so many strange things – so I went over and asked her if she was all right. The man she was with told me she was upset because she'd lost her favourite teddy bear, and he was going to buy her another one.'

'What time was this?' Beth asked.

'Early afternoon. Around one o'clock the first time I saw them. I was going into the shopping centre as they were coming out.'

'You saw them again?' Beth asked, her hopes building and adrenalin kicking in.

'No, it was just him the second time. He was alone in the shopping centre, having a coffee near the children's play area.'

'Oh,' Beth said, unable to hide her disappointment.

'I went over and asked him if he'd found his daughter's teddy bear. I was just being friendly. I know how upsetting it is for children to lose a favourite toy. But he seemed a bit put out that I'd spoken to him and was rather curt.'

'Which day was this?'

'Wednesday, the twenty-eighth of November. It would have been around three o'clock, perhaps a bit before.'

'Did he say whether they'd found the teddy bear?' Beth asked, taking notes.

'Yes, he said they had.'

'Did he have it with him?'

'No. I assumed he'd found it on a previous day.'

'And there was no sign of Leila?'

'No. It was clear he didn't want to talk to me, so I went back to sit with my friends. He left soon after.'

'Can you give me a description of the man?'

'Yes. Late forties. I guess five foot six or seven, average build. He had black hair but was bald on top. The first time I saw him he was wearing dark jeans and a navy zip-up jacket like the ones you get in Marks and Spencer, but I'm not sure the second time. He was sitting down. I didn't get a good view of him and he left soon after I spoke to him.'

'Would you be able to identify him in a line-up?'

'Yes, I think so.'

'Thank you. That's very helpful. Someone will be in touch to arrange that.'

'Have you found Leila?' she asked.

'No, not yet.'

'Oh dear. Her poor mother. Perhaps I should have done more when I first saw them together. I had a gut feeling something wasn't right, but then I told myself that lots of kids get upset over things they've lost.'

'You've been very helpful. I doubt there was any more you could have done.' Beth thanked her again, said goodbye and quickly updated DS Scrivener.

THIRTY-TWO

'We will be charging Colin Weaver with the abduction and murder of Leila,' Beth said to Kelsey, breaking the news as gently as she could. Kelsey's face immediately crumpled, and Sharon looked equally shocked. Beth had asked Sharon to be present when she spoke to Kelsey.

'But you haven't found her body yet,' Kelsey wept. 'There's a chance she might still be alive.'

'We don't think so,' Beth said gently. 'The circumstantial evidence is overwhelming. And the crown prosecution service wouldn't have given us the go ahead to take the case to court if they didn't agree.'

'Oh no. My poor darling Leila,' Kelsey cried. 'Please find her little body and bring her home, so I can at least bury her.' Beth's eyes filled, as did Sharon's.

For some moments, all that could be heard was the sound of Kelsey's uncontrollable sobbing. Sharon, still clearly in a state of shock, tried to comfort her sister. Eventually Kelsey's crying eased and Sharon asked Beth, 'Is Weaver pleading guilty?'

'At present he's pleading guilty to abducting Leila but not guilty to her murder,' Beth replied. 'However, that could change before the case goes to court. His solicitor may advise him to plead guilty to reduce his sentence.'

'Reduce his sentence?' Sharon quivered, appalled.

'It wouldn't be by much. Murder carries a life sentence,' Beth reassured her.

'Until then, he'll be kept in prison?' Kelsey asked, wiping her eyes.

'Yes,' Beth said.

'And you're still looking for Leila's grave on the moor, where Mrs Goodman suggested?' Kelsey whimpered.

'Yes, we are. But Mrs Goodman can only suggest places because of her knowledge of the area. She can't be exact. She's very upset by what has happened at her cottage, but apart from the one phone call Weaver made to her complaining about the cold, Mrs Goodman didn't hear from him while he was there.'

'He was complaining about the cold after he'd murdered my daughter!' Kelsey cried, her eyes filling again.

Beth gave a small nod. There was nothing more she could offer. She'd come here to tell them that Weaver would be charged before it was announced on the news. She now offered Kelsey and Sharon her condolences and made a move to go. She'd come alone – Matt was working on another case, as the team dedicated to finding Leila had been scaled down now Weaver had been caught.

'I'll see you out,' Sharon said, standing, and went with Beth to the front door. 'I was wondering,' Sharon said quietly so Kelsey couldn't hear, 'perhaps I should visit Colin Weaver in prison and try to persuade him to tell me where he's buried Leila?'

'I doubt his solicitor would agree to you seeing him before the trial,' Beth said. 'And it would be very upsetting for you and unlikely to achieve anything. Trained officers, including myself, skilled in interviewing techniques, have questioned

Mr Weaver and he's not ready to reveal where he's hidden Leila's body yet. Some people convicted of crimes like this never tell. Some boast in prison about what they've done, and others only tell after years in prison or on their death bed.'

'But wouldn't it be worth a try?' Sharon persisted. 'It might give my sister some hope.'

'My suggestion would be that you help your sister write a victim impact statement, which could be read out in court before Mr Weaver is sentenced.'

Sharon nodded, although to Beth it seemed half-hearted – as though she hadn't quite given up on the idea of visiting Weaver in prison.

'I'll let you know if there's any more news,' Beth said, and opened the front door.

'Thank you. Have a good Christmas,' Sharon said, her voice flat.

Beth nodded stiffly. 'Take care.' It didn't seem right to wish Sharon a happy Christmas, because clearly she and Kelsey wouldn't be having a happy Christmas this year or probably for many years to come, if ever.

The loss of a loved one was always worse at Christmas, Beth thought, as she made her way along the corridor towards the stairs. Her father had died just before Christmas ten years ago, but it still hung over her family at this time of year. It would be the same for Kelsey and Sharon. Beth hadn't asked them what they were doing on Christmas Day – it hadn't seemed appropriate – but she assumed the two of them would spend it together, locked in their misery. Some of the doors she passed had Christmas decorations, and a garland hung in the stairwell. Set against the backdrop of dismal grey concrete, it seemed pitiful rather than festive.

Beth got into the car and sat for a few moments, staring through the windscreen, deep in thought. When she started the engine, instead of going straight back to the police station, she drove around the ring road and parked outside Mrs Goodman's maisonette. Christmas fairy lights were draped across her living-room window, already switched on and twinkling in the murkiness of an overcast day. A holly wreath had been hung on the door. As Beth began up the path, the front door opened and Mrs Goodman appeared.

'What do you think?' she asked, stepping outside and pointing to the fairy lights. 'I wasn't sure if I should do it this year with Leila missing, but I thought it would be nice for the other children around here.'

'Yes, they're lovely,' Beth agreed, and went inside.

'Would you like a coffee and a mince pie?' Mrs Goodman asked, showing Beth into the front room. She seemed more relaxed than the last time Beth and Matt had visited her and was clearly in a festive mood.

'No, thank you,' Beth said. 'I'm due back at the station soon. I won't keep you long.' She sat opposite Mrs Goodman. 'I've just been to see Kelsey and Sharon to tell them that Colin Weaver is being charged with the abduction and murder of Leila.'

'Oh my! So you've found her body?' she asked, clearly shocked.

'No. But there's enough evidence to charge him without it. We're still searching the moors, but the search has been scaled down unless any new leads come in.'

'I'm so sorry, I've told you all I know,' she said.

'We appreciate your help, but I just wanted to run through the phone calls Colin Weaver made to you on the afternoon of Wednesday, the twenty-eighth of November.'

'Phone call,' Doris corrected. 'He only made one call.'

'According to Mr Weaver's phone records, which we've now looked at, he called you three times that afternoon, but

191

in quick succession. It appears you didn't answer the first two calls and they went through to your voicemail.'

'Oh yes, I see what you mean.'

'Did Mr Weaver leave a message?'

'No. I didn't get to my phone in time to answer it, and he called straight back as far as I remember.'

Beth nodded. 'That call lasted over six minutes. You said before when we asked you about it that he'd phoned to complain about the cottage being cold. What else did he talk about?'

Mrs Goodman looked thoughtful. 'Nothing, as far as I can remember. He was just complaining about the cold.'

'Six minutes is quite a long time. Did he give you any details? Where he was sleeping, for instance?'

She shook her head. 'In one of the beds, I assume.'

'Apparently not,' Beth said. 'While Leila was there, Mr Weaver slept on the sofa because the roof above one of the bedrooms was leaking so badly.'

'He might have mentioned that. Why? Is it important?'

'It could be, in pinpointing Leila's last movements. Mr Weaver was seen alone in Marsborough earlier that day, so we're now assuming Leila was already dead by that afternoon. If he was still sleeping on the sofa when he called you, though, it raises the possibility that she was alive then.'

'I'm really not sure,' Mrs Goodman replied.

'You said before that you advised Colin Weaver to go home if he was finding the cottage too cold?' Mrs Goodman nodded. 'Did you tell him we'd had to force entry into his flat so he wouldn't be able to let himself in as the door had been padlocked by us?'

Doris stared at Beth, clearly confused and a little flustered. 'I don't think I knew that then, did I?'

'I'd have thought so. The news would have quickly been general knowledge on the estate.'

'I'm sorry,' Doris said, drawing herself upright. 'Am I being accused of something? I know it was my cottage Colin used and I'm desperately sorry for what happened there. But I honestly had no idea what was going on. I feel bad enough without being made to feel more guilty.' She took a tissue from the sleeve of her cardigan and pressed it to her eyes.

'I'm not accusing you of anything,' Beth said evenly. 'Please don't upset yourself. I'm just trying to piece together Leila's last movements. If you do remember anything, no matter how small, let me or one of my colleagues know.'

'Of course I will. I've always helped the police before, haven't I?'

'Yes. And we're grateful for it.' Beth stood. 'Well, have a good Christmas.'

'And you.'

THIRTY-THREE

Colin Weaver sat glumly in his cell as sounds drifted in from other parts of the prison. Male voices – some raised, others with accents – movement, metal doors opening and clanging shut. He'd been there three weeks now, but he doubted he'd ever get used to it. The noise kept him awake at night, although he was being held in solitary confinement – for his own protection, a prison officer had told him.

The officer had taken him aside when he'd first arrived and explained that child abusers were often attacked by other prisoners with knives and sharp objects they'd smuggled in. Child abusers were looked upon as the lowest of the low, he'd said, the scum of the criminal world, and below them were child murderers – of which Colin was now one. He'd protested that he was on remand and hadn't been found guilty of anything yet but gave up his argument as another prisoner made a lunge at him right in front of the officer as they were on their way to his cell. Even his meals were brought on a tray, since other prisoners had been known to contaminate the food of child abusers and murderers with spit, urine and faeces. But however depressing all this was, Colin consoled himself that he wouldn't have to suffer it for much longer. As soon as what had really happened came out, he'd be released.

No, it shouldn't be much longer, Colin thought, before she phoned the police or his solicitor and explained everything, identifying herself as the accomplice Colin had referred to in his interview. She would describe how she'd masterminded the plan to take Leila and explain the mitigating circumstances that excused their actions. Yes, he was pleading guilty to abducting Leila, but it hadn't been against her will. Leila had readily gone with him and he'd done it to give her a better life. He'd tried to explain all this when the police had interviewed him, but when he'd said there'd been someone else involved whose identity he couldn't reveal, they'd dismissed it and referred him to a psychologist for an assessment. Just as they'd dismissed the two thousand pounds missing from his life savings as proof that Leila was alive. Morons. They were going to look very foolish when the truth came out.

Colin felt he'd been honest when the police had questioned him the second time, he felt, and had admitted that looking after Leila had proved far more of a challenge than he'd anticipated, and that he'd had to slap her a few times. But most parents slapped their children, didn't they? His father had often hit him for quite minor misdemeanours, and it hadn't done him any harm. He'd tried to tell DCs Mayes and Davis that he hadn't had any previous experience of looking after children and he'd been thrown in at the deep end, but they hadn't been interested. He'd also admitted that, with hindsight, he probably should have planned to take Leila a bit differently, but that would all come out once she phoned.

What was a few more days in prison compared to the life that awaited him once he was free?

It would of course help him enormously, Colin thought, standing and walking around his cell, if Leila was found, dead or alive. If she was dead, her body would show she'd died from natural causes. He'd told them where he'd searched and that his gut feeling was that she'd turned right instead of left out of the cottage and had got lost on the moors. If she'd died out there it was hardly his fault. She should have done as he'd told her and stayed in the cottage while he'd gone into town; then she'd still be alive. But DCs Mayes and Davis hadn't agreed with him and had kept asking where he'd buried Leila's body. He'd got angry and upset then and his solicitor had insisted on another break. When they'd returned, following her advice, he'd replied 'No comment' to all their questions. Which was probably what he should have done from the start.

It was Christmas Day tomorrow and he comforted himself with the thought that this time next year he would be enjoying his new life abroad.

THIRTY-FOUR

Kelsey woke the day after Christmas with a massive hangover. Her sister had insisted on being with her during Christmas Day but had gone home early evening, much to Kelsey's relief. Sharon had clearly felt she had a duty to be with her at what she'd called 'this very difficult time', but she had also looked relieved when Kelsey had told her she needed to be alone.

As soon as Sharon had left, Kelsey had opened the bottle of vodka she had hidden away, and she was now regretting it. Her mouth was parched dry, her head throbbed and she'd had terrifying dreams all night, most likely fuelled by all the alcohol.

The dreams had been so realistic – she'd been able to see clearly the dreadful mess she'd made of her life and the damage she'd done to her children. It was as though the Ghost of Christmas Past had visited her and forced her to see the reality of years of drink and drug abuse funded by prostitution. Did she have no self-respect? Apparently not. Four children taken into care and then adopted, and the last murdered by a paedophile and buried on the moors. It was all her fault and the regret burned into her like a red-hot branding iron. There'd been no Ghost of Christmas Future to give her hope. Kelsey was at rock bottom, with nothing to live for.

Now she was awake came the sickening realization that despite the abuse she'd suffered, her life needn't have been like this – fucked up and destroyed. She'd been given countless opportunities to get out of the mess: rehab, counselling, second chances. She'd blown them all, time and time again, and now it was too late. Ultimately, she was responsible for Leila's death, and she knew she couldn't stand many more days and nights like this with all hope gone.

Hauling herself up on the pillow, Kelsey checked the time on her phone: 10.14 a.m. Not that the time really mattered, since she had nothing to be up for. She needed a pee and a drink of water, though. Then, once she was dressed, she'd go out and buy herself another bottle of vodka – courtesy of her sister. With Leila being in the news so often and police visiting her flat, Kelsey's clients had been keeping away, so she didn't have any money. Sharon had realized and given her some more money.

'For food,' she'd said. Although Sharon must have known there was a good chance Kelsey would spend it on booze or drugs. She'd relapsed before and now that Leila was dead there was no reason for her to stay sober or off the drugs.

Easing herself from the bed, Kelsey pulled on the jumper, jeans and socks she'd taken off the night before and padded out of her bedroom to the bathroom. The flat was cold, but to her surprise the bathroom was tidy. Much cleaner and tidier than she remembered it. Sharon must have done it before she'd left, and Kelsey had been too pissed to notice last night. She'd better text Sharon and thank her.

Having flushed the toilet, Kelsey washed her hands and threw cold water on her face. She patted her cheeks dry with the towel that had been left neatly folded over the towel rail and then headed to the kitchen. This, too, was cleaner and tidier than she remembered. She'd let everything go since the last visit from the police. There was no point in keeping the place clean and tidy to impress Peter Harris, because now Leila wouldn't ever be coming back. Sharon must have cleared up in here as well and Kelsey had failed to notice. Not surprising, as she'd started drinking straight after Sharon had left and was out of it pretty quickly. Nice of her sister, though.

Kelsey searched the kitchen cupboards for something to eat. All she could find was a packet of biscuits, so she took those and a glass of water to the sofa. The coffee table was clear of debris and very clean – spotless, in fact. Which was odd. Where was the empty bottle of vodka and the glass from last night, plus any other rubbish she hadn't thrown in the bin? It couldn't have been Sharon, could it? Hadn't she left before Kelsey started drinking? Yes, she was sure of it – well, as sure as she could be after the amount she'd drunk. She must have thrown out the rubbish herself before she'd gone to bed and been too pissed to remember. It was odd, though – tidiness had never been a product of her drinking before. Just the opposite, in fact.

Kelsey returned to the kitchen where she pushed open the lid of the swing bin. Yes, there was the empty bottle of vodka and some other rubbish. So she *had* thrown everything away before going to bed, as if it mattered any more! She sat on the sofa again and absently ate a biscuit and drank some water. The other flats in the block were exceptionally quiet the day after Christmas as people slept in. Quiet as the grave, Kelsey thought. The day yawned before her, painful and raw. She needed to get some more alcohol. The twenty pounds her sister had given her would be enough to put her out for the day.

Suddenly, she froze. The hairs stood up on the back of her neck. She'd heard a noise that sounded as if it had come from inside the flat. Kelsey sat still and listened.

Yes, there it was again. Jesus! Had someone broken in during the night, and was now lying in wait for her, ready to spring out and attack? Another disgruntled client? Or maybe the pig returning? Her heart began drumming loudly as thoughts of her last beating flashed before her and fear gripped her. She needed something she could use for protection.

Quietly standing and with her legs unsteady, Kelsey crossed to the kitchen where she took a large kitchen knife from the drawer. She began silently along the hall. There it was again. The same noise. A floorboard creaking. It seemed to be coming from Leila's room. Her bedroom door was closed, like it always was now. After she'd gone missing Kelsey had closed the door and hadn't been in the room since. The memories were too painful.

She paused outside Leila's room and listened. The front door was only a few steps away. Should she make a dash for it and cry out for help? But who would answer her cries? She doubted anyone would come to her assistance. She'd have to deal with this alone, just as she had done most of her adult life. Another creak and the handle on Leila's bedroom door began to turn. Kelsey flattened herself against the wall, knife at the ready, and watched in terror as the door slowly opened.

'Stay away!' she cried, raising the knife, ready to bring it down.

'Don't!' A child appeared. 'It's me.'

'Leila?' Kelsey stared in disbelief. 'It can't be,' she gasped.

'Yes, it is. Put the knife down, Mum, you're scaring me.'

Kelsey lowered her arm. 'Is it really you, Leila?'

'Yes, I've come home.'

But it wasn't until Kelsey felt her daughter's arms slip around her waist that she truly believed it was her. Then she began to cry, and couldn't stop.

THIRTY-FIVE

'Don't cry,' Leila said, holding her mother. 'I wanted to surprise you, not make you cry. I thought you'd be happy.'

'I am happy,' Kelsey said through her tears. 'But you scared me half to death. The police told me you were dead and that they were looking for your grave on the moors. You look so different with your hair short and those fancy clothes. I didn't recognize you.'

'I bought them, Mum, and I'm going to buy you lots of nice things too now. I've got money.'

'How did you get money?' Kelsey asked, a new fear gripping her. 'Where've you been all this time? I have so many questions. Start at the beginning and tell me what happened. I've been going out of my mind.'

'I'll tell you, but you have to promise you won't be angry with me.'

'I promise, of course I won't be angry with you,' Kelsey said, with a small nervous laugh. 'I'm just grateful you're alive.' But she steeled herself for what she was about to be told.

Leila wiped away her mother's tears and sat very close as she began her story. Kelsey held her daughter's hand, unable to believe she was really here. 'Colin who lives in the flat below took me,' Leila said.

'I know. The police told me.'

'He seemed nice to begin with. He used to talk to me and buy me presents, and he let me wait in his flat when it was raining and I couldn't come here because you had a man in your bedroom.'

Kelsey flinched with guilt.

'Colin told me I deserved a better mother than you and I thought he was right. I was angry with you for not looking after me like other parents do. Colin said I could trust him and that he had a plan to teach you a lesson. I didn't think you would care if I came home or not. It seemed as if I was just in your way.'

Kelsey's eyes filled and she squeezed her daughter's hand. 'I'm so sorry.'

'Running away was like a game to begin with,' Leila continued. 'Colin told me not to take anything from here because he would buy me new clothes. I'd never had new things before, so I was happy. But the first night I was at his flat I realized I didn't have Buttons, so we came back here to get him.'

'I thought I heard you,' Kelsey said.

'Did you? You seemed to be asleep. It was funny then, the two of us in the middle of the night creeping into the flat. You were snoring and I laughed. Colin told me to be quiet. I got Buttons and we left. But the next day Colin went to work and locked me in the bedroom in his flat. It was then I started to get scared. I didn't like being locked in and I had to use a potty like a baby. He threatened to tie me up and gag me if I made a noise.'

'Did he touch you ...?' Kelsey began but had to stop and try again. 'Did he touch your privates?'

'No. But he slapped me and shouted a lot, and he was

203

really scary if I didn't do as he said or if I didn't like the food or the clothes he bought. He wasn't at all like the person I knew from before, and I wanted to come home. I could hear you being hurt and crying in here and I told him you needed help, but he wouldn't let me come. He said you could take care of yourself and you didn't really want me anyway. Which I sort of knew.'

'That's not true!' Kelsey cried, upset. 'I did want you, but I was a mess.'

'I know that, and from now on I'm going to help you, so I can stay here.'

Kelsey didn't say what she was thinking – that it wasn't possible for her to stay as the social services had a care order. For now, she needed to hear Leila's story, and waited for her to continue.

'Colin gave me new clothes so I wouldn't be recognized and threw away my old ones. He took me in his car to Granny Goodman's cottage. It was horrible – freezing cold, and there was no television. I don't think he liked being there either. He moaned a lot and got more angry. He cut my hair so he could take me out. All the time I was looking for a way to run off, but I knew he would catch me. Then one day he left me in the cottage by myself and I knew that was my chance. I took some of his money – he had loads in a carrier bag – and I forced open a window and climbed out. There was thick fog and I could hardly see anything, but I walked all the way along the lane. It was scary but not as scary as staying with him. I knew the way the lane bent from seeing it when he took me out in the car. Eventually I came to the village and found a bus stop. I had money to pay, but when I got on the bus the driver asked where my mummy was and I said I was meeting her in town. When we arrived I'd no idea where I was and it was dark and cold. I knew I needed to find somewhere warm to sleep. I had plenty of money, but I knew I couldn't book into a hotel by myself. Then I saw a woman sleeping rough in a shop doorway and I asked her if she would like to go to a hotel for the night. She thought I was joking to begin with, until I showed her the money. She found us a cheap hotel and spoke to the receptionist and signed us in.'

Kelsey looked at her daughter with admiration. 'That was good thinking.'

Leila smiled. 'It was lovely and warm, Mum, not like the cottage, and Misha was nice. We had a bed each. She told me she was eighteen and used to work in a hotel but had lost her job and ended up sleeping on the streets. There was a phone in the room and she used it to call home. I thought about calling you, but I wasn't sure you wanted to hear from me. I was still thinking Colin was right when he said you didn't want me, and I thought you'd be angry if I got in touch.'

'Oh, love, I'm so sorry you should think that.' Kelsey's eyes filled again, and she held her daughter close.

'Misha and I stayed there for two weeks.'

'You were there all this time?' Kelsey asked incredulously.

Leila nodded. 'Misha was kind to me. We talked a lot. She was lovely and I told her about what had happened to me. She said I should come back home to you and tell you about Colin, because he was a bad man and the police needed to know, as he might come after me.'

'He can't come after you – he's in prison now,' Kelsey reassured her.

'Good. Misha finally got another job in a hotel that was fifty miles away, so we had to say goodbye and leave.'

'So then where have you been since then?' Kelsey asked, amazed.

'Trying to get back here. I thought about what Misha said and I decided Colin had been wrong and you did love me. And anyway, you are my only mummy and I wanted

205

to be with you. I knew the cottage was a long way from here, but I began getting on buses, trying to find my way back. I used those maps at the bus stops and asked people if I didn't know. I kept my hoody up so people couldn't see my face very well. I had to be careful and I couldn't stay on the same bus for long just in case. I always got on with an adult and chose a bus that was crowded so no one noticed me. Then at night I found a homeless woman and asked her if she would like to book us into a hotel. They always said yes when I showed them I could pay. They were nice apart from one who got very drunk. I cleared off early in the morning while she was still asleep and left her to pay the bill.'

Kelsey laughed.

'Some of them wanted to talk and tell me why they were on the streets and others just wanted to shower and sleep. I never told anyone else about Colin and just said I was twelve and had run away but I was going home.'

Kelsey looked at her daughter, impressed by her resourcefulness. 'You did well. When did you get back to Coleshaw?'

'Late last night, Christmas Day, but there weren't many people out. I guess they were all at home having a nice Christmas. I was excited coming back and a bit nervous. I was careful no one saw me. I still had my front door key. I kept it safe. But when I let myself in and found you'd been drinking again I was very sad. I thought things might be different, like you'd learnt your lesson, but it seemed nothing had changed. I cleared up and went to bed.'

'I'm sorry you found me like that, but I have changed, honestly,' Kelsey said, taking her daughter's hand. 'Last night was a mistake, a relapse. I've been off the booze and drugs for weeks. I drank last night to try to forget.'

'Forget me?' Leila asked.

'No. Not you, love. The pain of losing you. I thought you

were dead. I'm sorry I was such a shit mother. Can you ever forgive me?'

'Yes, I can, and I'm sorry I wasn't a better daughter. I should have helped you more. We can work together now so I can stay here.'

Kelsey looked at her daughter. There was no easy way to say this.

'There's something you need to know,' she said quietly, her voice faltering. 'Peter, our social worker, took out a care order when he thought you'd run away. It still applies. You're going to have to live with Aunty Sharon for now.'

'But I don't want to live with her! I want to stay with you.'

'I know, and I want you here too, but it's not possible right away – the court has decided. And it's better you go to Aunty Sharon than a foster carer you don't know or a children's home. We'll be able to see each other whenever we want. She promised.'

'Will you try to get me back so I can live here?'

'Yes, of course.'

'And we don't have to tell Peter I'm home straight away, do we?'

'I suppose not,' Kelsey agreed.

'So we can spend a few days together, just the two of us, like a proper mother and daughter.'

Kelsey's eyes filled again. 'Yes, love, we can. But stay out of sight. If anyone finds you here, I'll be in big trouble.'

'I'll hide if anyone comes. I'm good at hiding.' Throwing her arms around her mother, she hugged her for all she was worth.

THIRTY-SIX

Sharon was watching the news.

'In an astonishing turn of events, schoolgirl Leila Smith, missing since the thirteenth of November and presumed dead, has been found alive and well at the home of her mother,' the news reporter said, looking earnestly into the camera. She was giving her report standing in front of the block of flats where Kelsey lived. 'The exact details of Leila's miraculous return are as yet unclear, but she was taken from her mother's flat by two social workers earlier today. Mrs Kelsey Smith left with police officers a few minutes later to be questioned, it is understood, about the disappearance of her daughter.'

The camera panned to the entrance to the flats where other reporters and a group of onlookers were waiting. 'It's over six weeks since eight-year-old Leila disappeared without trace, sparking a nationwide hunt,' the reporter continued. 'The obvious question now is: where has she been all that time? Mr Colin Weaver, who lives in the flat directly below Leila and her mother, was charged with Leila's abduction and murder. Clearly the murder charge will have to be dropped now, but what was his involvement in Leila's disappearance, if any? Could it be that the police made a dreadful mistake and he is completely innocent? Leila's aunt, who is close to the family, was unavailable for comment, but a neighbour and friend of Kelsey Smith's said she wouldn't be surprised if Mrs Smith had been hiding Leila all along.

'Is that really possible? That for six weeks, while police forces across the UK were looking for Leila, she was in fact living in the flat you can see behind me all along?'

'No, of course she wasn't, you stupid woman!' Sharon said angrily and switched off the television. They should get their facts right. The police searched Kelsey's flat and had been there countless times since, as had she. Leila wasn't there. She was abducted by Colin Weaver just as the police said. OK, he didn't murder her, but he was still the one who took her.

Sharon went through to the kitchen and poured herself a large gin and tonic to steady her nerves. It had been a long, gruelling day and it wasn't over yet. Around three o'clock that afternoon, Peter Harris had unexpectedly phoned with the news that Leila had been found at her mother's home. Sharon had been too shocked to speak. Apparently Kelsey had called him at ten-thirty that morning, saying Leila had just turned up. He'd gone to Kelsey's flat with a colleague and the police. He said Leila appeared to be physically unharmed, but she would need to have a medical, and then he would bring her to Sharon's. He'd said that, as yet, he didn't know any more about what had happened to Leila. He'd tried talking to her but she was too traumatized to say anything other than Colin Weaver had taken her. He'd told Sharon she shouldn't press Leila for details. It could take weeks, months, even years before she was able to talk about her abduction. However, if Leila *did* disclose anything, Sharon should write it down and tell him.

Now at five o'clock Sharon was anxiously waiting for

Peter Harris and Leila to arrive. Coleshaw was over an hour's drive from her house – Leila's new home.

Sharon refilled her glass and wandered into what would shortly be Leila's bedroom. Peter had been impressed when he'd first seen it – freshly decorated and well equipped. 'Just like a child's bedroom should be,' he'd said. This would be a new start for them both. Leila would quickly see how much her life had improved and would love her as she'd never loved her own mother. Kelsey hadn't appreciated the gift of children – but Sharon would.

The doorbell rang, jolting Sharon from her thoughts. She quickly downed the last of her gin and tonic and, leaving the glass out of sight in the kitchen, went to answer the front door. Leila was standing between two social workers.

'Hello, love,' she said, smiling. The child scowled back.

'This is my colleague, Rana Philips,' Peter said, introducing the woman standing next to him.

Sharon forced a smile and stood aside to let them in. She hadn't expected Peter to bring another social worker with him. He hadn't mentioned it when he'd phoned and had come alone on his previous visits. Rana offered her hand for shaking and Sharon felt obliged to take it. She was a large woman with a firm handshake, someone with presence who wouldn't be bullshitted, Sharon thought. Unlike Peter Harris, who Sharon had eating out of her hand. He was so grateful to her for taking Leila, it was embarrassing.

'Come through,' Sharon said, leading the way into her immaculate off-white living room. 'Would you like a coffee or a tea?'

'No, thank you.' Both social workers declined.

'I want a drink,' Leila demanded, flopping into the armchair that Sharon usually sat in.

'Of course you do,' Sharon said sweetly. 'What would you like? Water, juice or milk?'

'Cola or Fanta,' Leila replied, drawing her feet, shoes still on, onto the cream chair.

'I don't have fizzy drinks, I'm afraid,' Sharon said patiently. 'I thought they were bad for children.'

'All things in moderation,' Rana said, which seemed to suggest she was siding with Leila.

'I have fizzy drinks at my mum's,' Leila added, pulling a face.

'I'll get you a juice,' Sharon said brightly, swallowing what she really wanted to say.

She went into the kitchen and poured a glass of juice. Returning to the living room, she positioned it on a coaster on the coffee table just in front of Leila, then brought in a dining chair to sit on.

'Well, here you are at last,' she enthused. Leila continued to scowl as she drank some of the juice.

'It's bound to take her a while to settle in,' Rana said.

Sharon smiled and nodded.

'So, a few formalities,' Peter said, taking a wodge of papers from his briefcase. 'Here is a copy of the Essential Information Forms.' He passed her the set of printed forms. 'You can read them later, although I expect you'll know most of it already, as you're a relative.'

Sharon nodded and put the papers to one side. Rana was looking around, scrutinizing the room. Sharon thought she'd be impressed.

'You need to sign this form,' Peter said, holding out a pen and another form. 'It gives you the right to foster Leila. I'll leave a copy here.' Sharon signed the form and handed it back.

'Will Leila be allowed to play in this room?' Rana asked.

The short answer was no, but Sharon knew that wasn't what they wanted to hear. 'She has a gorgeous bedroom that Peter has already seen,' she replied.

'It's nice for children to have some of their toys in the

family's main living room,' Rana said. 'It gives them a sense of belonging – of being part of the family.'

'Yes, of course,' Sharon said, bristling at being told what to do in her own home.

'Leila hasn't come with any toys or clothes from home,' Peter said. 'I'll ask Kelsey if she can let you have some.'

'No need,' Sharon replied. 'There was never much there. I've bought Leila clothes as well as some toys, books and games.'

'But it's nice for the child to have some of their own belongings,' Rana said. 'It's reassuring for them to have something familiar when everything else in their life is unfamiliar. The smell of a washing powder, for example, can be a poignant reminder of their home and the loved ones they miss.'

Sharon set her expression to convivial and swallowed the retort biting at her tongue. She would have thought that the fewer reminders Leila had of home, the better.

'Your foster carer payments should start next week,' Peter continued, going through a checklist of matters he needed to raise.

'You get paid for looking after me?' Leila asked, surprised, her juice slopping onto the coffee table as she set down the glass.

Sharon gave a small nod and wondered why the social worker needed to bring this up now in front of Leila. Life was going to be difficult enough without Leila resenting her for being paid to look after her.

'My mum didn't get paid for looking after me,' Leila said. 'And we needed money badly, more than you do.'

Rana smiled knowingly at Sharon. 'It's an inconsistency many of our older children in care pick up on,' she said.

'Really?' Sharon replied, unable to keep the edge from her voice. 'If her mother hadn't had a drink-and-drug problem, they'd have had money. I'm guessing it's the same for many of the children in care.' She knew immediately it was the wrong thing to say. Peter had looked up from his paperwork.

'We mustn't demonize the parents,' Rana said patronizingly. 'Children in care need to maintain a positive image of their birth families.'

Sharon nodded and felt Leila's gaze bore into her as if she'd just scored a point and Sharon had failed the first test.

'Contact,' Peter continued, glancing at his notes. 'I understand from Kelsey that you and she have already discussed Leila seeing her mother. If you are both happy to make your own arrangements, that's fine with me.'

'Good,' Sharon said. 'We are.'

'How often can I see my mummy?' Leila asked.

'I would suggest three times a week to begin with,' Peter replied. 'And phone contact on the days they don't see each other.'

'That's a lot, isn't it?' Sharon said. 'I mean, Leila will be going to school in a few days and she'll have homework. I work and it's an hour's drive each way to Kelsey's flat.'

Peter looked thoughtful. 'If you make one of the contacts at the weekend and two during the week – say, Tuesday and Thursday – then it won't be so disruptive or tiring for you all.'

'It is important Leila sees her mother regularly,' Rana put in. 'Some of our younger children see their parents every day when they first come into care. If you prefer, *we* could set the arrangements for contact ourselves.'

'No, it'll be fine,' Sharon said tightly. 'We'll work it out.'

'Good.' Peter made a note. 'We can always review the arrangements in a month or so,' he added. 'Do you have any other questions? If not, we'll have a look around the house and then leave you to it. I'll phone you tomorrow and then visit again in a couple of days.'

'I don't have any questions,' Sharon said.

'I do,' Leila said, slopping more sticky juice on the table.

'Yes, love?' Rana asked.

'When can I go home?'

There was a short silence, as if the social workers were deciding who should answer.

'Do you remember what we said in the car?' Rana asked with an intensity Sharon found quite nauseating. 'That we need to keep you safe? At present your Aunty Sharon is the best person to do that.'

'You also said I'd get pocket money,' Leila replied tartly.

Rana laughed, although Sharon thought she should be telling Leila not to be so bloody rude and demanding.

'That's right,' Peter said brightly. 'Aunty Sharon will give you pocket money each week.' Then to Sharon: 'At Leila's age it's five pounds a week, which is included in your allowance.'

Sharon nodded stiffly and moved the glass of half-drunk juice that Leila had left near the edge of the table further away so it wouldn't get knocked over.

'I haven't finished that yet!' Leila cried and snatched it back, slopping juice everywhere.

'I'll get a cloth,' Sharon said, and disappeared into the kitchen.

As she mopped up the juice, she saw Rana's judgemental expression, but sod it, it was her house.

'So maybe you could show us around now,' Rana said, standing as Sharon finished wiping up the mess. 'Let's start with the kitchen.'

Sharon knew her kitchen was very different to her sister's and probably most others they saw – spotlessly white with sparkling granite worksurfaces. She was sure at least one of the social workers would comment. But they watched her put the cloth into the washing machine, glanced around, then headed out, upstairs and to Leila's room.

After Rana's remarks about the importance of Leila having her old belongings, Sharon decided not to make too much of all the new clothes she'd bought Leila, which were now hanging in the wardrobe. She just opened the door to show them. Peter nodded, but Rana opened the chest of drawers where Sharon had neatly folded Leila's new underwear, pyjamas, socks, vests and T-shirts. Again, there were no comments and Sharon sensed disapproval of her neat, orderly arrangements.

'Do you like your desk and chair?' Sharon asked Leila, drawing them to her attention.

'Where's the television?' Leila asked.

'There isn't one in here, love,' Sharon replied. 'It's downstairs in the living room.'

Leila pulled a face. 'All the kids at school have televisions in their bedrooms, and iPads. Have you got me an iPad?'

Sharon stared at her, incredulous. She didn't seem to be joking, and the social workers were looking at her expectantly too.

'Children nowadays need access to a laptop or tablet,' Rana said. 'With suitable parental controls in place, of course.'

'But she's only eight,' Sharon said as Leila stared at her.

'They learn how to use them at school in reception class,' Peter said.

'Fine,' Sharon said brusquely. 'But it's nice to play traditional games too, like Cluedo and Scrabble, isn't it?'

'You sound just like Colin,' Leila said.

Sharon froze. Both social workers were looking at Leila to see if she would say any more about her abductor, but Leila had moved on and was now rummaging in the toy box. Sharon breathed a sigh of relief.

'It's all baby stuff,' Leila said, tipping the box upside down.

'We can go shopping tomorrow and buy some more toys,' Sharon replied, throwing the social workers a rueful smile. 'I've got a lot to learn.'

'That's what Mum said about you,' Leila replied, as sharp as a knife – just like her mother. 'She said you know jack shit about kids, but I'd soon teach you.'

Sharon resisted the urge to slap her and went instead to the bed.

'Have you seen these?' she asked, picking up the soft toys she'd bought and carefully arranged on the pillow. These would surely impress them all, she thought. 'Peter Rabbit, Rainbow Fish, a Care Bear and a soft furry elephant,' she said, stroking each one. 'Aren't they cute?' Then to the social workers she said, 'All I need to buy now is her new school uniform.'

'Can't I go to my old school?' Leila asked, snatching the Care Bear from her aunt.

'It's too far away,' Peter said. 'You'll soon make new friends.'

Sharon saw Leila's face lose its harshness and she appeared almost vulnerable. 'Have you found Buttons yet?' she asked, her voice slight.

'I'm afraid not,' Peter said gently.

Sharon had been prepared for this and, lifting up the duvet, she took out her pièce de résistance – the teddy bear that was an exact replica of Buttons – and placed it in Leila's arms.

'That's not Buttons!' Leila declared angrily, hurling it against the wall. 'You're trying to trick me just like Colin did!'

'She's been through a lot,' Rana said.

'I expect she's tired,' Peter added. 'We'll have a quick look round the rest of the house and then leave you to it.'

Sharon showed them the spare room, then the bathroom. She was about to go downstairs when Rana opened Sharon's bedroom door and went in. Peter followed her and Leila tried to push past Sharon to go in as if she owned the place.

Sharon stuck out her elbow and then pretended it was an accident when she squealed. This was her bedroom, her own personal space, and it would be the first and last time Leila entered it. She waited by the door while the three of them traipsed in and then came out.

Downstairs, Peter wished them a pleasant evening and both social workers said goodbye and left. As soon as Sharon closed the front door, Leila looked at her accusingly. 'You've been drinking,' she said. 'I can smell it on your breath, just like I used to smell it on my mum's. You're no better than she is. How much will you give me to stop me telling the social worker?'

'Nothing. You're a rude, ungrateful little cow! And if we're going to get on, you need to start doing as you're told.'

'That's just what Colin said, and I don't like him either!'

THIRTY-SEVEN

At six o'clock it was pitch black as Kelsey got off the bus and entered the Hawthorn Estate. She'd spent the whole afternoon at Coleshaw Police Station, answering questions about Leila's disappearance while officers had searched her flat looking for evidence that she may have been harbouring Leila while she'd been missing, or had known where she was. They'd found nothing, of course.

Throughout the questioning Kelsey had kept to the story she and Leila had agreed upon: that Leila had come back that morning, not the day after Christmas, and that Kelsey had phoned the police straight away. She'd said Leila had told her Colin had taken her from the play area and then kept her in his flat and then at Mrs Goodman's cottage, but other than that she'd been too traumatized to say anything else. Eventually they'd released her without charge and now she was looking forward to getting home and phoning Leila at Sharon's house.

Hands deep in her pockets and head drawn in to protect her from the cold, Kelsey continued across the estate, wondering how Leila had got on when Peter Harris and the police had spoken to her. She and Leila had agreed that it was safer if she didn't give too many details about her disappearance and return so there was less chance of her slipping up and giving them away. They'd agreed that she wouldn't tell them she'd taken Colin Weaver's money, although Kelsey doubted Leila would get into much trouble for that, considering what he'd done to her. Kelsey had also told Leila not to admit she'd gone with Colin Weaver of her own free will, as it could complicate matters and might lead to a more lenient sentence for him. He had abducted her, causing them both unbelievable agony – so he deserved whatever he got. Leila had told her mother he hadn't sexually abused her, but Kelsey still had her doubts, because why else would he have taken her? It didn't make sense and she told the police that.

The time she'd spent with her daughter had been wonderful, she thought as she walked. Two whole days – talking, laughing, crying, watching television, ordering take-aways, doing silly things, making up for lost time, and creating the mother-and-daughter relationship they'd never had. Kelsey had wished it could last forever, but that wasn't possible. One day, she told Leila, if she kept off the drink and drugs, they could do it again, for good. She promised she would do everything possible to win her back. She'd lost her older children for good. Her only hope of seeing them again was if, as adults, they decided to contact her. But she still had a chance with Leila.

Others walking on the estate after dark kept to the paths where the lighting was better, but, eager to be home, Kelsey took the shortcut towards the play area. It had emptied now of children and a group of teenagers were hanging around as usual, but other than looking over they paid her little attention. It was too early for Kevin, Jason and Mike to be out dealing. With relief, Kelsey acknowledged that those days when she'd waited anxiously for them to arrive, ticking off the minutes till her next fix, had passed. She had no need for them now and she would make sure she never did again.

Kelsey heard Doris Goodman's door open behind her, followed by children's voices saying goodbye and thanking her for dinner.

'You're welcome. Good boy. Make sure you go straight home,' Doris said.

Kelsey supposed she wasn't so bad really. Her heart was in the right place. She'd often taken Leila in, although Kelsey had resented it. Now her mind was clearer, she was starting to see she'd probably deserved all those lectures. The police had said Mrs Goodman felt really bad that Colin Weaver had used her cottage to hide Leila. Kelsey thought she might call in on her sometime and tell her it wasn't her fault and that she didn't hold her responsible. Now Leila had been found safe and well, Kelsey was feeling very magnanimous and forgiving.

As she entered her block of flats, her neighbour Brooke was leaving with her two youngest children, but instead of saying hello or even smiling, she pushed past her. 'You want to be ashamed of yourself!' she hissed. 'Women like you shouldn't be allowed to have kids.'

'And you need to mind your own fucking business!' Kelsey returned angrily. 'I know it was you who spoke to the press. Concentrate on your own problems. I've heard what goes on in your place through the walls.'

Ignoring Brooke's middle-finger sign, Kelsey continued up the stairs to her flat. As she rounded the corner, her heart sank. Her front door had been graffitied in black paint. *Whore! Liar! Slag! Bitch!* The council had only just removed the last lot. There were plenty of people on the estate who could have been responsible – ready to condemn others while ignoring their own failings.

Opening her front door, Kelsey was immediately hit by

the emptiness inside the flat. Just those couple of days of Leila being there had injected life into it – her laughing and messing around, trying to recover the childhood she should have had. Now it was gone again – as if it never existed. As she went in and closed the door, Kelsey vowed once more to do whatever it took to bring Leila back. In the meantime, she'd make the most of contact. Peter had said she could phone Leila on the days she didn't see her. But first she needed a hot drink.

Kelsey filled the kettle and made herself a cup of tea, marvelling at all the food in the cupboards, fridge and freezer. While Leila had been there she'd given Kelsey some of Colin Weaver's money and told her to go out and get what they needed. Kelsey would have loved to take Leila with her shopping, but it was too risky – she would have been spotted. So she'd taken the hundred pounds Leila had counted out and called a taxi – there and back. She wouldn't normally have spent the money on taxis, but she wanted to be as quick as possible so she didn't miss any time with Leila. She'd returned laden with bags of groceries. There was still over five hundred pounds left, which Leila had told her mother to keep. Kelsey had promised none of it would go on drugs or alcohol, and Leila had said she trusted her.

Taking the mug of steaming tea and a savoury pastry to the sofa, Kelsey pressed the number for Sharon's mobile. She'd told Leila she'd buy her a phone of her own with some of Weaver's money so they could talk whenever they wanted to, but for now their calls would have to go through Sharon. Her phone rang a few times and then went through to voice-mail. Typical Sharon, Kelsey thought; she often left her phone in her handbag where she couldn't hear it. She tried again with the same result and then called Sharon's landline, which she was sure to hear. She took another sip of her tea and waited for Sharon to answer. The phone rang and rang.

Strange she wasn't picking up. Peter had said he'd make a point of telling Sharon that she would phone. Perhaps they'd gone out. Yes, that must be it.

Kelsey finished her tea, ate the pastry, waited fifteen minutes, then tried Sharon's landline again. As before, it rang and rang and no answerphone cut in. She tried her mobile and this time she left a message. 'Hi, Sharon, it's me. I guess the two of you are out. Can you give me a ring when you're free so I can talk to Leila? Thanks.'

If felt strange having to ask her younger sister if she could speak to Leila, but she supposed she'd have to get used to it. It was probably difficult for Sharon too – assuming parental duties for her niece when she'd had no experience of looking after a child, and with Kelsey looking on. Or perhaps it wasn't. Sharon could be a dark horse sometimes, never letting on or talking about her feelings. It had surprised Kelsey that she'd wanted to look after Leila.

Kelsey made herself another mug of tea and returned to the sofa. She'd cook something proper to eat, just as soon as she'd spoken to Leila. She ached to speak to her, to hear the sound of her voice again, and find out how she'd got on since they'd parted earlier. Hopefully Leila would be able to take Sharon's mobile somewhere so they could talk in private – the landline was in the living room. She'd told Leila not to give her aunt any more details of her return than she'd given the police and her social worker, because Sharon was sure to feel duty bound to pass it on.

'She's not like me,' Kelsey had said. 'She's got better morals.'

They'd laughed conspiratorially and Leila had kissed her cheek and said, 'I love you, Mum. You're far better than Sharon. You're not stuck up like she is.'

They'd laughed again and Kelsey had appreciated Leila's loyalty. Having let her daughter down so badly in the past, it meant a lot to Kelsey to know she still had her on-side. If she was honest, she felt jealous that Sharon was looking after Leila, but there'd been no alternative if she wasn't to go to a foster carer or a children's home.

Half an hour passed and Sharon didn't return her call. It was 7.30 p.m. Surely they were back from wherever they'd been by now? Kelsey didn't want to make a nuisance of herself by phoning repeatedly, but she couldn't settle to anything until she'd spoken to Leila. First thing in the morning she'd go out and buy Leila the mobile phone she'd promised her; then they wouldn't have this problem. She should have bought her a phone of her own months ago when she'd first wanted to – then none of this would have happened!

Kelsey waited another ten minutes and called Sharon's mobile again. As before, it rang and then went through to voicemail. 'Hi, it's me again. Can you phone, please, so I can talk to Leila? Thanks.'

She tried the landline, but still no luck. Where were they at this time? What could they possibly be doing? Surely Sharon had checked her mobile by now and seen the missed calls and listened to her voice message?

Suddenly her phone bleeped with a text message. It was from Sharon: *Leila is asleep. Will phone tomorrow. x*

Of course. Relief. That was it. Leila was asleep. She texted back: *OK. Speak tomorrow x*. Leila would have been exhausted with everything that she'd been through today. But why hadn't Sharon answered her landline? If Leila was in bed asleep, surely she would have answered it quickly so the sound of it ringing didn't wake her?

For reasons Kelsey couldn't quite say, she felt a pang of unease, which she dismissed as anxiety. She'd lost her daughter once through her own stupidity and neglect, and now she was being overprotective. Naturally Sharon would take good care of Leila. Why shouldn't she?

THIRTY-EIGHT

'You're not going to like this,' Beth said as Matt slid into his office chair the following morning. 'Colin Weaver's solicitor is going back to court this morning to apply for bail.'

'He won't get it, will he?'

'The DS says he's in with a chance now the murder charge has been dropped. We're opposing the application, but Weaver has no previous convictions, and until all of this he was considered of good character. Forensics couldn't find anything on his computer to suggest paedophile activity and Leila isn't saying he molested her. In fact, she's saying very little. The judge might decide he isn't a threat to the public and grant him bail.'

'But he's pleading guilty to abducting Leila,' Matt said.

'Yes, with mitigating circumstances. He's still claiming he was acting in Leila's best interests and that she agreed to go with him. He says he was like a father figure to her and only did what he did to keep her safe, because the social services weren't doing their job and her mother was useless. He's claiming he planned to start a new life with her, which is why he took out all his savings.'

Matt pulled a face. 'The judge won't buy that.'

'Possibly not, but there might be enough to grant him bail – innocent until proven guilty, after all. And as his solicitor pointed out, some of our case – namely the murder charge – has already been disproved. Forensics have shown that the blood found in the cottage was his and likely to be from when he cut himself opening a can of food as he claimed. The psychiatrist says he's not delusional and appears to have a good grasp of reality. He was depressed, but no more than one would expect from being in prison.'

'If he is granted bail,' Matt said, 'it will come with conditions attached. He won't be allowed to contact Leila or Kelsey, or leave the area, and we have his passport.'

'Yes, apparently his solicitor asked for a safe house for him but was told there weren't enough safe houses to go round for those in the witness protection scheme, let alone a defendant awaiting trial. If he's released on bail, he'll be expected to make his own arrangements if he doesn't want to go back to his flat.'

'He could stay with his imaginary friend,' Matt suggested with a smile.

'He hasn't mentioned her again,' Beth said. 'I expect his solicitor told him he wasn't doing himself any favours unless he named the person.'

'He hasn't had any visitors while he's been held on remand,' Matt said. 'I checked.'

'What about phone calls?' Beth asked.

Matt shook his head. 'You'd have thought that if he really did have an accomplice, they might have been in contact while he was in prison.'

'Although they would know all phone numbers are checked by the prison authorities first, so they would know who he was speaking to,' Beth said. 'There is one number in Weaver's phone that hasn't been accounted for yet. It's a pay-as-you-go and not registered to anyone. It was used for about a year prior to Leila going missing. I've tried phoning it, but it goes through to voicemail. It could be anyone.'

'Or someone of interest,' Matt said. 'If he's released on bail it might be worth a trip to see if anyone collects him. Do you fancy a ride out to Sleaseford Prison?'

'Yes, why not? We can call on Kelsey afterwards and inform her. Sharon will need to be told too if he is released.'

At midday, DS Bert Scrivener stood up and announced that Colin Weaver had been granted bail and would be returning to his flat to live until his trial, as he didn't have anywhere else to go. 'His solicitor has requested that the key to the padlock we've put on his door be taken to him,' he said. 'Beth, Matt, go to Sleaseford and tail Weaver when he comes out. Then meet him at his flat and give him the key.'

'Yes, sir,' Matt said, standing. 'We'll also inform Kelsey Smith and the aunt Leila is staying with that he's out.'

The DS nodded. 'I suggest you two leave now or Weaver will have been processed and let out by the time you get there.'

'Yes, sir,' Beth said, also standing. 'We're on our way.'

An hour later, Beth and Matt were sitting in the unmarked police car down a side road opposite Sleaseford Prison, watching the main gate and eating a sandwich lunch. The prison, built in the 1950s, was on the outskirts of the old part of town and flanked by streets of Victorian terraced housing. Matt had finished his BLT and was downing a large Americano as Beth sipped her latte before starting on her cheese and cress roll. Suddenly the integral metal door of the prison opened and Colin Weaver stepped out, carrying his belongings in a plastic bag. Beth and Matt quickly set aside their food as Weaver immediately turned right and hurried down a side street.

'I'll follow him on foot,' Matt said, and got out.

Beth started the car and headed off after them, following at a safe distance so that if Weaver turned, he wouldn't see her. Matt, head down, was walking unobtrusively a few people behind Weaver as he navigated the back streets, heading for the town centre.

Ten minutes later, Weaver entered the bus and coach station where he bought a ticket. Beth parked in one of the designated pick-up/drop-off bays where she could see them. Weaver had gone into the waiting room and sat down, while Matt stood outside at a bus stop as if he were waiting for a bus, where he could see Weaver. Beth could see Matt was getting cold, but it was his own fault as he never wore a coat in winter, just a light jacket. She finished her lunch as buses and coaches came and went. Then a coach pulled in with the destination sign showing Coleshaw.

Weaver stood, came out of the waiting room, showed his ticket to the driver and embarked. Matt remained where he was until the coach pulled away and then returned to the car.

'I think we can assume he's going to Coleshaw,' Matt said, rubbing his hands to try to warm them. 'The coach makes one stop and doesn't arrive for another ninety minutes. As Weaver hasn't made contact with anyone we may as well head back and see Kelsey first. I'll update the DS as we go, and call Leila's aunt.' His teeth chattered from cold.

Beth turned up the heating in the car and headed for the motorway.

Forty-five minutes later they were outside Kelsey Smith's front door, which was covered in graffiti. She answered the bell on the second ring, dressed smartly in what looked like new clothes, and with freshly washed and styled hair.

'Hello, Kelsey,' Beth said. 'How are you? You look good.'

'I'm doing OK, thanks.'

They followed her into the living room, which was clean and tidy.

'Something smells tasty,' Matt said, sniffing the air.

'I made myself a steak sandwich for lunch,' Kelsey said. 'I would offer you some, but I ate the lot.'

'Well done you,' Beth said with a smile. As far as she knew, it was the first time Kelsey had cooked anything beyond oven chips. 'How is Leila?' she asked, sitting on the sofa beside Kelsey. Matt positioned himself by the window. It didn't matter that they weren't in a patrol car – thugs could spot an unmarked police car.

'Leila's fine as far as I know,' Kelsey said, a little subdued. 'I didn't get to speak to her last night. She was tired and was in bed when I phoned, but I'm hoping to see her later today. Sharon lives over thirty miles away and I don't drive, so Peter said they should come here.'

Beth nodded. 'Has Leila said anything more about the time she was missing?'

'Not as far as I know, but I haven't spoken to her since Peter took her.'

Beth held her gaze. There was no easy way to say what she had to. Kelsey was sure to be angry, upset and frightened. Victims usually were when they learned the accused was out on bail. They assumed – as did many members of the public – they would be locked up until their trial. 'Kelsey, there's something we need to tell you,' Beth said. 'Colin Weaver has been granted bail and will be returning to live in his flat until his trial.'

'What the—!' Kelsey's face immediately registered shock and anger. 'But he's dangerous! He could snatch another child.'

'The judge has decided otherwise.'

'Idiot!' Kelsey snapped.

'Try not to worry,' Beth said. 'Mr Weaver isn't allowed to come anywhere near you or Leila. It's one of the conditions of his bail. We've told Sharon too.'

'You spoke to her today?'

'Yes.'

'When?'

'About half an hour ago.'

Kelsey looked thoughtful and then asked, 'Weaver doesn't know where Leila is, does he?'

'No. And if he approaches you, call us and he'll be straight back to prison for breaching the terms of his bail. I appreciate it's going to be difficult for you with him living in the flat below, but the judge felt it was reasonable that he should be allowed to go home, as he didn't have anywhere else to go.'

'I'll show him where to go!' Kelsey said angrily.

'No, you won't,' Matt warned. 'If you see Weaver, which is quite possible, just walk on by. If you assault him, you will be in the wrong and you could be arrested.'

'It might be worth it,' Kelsey said. 'Teach him a lesson. I have nightmares about what he did to Leila.'

'I know, and he will be punished,' Beth reassured her.

'So what happens now?' Kelsey asked. 'The trial isn't for another three months.'

'You try to get on with your life,' Beth said. 'Nearer the trial date, I can go through with you what to expect in court.'

'Leila won't have to go to court, will she?' Kelsey asked anxiously.

'No. Not at her age. She will be able to give her evidence on tape when she feels up to it.'

'Supposing she never feels up to it. Will he get off?'

'There's plenty of circumstantial and forensic evidence,' Matt said. 'And remember that Weaver is still pleading guilty to abducting Leila.'

Kelsey gave a half-hearted nod.

'Do you have any questions?' Beth asked.

'Did my sister say anything to you about Leila when you spoke to her?'

'No. We just informed her that Mr Weaver was out on bail and that was it, really.'

Kelsey picked up her phone and checked the caller display. Sharon hadn't called.

'We'll be in touch soon, then,' Beth said, standing.

Matt came over from the window.

'Take care,' Beth said. 'We'll let ourselves out.'

'Yes, make sure you close the door properly, please. I don't feel safe with him out of prison.'

As Matt and Beth let themselves out, Kelsey studied her phone. Sharon had been able to answer the call from the police, so why hadn't she returned any of her calls? She'd been phoning about every half-hour, and had left two messages, but she'd heard nothing, not even a text. It was frustrating, worrying and annoying. She'd gone out early when the shops had opened and bought Leila a pay-as-you-go phone and was planning to give it to her later that day when she saw her. Sharon wasn't in work until school started the following week, so Kelsey couldn't imagine what was so important that she couldn't ring her back.

With mounting concern and annoyance, she pressed Sharon's mobile number again, half expecting it to go through to voicemail. She was surprised when it was answered immediately.

'Hi, I was just about to call you,' Sharon said chirpily. 'Sorry I haven't been in touch. It's been non-stop here. I've been running to stand still. Parenting is a sharp learning curve for me.' She gave a little laugh. With Sharon so chatty and friendly, Kelsey felt guilty for thinking badly of her sister. 'I'll fetch Leila so you can talk to her.'

230

'Thanks, but when will I see her?'

'Tomorrow. I'm taking her to a pantomime later this afternoon.'

'Oh, OK,' Kelsey said, disappointed.

'It's New Year's Eve tomorrow so I'll bring a bottle of bubbly and we can celebrate the new year together as a family.'

'That would be lovely,' Kelsey said, putting aside her disappointment at not seeing Leila. 'Although I won't have much to drink; I don't want to relapse again.'

'Of course not, just a little one to see in the new year. Here's Leila, she's dying to talk to you.'

'Thank you, and thanks for everything, Sharon.'

'You're welcome.'

Leila came on the phone. 'Hi, Mummy, I miss you.'

'I miss you too, love. We're seeing each other tomorrow. And I've bought you a phone.'

'Great! I'll be able to speak to you whenever I want and not ...' She stopped.

'Can Sharon hear you?' Kelsey asked.

'Yes.'

'OK, don't mention it again. The phone will be our secret. When I see you tomorrow I'll slip it to you quietly when she's not looking.' Kelsey laughed conspiratorially. 'I've put plenty of credit on it so we can phone each other whenever we want.'

'Fantastic. We can phone at night,' Leila chuckled.

'Yes, but don't say any more. How are you?'

'OK, I guess,' Leila said, dropping her voice. 'It's very different here.'

'I know, but Aunty Sharon is looking after you?'

'I suppose so.'

'And you're going to a pantomime this afternoon.'

'Yes. I wish you were coming too.'

'So do I, love.'

Kelsey heard her sister's voice in the background, calling Leila.

'I have to go now, Mum, and get ready,' Leila said.

'OK, have a good time and see you tomorrow.'

'Love you.'

'Love you too.'

The call ended. Kelsey couldn't help feeling jealous that it was Sharon taking Leila to her first pantomime and not her, but she dismissed it as selfish. It would have been nice if Sharon had included her and they could all have gone together, but she guessed that wasn't practical given the distance and that she didn't drive. Sharon was clearly looking after Leila and she should be grateful. She needed to put all her efforts into proving to Peter Harris that she really had got her life on track and was capable of looking after Leila herself.

THIRTY-NINE

After leaving Kelsey Smith's flat, Matt and Beth checked that Colin Weaver wasn't already waiting for them outside his flat, and then returned to their car to wait for him. They were parked directly in front of the one main door in and out of the flats, and were expecting him any time, assuming of course he'd come straight home as he'd told his solicitor.

'Kelsey seems to be doing all right,' Beth said as she gazed through the windscreen.

'She does,' Matt agreed. 'Better than I would have expected. Not sure it will do her any good, though.'

'There seems to be a determination about her this time. I think Leila's abduction has given her a wake-up call.'

'And having all her other children taken into care didn't?' Matt asked cynically.

'Sometimes it just isn't the right time to turn your life around,' Beth said. 'Pity. In another life I think she would have made a good mother. Look, here comes Mr Weaver.'

They both looked through the windscreen as the lone figure, grey overcoat flapping in the wind and plastic bag over his arm, plodded towards his flat. Small in stature, head down, he appeared an insignificant character and not one you would immediately associate with a carefully executed plan to abduct a child and then evade a nationwide police search.

'Someone is sure to have a go at him,' Matt said. 'If not Kelsey, there are plenty of others on the estate who will.'

'I know. It's crazy him coming back here. He'd have been safer staying in prison.'

As he approached, they got out of the car and then waited by the entrance to the flats. Colin Weaver continued along the path towards them and looked up at the last moment. 'Oh, it's you,' he said, startled.

'Good afternoon,' Matt said. 'We've brought the key to unlock your front door as your solicitor requested.'

'Oh, yes, I see, thank you.'

They followed him through the main door. 'You'll need to get a locksmith to fit a new lock,' Matt said as they climbed the stairs.

'And who's going to pay for that?' Weaver asked. 'You've got all my money.'

'You can apply to have it returned. Also, try putting in a claim to your insurance company,' Matt said. 'Your solicitor should be able to advise you.'

Weaver huffed. 'Why does it take two of you to bring me a key?' he asked as they arrived at his floor. 'It's intimidating.'

'It wasn't our intention to be intimidating,' Beth said in a consolatory tone. 'We often work in pairs and we've just come from seeing Mrs Smith.'

They went along the corridor to his flat, 317. 'Jesus! You've made a right bloody mess of my door,' Weaver exclaimed.

'Nothing that can't be put right,' Matt said. He unlocked the padlock and handed the key to Weaver. 'You'll have to jam the door shut from the inside until you get the lock replaced,' he said helpfully.

Weaver hesitated. 'Are you coming in?'

'Briefly,' Matt said. 'Just to make sure everything's OK.'

Beth and Matt stood aside to let Weaver go in first. The flat was cold and smelt shut-up. They watched as Weaver turned on the heating and then went from room to room, looking in and tutting. It was obvious the place had been thoroughly searched and that the crime-scene officers had been in, but the disruption was minimal and could have been far worse, Beth thought.

'You could wedge the front door to with one of those dining chairs for now,' Matt suggested as they stood in the living room. 'For your own protection.'

'Why would I need protecting?' Weaver asked, apparently genuinely not understanding the situation he was in.

'Feelings can run high in cases like this,' Matt said. 'Phone us if you have any problems or 999 if the situation is life-threatening.'

'Life-threatening! But I'm innocent,' Weaver exclaimed, horrified.

Beth and Matt ignored this. 'Your solicitor explained the terms of your bail?' Beth asked. 'You know you mustn't contact Leila, Mrs Smith or her sister, either in person, by phone, text or email.'

'Yes, I know,' he said testily. 'As if I'm going to contact them after all the trouble they've caused me.'

'That's fine then,' Matt said, throwing Beth a glance.

Colin Weaver began opening and closing the kitchen cupboard doors, checking what was in them. A strong smell of rotting food escaped as he opened the fridge door. 'I'm going to have to throw all this away and go shopping,' he moaned. 'Hopefully my credit card still works.'

'I would call the locksmith first,' Beth said, and she and Matt headed to the door.

'I'd have thought rotting food would be the least of his worries,' Matt said once they were outside.

'So would I. I still don't think he's got the measure of the seriousness of what he's done.'

Meanwhile, inside his flat, Colin was doing as Matt had suggested and dragging a dining chair to wedge against the front door to keep it closed before the lock was replaced. He was angry he'd been put in this position when none of this was his fault. He felt violated and humiliated: arrested, interrogated, locked up in prison, and then coming back to this. It wasn't fair. It wasn't supposed to be like this. He should have been far away from here by now, enjoying his new life abroad. Why hadn't she phoned the police and explained? Had something gone badly wrong that had stopped her? But first things first – he needed to get a new lock fitted to his front door.

Colin sat on the sofa, coat still on, and took his wallet from his pocket. The police still had his bag of money containing his life savings, mobile and laptop, but his wallet with his credit cards had been returned to him. He picked up the landline phone, which thankfully was still working, and began by phoning directory enquiries. 'I need the number of an emergency locksmith,' he said.

He was put through and booked an appointment for them to come in an hour and a half. Before they arrived he would go out and buy some food and a new mobile – pay-as-you-go, so it couldn't be traced. Then he would call her and find out exactly what was going on. It had been too risky in prison to phone, as they monitored all calls in and out. She needed to speak out quickly or it might be time for him to tell the police everything. He wasn't going to take the blame for all of this any longer. His solicitor had told him that he could get fourteen years for child abduction, so she had to tell them the truth now – or he would.

FORTY

Kelsey didn't sleep at all well knowing Colin Weaver was in the flat below. She tossed and turned, imagining she could hear his voice close by as she had done on the night he'd abducted Leila. She shivered at the thought of him being down there. It made her skin crawl. Although he couldn't get in now, it was as though his evil was permeating up through the floor from the flat below.

During the evening she'd heard his door being repaired, but prior to that – when he'd lived there before – she'd hardly heard a thing from his flat, unlike those of some of her neighbours, where the ups and downs of their daily lives were broadcast through the walls and echoed along the corridors. Even if she had heard anything coming from his flat, she hadn't taken any notice. But now it seemed that every noise in the block – footstep, groan, cry or conversation – could be coming from Colin Weaver's flat. At one point in the early hours Kelsey had got out of bed and been about to go down when she remembered what Matt had told her about confronting him, and thought better of it. She needed to stay out of trouble if she stood any chance of getting Leila back.

It was a relief when morning came and the torturous

thoughts of the night receded. It was New Year's Eve; a new year was about to start, full of hope and possibility. Even if she didn't get Leila back this year – which Kelsey had to admit was unlikely, given her track record – she'd make the most of every minute they spent together and make sure Leila grew to be proud of her. At some point, when Leila was old enough, she'd be able to decide where she wanted to live and Kelsey would make sure it was with her.

As she showered and dressed, Kelsey pictured the little party they would be having that evening to see in the new year. *Celebrate together as a family*, Sharon had said, which had made Kelsey feel warm and wanted. She'd texted: *I'm making us supper. Come as soon as you can in the afternoon, and stay the night.* Sharon had replied with a smiling emoji saying they'd be there as soon as they could. The flat was clean and tidy – Sharon could have Kelsey's bed and she'd sleep on the sofa. Leila would have her old room. She was very excited.

Dressed in clean jeans and a jumper, Kelsey made herself some breakfast – coffee and toast – and then filled the washing machine and left it to do its job. She needed to go shopping to buy supplies for their party tonight. Feeling more positive than she had done in years, she let herself out, ignored the graffiti still on her door, which she'd see to later, then caught a bus into town. She had made a list of all the things she needed to buy, and the first stop was the toy shop. At 9.10 a.m. it had just opened and the sales were on. Kelsey was like a kid in a sweet shop and bought a selection of games, including Monopoly and Jenga – not only to play that evening but whenever Leila visited. It was to her shame, Kelsey thought, that she didn't already have games, but in the past she'd never played with Leila. Not at all. But all that had changed. They were going to have fun tonight and every time she and Leila were together from now on.

Leaving the toy shop, Kelsey went to the supermarket where she bought a strong detergent and wire wool for cleaning the front door, party food and soft drinks. She'd have one glass of the bubbly Sharon was bringing but that would be all. There certainly wouldn't be a repetition of Christmas Day evening, when she'd drunk herself into oblivion. She still felt ashamed of that.

Shopping done, Kelsey caught the bus home and then struggled up the stairs with all the bags. She paused on the landing of the floor below hers and looked along the corridor towards Colin Weaver's flat. The padlock had gone and there was no sign of him, but how she would have liked to have told him it was his money that was funding their party this evening. Payback, she thought; a small retribution for what he'd done.

Resisting the urge to knock on his door, she continued up the stairs to her flat where she unpacked the bags and put the party food in the fridge to cook later. She arranged the paper plates, party poppers, whistles and boxes of games on the coffee table, then stood back and admired her work. What a surprise Leila would have when she came in and saw all this. So, too, would Sharon. She could only remember one occasion when she and her sister had sat around a table playing games as a family. It was the night their stepfather had started to abuse her – touching her under the table. After that there'd been no more games or laughter. But that was the past. He'd done enough damage; the future was theirs.

Now to clean the front door. Kelsey wanted it looking decent and all those foul words gone for when Leila and Sharon arrived. She filled a bucket with hot water, added detergent, then took the wire wool outside. Hopefully, once news spread that she'd had nothing to do with Leila going missing, she wouldn't be targeted any more. She scrubbed, her hands growing red and sore, but half an hour later the graffiti had gone. So, too, had large patches of paint. But it looked much better. As she finished, Brooke came out of her flat. Kelsey glanced at her suspiciously. 'Hi,' Brooke said as an ice-breaker.

'Hi,' Kelsey replied, relieved. It wouldn't be long before they were on good terms again.

The door clean, Kelsey returned indoors, emptied the bucket of dirty water down the toilet, then changed into a new dress – courtesy of Weaver – combed her hair and put on some make-up. Trying to curb her excitement, she went to the living room and looked out of the window, hoping to see Sharon's car arrive. It was nearly three o'clock and Kelsey had told her to come in the afternoon as soon as she wanted, so she was expecting them any time now.

It was a bright, cold day and children were in the play area, many of them accompanied by a parent. Parents on the estate were being more vigilant since Leila had been taken. Her gaze shifted to Doris Goodman's flat – the Christmas fairy lights were on. At some point she would go over and make peace with her. Maybe even invite her into her flat so she could see for herself the improvements she'd made and show her she was turning her life around. She would make it a New Year's resolution.

Kelsey stayed by the window, gazing out, looking for Sharon's car. An hour passed. The daylight began to fade and the children disappeared from the play area. Her phone bleeped with a text message and she quickly picked it up, hoping it was Sharon to say they were on their way. But it was from an old client who'd been working abroad for the last four months and probably hadn't heard about all the fuss of Leila going missing. Or perhaps he had but was desperate for a bit of what he liked before he returned to his family. *Just landed. Can I pop in on my way home?*

No. Sorry, I have other plans, Kelsey texted.

When then? he replied.

She hesitated, her fingers hovering over the keypad. Weaver's money wouldn't last forever, but she needed to stay off the game and find herself a proper job if she stood any chance of regaining custody of Leila.

I've had a career change so no longer available, she texted. *Good luck x*

He'd been one of the nicer ones, who'd treated her with respect.

By five o'clock Kelsey couldn't stand the wait any longer and texted Sharon. *How long before you get here?*

There was no reply, so Kelsey assumed she must be driving and they were therefore on their way. Excited and unable to settle, she paced the room, waiting for them. Another hour passed and it was dark outside. She realized they couldn't have been on their way when she'd texted or they would have arrived by now. She tried phoning Sharon's mobile but it went through to voicemail, so she left a message, again assuming they must be on their way. 'Hi. Looking forward to seeing you both.'

Another thirty minutes passed, during which time Kelsey thought every sound in the corridor was them arriving and she rushed to the door only to be disappointed. She couldn't imagine why it was taking so long. At six-thirty she tried phoning again and left another message. 'What time will you be here?'

Then she tried Sharon's home phone, which just rang and rang, so at least they must have left and were on their way.

She was like a cat on a hot tin roof, walking up and down her flat, listening out, the living-room curtains closed against the night sky. Sharon probably didn't realize how much this evening meant to her; how much she was looking forward to it and all the trouble she'd gone to. Just as well there wasn't any alcohol in the flat, Kelsey thought, because she'd have been tempted to have a glass to calm herself down.

Perhaps she hadn't made it clear to her sister what time she was expecting them? Yes, that must be it. Instead of saying afternoon she should have given a specific time. But it was evening now, not afternoon. Disappointed but still expecting them at any moment, Kelsey decided to start cooking the party food so it would be ready for when they arrived. They'd be hungry. She arranged the food on trays and placed them in the oven, but – preoccupied and not used to cooking – she forgot all about them until the smell of burning food hit her.

Rushing to the oven, Kelsey pulled open the door, but it was too late. Most of the delicate filo pastry savouries were ruined. Tears sprang to her eyes. It seemed that no matter how hard she tried, nothing ever went her way. Suddenly the front doorbell rang and she ran to answer it, wiping her eyes as she went. Leila and Sharon, laden down with bags, stood smiling before her.

'Sorry we're late,' Sharon said. 'The traffic was awful and we stopped off to pick up some food.'

'Have you burnt something, Mummy?' Leila asked as they came in, placing the bunch of flowers she was carrying in Kelsey's arms.

'They're lovely,' Kelsey said, blinking back fresh tears. Then with a small laugh, she said, 'Just as well you brought some more food – I'm afraid I've burnt what I had.'

'No worries,' Sharon said positively. 'There's plenty here to eat and drink. You look like you could do with a glass of something.'

'Too right,' Kelsey said, relieved that they were here and the evening was salvageable.

She followed her sister and Leila into the kitchen where they took control. She watched them as they worked together, putting the flowers in water and setting out the already-cooked platters of food and dips they'd brought with them. 'Thank you so much,' she said gratefully.

'You're welcome,' Sharon said, and put a drink into Kelsey's hand. 'To us,' Sharon said, raising her glass of lemonade.

'To us,' Leila and Kelsey repeated.

Immediately Kelsey started to feel better as the alcohol took effect, warming and relaxing her. It wasn't the bottle of bubbly her sister had said she'd bring but gin topped up with lemonade. The sweetness of the lemonade masked the strength of the gin, so it was easy to accept a refill.

'Let's play Jenga,' Kelsey suggested, going to the table.

'Yes!' Leila exclaimed excitedly. 'Aunty Sharon and I play it at her house.'

Kelsey banished the twinge of jealousy she felt at Leila being already familiar with the game from playing it with Sharon, and homed in on the fact that Leila hadn't referred to her aunt's house as home, which would have really hurt. The three of them grouped around the table and sipped their drinks as they began to play, taking turns to carefully slide out one of the wooden bricks from the tower, hoping it wouldn't topple over. It was fun, they laughed a lot, and paused from playing only when Sharon went to refill their glasses again. Kelsey noticed she appeared to be drinking only lemonade.

'Have a proper drink,' Kelsey said, swinging her glass gaily. 'You don't have to drive; you can both stay the night.'

'I will later to see in the new year,' Sharon said.

Moderation in all things – typical of her sister, Kelsey thought.

Leila glanced at her mother and then took her turn and pulled out a brick from the Jenga tower. It went crashing to the floor. She and Kelsey hooted with laughter, clapped and then blew party whistles.

'Sshh,' Sharon said, pressing her finger to her lips. 'He might hear us.'

'Who?' Kelsey asked, hiccupping and finishing her drink. She was definitely tipsy.

'Him below,' Sharon said, looking down to Colin Weaver's flat.

'I don't give a fuck what he hears,' Kelsey said, then apologized to Leila for swearing.

They helped themselves to party food and Sharon refilled their glasses again. 'I mustn't have any more after this one,' Kelsey said unsteadily.

'You're OK. It's New Year's Eve,' Sharon replied indulgently, although Kelsey saw Leila watching her carefully.

The evening continued just as Kelsey had imagined it, with lots of fun and laughter. But at eleven o'clock, as Kelsey tried to stand, she realized she'd overdone the drink. She took a step, the room swayed, and she would have fallen over had Sharon not grabbed her.

'Oh, Mum,' Leila cried, rushing to her.

'I think you need to have a lie down,' Sharon said.

'But it's only eleven o'clock,' Kelsey protested, slurring her words. 'I want to see in the new year.'

'We'll wake you when it's time, Mum,' Leila said.

'Thank you, love.' She kissed her cheek. 'Glad I've got you two.'

With Sharon on one side and Leila on the other supporting her, she went unsteadily into her bedroom. 'Thanks,' she said again, because without doubt she would never have made it without them.

Once she was sitting on the edge of the bed, Sharon sent Leila out of her room, then Kelsey became aware that her sister was taking off her shoes and helping her into bed.

'Don't forget to wake me when it's midnight,' Kelsey mumbled, her eyes already closing.

'I won't,' came Sharon's voice. Just before she left, Kelsey thought she saw the flash of a camera, but it was most probably from all the drink. A second later she heard the bedroom door click shut and darkness engulfed her.

FORTY-ONE

Shit! As Kelsey surfaced, her first thought was that she'd forgotten to give Leila the pay-as-you-go phone she'd bought for her. She'd been looking for an opportunity to slip it to her without Sharon seeing, but her sister hadn't left the room. But just a minute – what room was she in? Where was she? Her head throbbed, her stomach churned and bile rose in her throat. She opened her eyes and saw the ceiling of her bedroom. She was in bed with her best dress still on! Then she began to remember.

It was New Year's Eve. What time was it? She gingerly turned her head and reached for her phone. It was where she'd left it the evening before, charging. She squinted at the bright light of the screen. Jesus! It was 9.05 a.m. on 1 January. She'd missed New Year. But why hadn't Leila and Sharon woken her? She was sure they'd promised they would. Or had she imagined it?

Bitterly disappointed and ashamed of herself, Kelsey slowly eased herself upright on the pillow. She remembered Sharon and Leila bringing her to bed and then nothing. They probably hadn't been able to wake her to see in the new year so had seen it in together – just the two of them. Her heart fell

246

and guilt engulfed her. She assumed they were still asleep. Sharon was supposed to be sleeping in her bed, but clearly she wasn't, so she must have taken the sofa. She'd have to apologize to them both.

As she stood, the room tilted. God, she'd had a hell of a lot to drink. What had she been drinking? Oh yes, gin and lemonade. She had a vague recollection of Sharon refilling her glass, even when she'd told her not to. No good blaming her, Kelsey thought. It was her own stupid fault. Pissed again and in front of Leila! She felt wretched. What sort of example was that from someone who had supposedly turned their life around? Would they forgive her? It would serve her right if they didn't.

Kelsey walked carefully to her bedroom door and then to the bathroom. She made it just in time and threw up in the sink. She hoped she hadn't woken Leila and Sharon. They'd be even more annoyed with her. Rinsing her mouth with cold water, she then used the toilet and went along the hall to the living room. The sofa was empty. Where was Sharon? Had she shared Leila's bed? She went into Leila's bedroom. Her bed was empty too. So they hadn't stayed the night, and all because of her! Kelsey felt the crushing weight of her failings both as a mother and a sister. She'd let them both down again! What a start to the new year. How was she going to make amends this time? She had no idea.

Dejected and despising herself, she returned to the kitchen for a drink of water. She was badly dehydrated from all the alcohol. The kitchen was clean and tidy. No empty bottles, unwashed glasses or paper plates of half-eaten food as she would have expected. Everything had been put away and the vase containing the flowers Leila had given to her had been positioned in the centre of the table. She guessed that was Sharon's touch. Kelsey felt even more of a failure and envious of her sister. She could picture her and Leila united in clearing up while she lay unconscious from alcohol. It would add to their perception of her as an unfit mother, a waste of space, and strengthen the bond between them. She stamped her foot in anger.

But it was really his fault! Him down there! Fucking Colin Weaver! If he hadn't taken Leila and highlighted her neglect, they might have survived as they had been doing. Not perfect, but getting by. He'd set in motion a chain of events that had resulted in her losing the last of her children. Her anger and frustration flared. She stamped her foot again on the tiled floor of the kitchen, but barefoot it made little impact. Furious and looking for an outlet for her anger, she grabbed a metal pan from the cooker and began hitting the floor with it. 'It's your fucking fault, Weaver!' she shouted. 'You should have minded your own bleeding business. You'll pay for it, I promise.'

Over and over again she beat the floor, shouting and crying, venting her anger. He would be able to hear her for sure, assuming he was in. Leila had said she had heard her when he'd held her hostage there. She had heard her crying out for help when the pig had beaten her. Bang, bang! The noise would drive him mad. Good.

When he couldn't stand it any longer he'd come up and then she'd have him.

The doorbell rang. Weaver? Perfect. Dropping the pan, Kelsey yanked open a kitchen drawer and took out the carving knife. With no thought for her future – she didn't have one without Leila – but blind with hatred and revenge, she continued towards the door. Her opportunity to get her own back and make him pay for what he'd done had arrived. She raised the knife and opened the front door. It wasn't Weaver, but her neighbour, Brooke.

'Kelsey, what the hell is going on? Put that knife down. You're upsetting my kids with all your noise.'

248

Embarrassed, Kelsey lowered the knife.

'You're still in your party clothes so I'm guessing you had a rough night,' Brooke said. 'Shall I come in and you can tell me what happened? The kids' dad is with them.'

Kelsey nodded dumbly and stood aside to let Brooke in.

'I'll make us a coffee,' Brooke suggested.

'Yes, please.'

A few minutes later, Brooke set two mugs of instant coffee on the table in the living room and drew up a chair to sit opposite Kelsey, ready to listen. 'I know we've had our differences, love, but you look like you need to share what's going on.'

'I do,' Kelsey admitted quietly. She took a few sips of her coffee and began. 'Leila is living with my sister, Sharon. I'm supposed to be staying clean and making improvements to my life so I stand a chance of regaining custody of Leila. But no matter how hard I try, I fail.' Kelsey then told Brooke her life story. How she'd been sexually abused by her stepfather, had married young to escape him, but her husband had beaten her and cleared off, leaving her with two kids, Shane and Rory. How she'd got into drink and drugs to blot out the pain and had ended up having another two kids, Poppy and Mia, by different men who'd treated her no better. She found that, once she'd begun, it was easy to continue, as Brooke listened non-judgementally without interrupting. She finished with last night's New Year's Eve party when she'd passed out from the gin Sharon had brought. It was a relief to tell someone everything.

'OK, girl, so you messed up again, but it's not the end of the world,' Brooke said. 'Phone Leila and apologize. But whose side is that sister of yours really on?'

'What do you mean?' Kelsey asked.

'She should have known better than to give a recovering alcoholic even one drink.'

'So you think it wasn't all my fault?'

'I know so. With friends like your sister, who needs enemies? It sounds like she's working to a different agenda.'

Brooke left twenty minutes later, after giving Kelsey a good talking to. Feeling more positive, Kelsey phoned Sharon's landline as Brooke had suggested. It rang and rang, so she assumed she and Leila must be having a lie-in after their late night. She tried Sharon's mobile and it went through to voicemail, so she left a message. 'It's me, Kelsey. Sorry about last night. I feel really bad. We were having so much fun and then I blew it. My fault, but it would really help me if in future you didn't give me alcohol. I need to apologize to Leila, too, so please phone as soon as you can. Thank you. Oh yes, and Happy New Year.'

Satisfied she'd pitched the message right, Kelsey made herself another coffee and then checked the kitchen cupboards for something to eat. Next to the cereal she'd bought for Leila's breakfast was an open bottle of gin. Sharon must have left it. Brooke's words came back to her as Kelsey realized she must have drunk a whole bottle of gin by herself and then started on the second. Little wonder she'd passed out! Well, never again. She'd learnt her lesson. Unscrewing the cap, she tipped the contents of the bottle down the sink and threw it into the bin.

She swallowed two paracetamol for her headache and took the coffee she'd made to the sofa where she switched on the television and waited for Sharon to return her call. Since Leila had gone to live with her, it seemed Kelsey had spent most of her time waiting for Sharon to return her calls.

An hour later, with no text or call from Sharon, Kelsey tried both phones again, and then showered, dressed in jeans and a jumper and put her party dress in the wash. At midday, losing patience, she phoned Sharon's mobile and left a message asking her to call ASAP. She could have kicked herself for not remembering to give Leila the phone she'd bought for her while she'd been sober enough to slip it to her – then there wouldn't have been all this waiting for Sharon to return her calls. It was really getting to her now. Peter Harris had said she could have phone contact on the days she didn't see Leila, so for once she was in the right.

At one o'clock Kelsey had had enough and phoned Sharon's mobile again. It went through to voicemail and this time the message she left was demanding and assertive. 'It's Kelsey. If you don't return my call so I can speak to Leila, I will get in a taxi and come straight over. I need to speak to my daughter to apologize to her. It's important.'

As she ended the call she wondered if she'd sounded rude, and was thinking about calling again and apologizing when her phone rang, making her start. The caller display showed Sharon's mobile number. 'Hi, Kelsey, sorry I missed your call,' she began brightly, unfazed. 'We went for a country walk to clear away the cobwebs from last night. I left my phone in the car. Happy New Year.'

Kelsey cringed and felt awful. Of course – lots of people went for a walk on New Year's Day. 'Sorry if my message sounded a bit off,' she said. 'I feel bad about last night.'

'OK. I thought it best to bring Leila home. I knew you wouldn't want her seeing you in that state.' Which made Kelsey feel a whole lot worse.

'I need to apologize to Leila,' Kelsey said, subdued and chastened. 'Can you put her on, please?'

'Sure, here she is.'

'Hi, love,' Kelsey said. 'I am so sorry about last night. Can you forgive me?'

She was expecting Leila to be angry with her, as she'd been in the past for drinking, but instead she said, 'It's OK, Mum. It wasn't your fault.'

'It was, love, and I'm so sorry. I promise it won't happen again.' How many times had she said that! 'I had your phone all ready to give to you, too, but I forgot.'

'When will I next see you?'

'I'll have to arrange it with Aunty Sharon.'

'We're not doing anything this afternoon.'

'OK. Put her back on.'

'Can you come over here today?' Kelsey asked. 'I'll make up for last night.'

'I'm afraid not,' Sharon said, her voice controlled and business-like. 'Peter Harris was most specific that contact should only take place three times a week so that Leila has a chance to settle with me.'

'But he needn't know,' Kelsey said.

'If he found out I was deceiving him and collaborating with you, he'd take Leila from me. We can't allow that to happen, can we?'

'I suppose not. So when can I see her?'

'Tomorrow – that seems fair as you saw her yesterday.'

'OK,' Kelsey agreed.

'I'll text you the time. And Kelsey, please try to stay sober. It's not nice for Leila to see you like that, and she's bound to tell Peter. Goodbye.' The line went dead.

Kelsey sat for a moment, stunned. Her instinct was to phone her sister straight back and ask her whose side she was on, as Brooke had. But deep down she knew Sharon was right, just as she always was. If Leila was to be allowed to stay with her and not taken into foster care then they needed to abide by the rules. And when all was said and done, while Sharon had brought the gin, Kelsey was the one who'd drunk it.

FORTY-TWO

The following afternoon, Kelsey found herself once again standing at her living-room window, watching out for Sharon's car. It was a grey, overcast day and the persistent drizzle cast the estate in its worse light, but that didn't diminish Kelsey's feelings of joy and positivity. After the disappointment of New Year, Kelsey felt tentatively in control again. Sharon had texted saying she'd bring Leila to see her around two o'clock and it was exactly that now. This time nothing would go wrong.

There was no alcohol in the flat and Kelsey had gone shopping that morning and bought cheese and ham to make sandwiches, and some cupcakes too. Leila's phone was ready in her bedroom and Kelsey would take her in there on the pretext of her trying on some of her old clothes to see if they still fitted. Quite why it was so important Sharon didn't know Leila had a phone Kelsey couldn't say. It just felt better that way; her and Leila having the means to communicate whenever they wished without being overheard. With mounting excitement, Kelsey looked through her living-room window, willing Sharon's car to arrive.

*

Three miles away, Colin Weaver was entering Coleshaw Police Station with his solicitor, Deborah Harold. Wednesday, 2 January, was the first day back at work for many after Christmas and New Year, and Colin had telephoned his solicitor that morning as soon as the firm had opened. He said he had something very important to tell her: he was going to the police station to change his statement, and what he had to say would help his defence, even clear his name.

'What is it?' Deborah Harold had asked, concerned. 'You need to come to my office first to discuss it.'

'No. I'm going straight to the police,' he persisted. 'This has gone on for long enough. I can't leave my flat for fear of being attacked by yobs on the estate who think I'm a paedophile. Someone pushed shit through my letter box last night and I've had death threats. I need to clear my name.'

'Very well, I'll meet you at Coleshaw Police Station at one-thirty,' Deborah Harold said. 'I'll tell them to expect us, but if you arrive early, don't talk to anyone until I'm there.'

'All right. But you won't change my mind. I'm not carrying the can for this any longer.'

Now, Colin and his solicitor were waiting for an interview room to become free so he could tell the police what he'd just told her. From Deborah Harold's expression, it was obvious she thought her client was making a huge error of judgement. She sat upright on the bench and was writing furiously, using her briefcase to rest on.

DC Matt Davis came through the security door into reception.

'Sorry to keep you waiting,' he said. 'We have a room free now. Come this way, please.' He glanced at Weaver as he and his solicitor stood. He looked even rougher than the last time Matt had seen him, on his release from prison. There were dark rings around his eyes, as though he hadn't slept, and his forehead had broken out in acne.

'Did you have a good Christmas?' Matt asked Ms Harold politely, holding the security door open for her and Weaver to go through.

'Yes, thank you,' she replied crisply.

Matt showed them into Interview Room 3, where Beth was already seated at the table, a folder of printed papers and a notepad and pen in front of her. DS Scrivener had given them the job of hearing what Weaver had to say since they'd interviewed him before and taken his previous statement.

'Good afternoon,' Beth said.

'Good afternoon,' Ms Harold said stiffly.

Beth waited until everyone was seated, with Colin Weaver sitting opposite her, and then went through the formalities, stating the date, time, those present and the reason for the interview.

Beth concentrated on Colin Weaver. He was staring at his hands, clasped together on the table in front of him. 'Mr Weaver,' she began. 'We understand from your solicitor you wish to change your statement?'

'Yes, I do,' he said, looking up sharply. 'I should have told you the truth at the beginning instead of covering up for her. It wasn't my idea to take Leila Smith. I just went along with it.' He stopped and Beth glanced at his solicitor, who was writing. This wasn't anything new.

'I think you said something similar the last time we interviewed you,' Beth said. 'That you had an accomplice, but you couldn't give us their details, so I'm afraid we weren't able to progress with that.'

'Well, I'm willing to give you the details now,' he said, determination on his face. 'I've thought long and hard about it and I think I've been duped.'

'OK,' Beth said, pen ready. 'Who is this person?'

Matt and his solicitor were also looking carefully at Weaver.

'Sharon Kern,' Weaver said.

Beth made a note of the name. 'And what's her relationship to you?'

'She's my friend – or was, you know, my girlfriend, or I thought so.'

Beth saw Matt shift beside her and knew what he was thinking. Weaver was going to have to do a lot better than this.

'Do you have the contact details for this Sharon Kern?' Beth asked.

'Yes, of course, and so do you.'

Beth looked at him carefully. 'She has a criminal record?' It seemed the most likely explanation.

'No. Well, not as far as I know, although anything is possible. You've met her. Sharon is Kelsey Smith's sister. She never married, so she has her maiden name still.'

'You know Sharon?' Beth asked, amazed.

'Yes. I have done for about nine months. I thought I could trust her, but I now realize I made a big mistake.'

'In what way?'

'We had plans for a future together, but she's let me down badly and now my life is in ruins.'

Matt was staring at Weaver, trying to hide his scepticism, as Ms Harold continued writing.

'Perhaps we could go back a bit,' Beth said. 'Can you tell us how you met Sharon?' It was highly likely Weaver was making all this up, she thought, and being asked for details would catch him out. Beth was sure Sharon would have told them if she'd had anything to do with Weaver.

'I first met Sharon in March last year,' Colin began. 'I bumped into her as she was coming out of the flats and I was going in. I recognized her because I'd seen her before visiting Kelsey and Leila. I introduced myself and said I was very worried about Leila. That I heard a lot living in the flat

256

below and I knew Leila was often left there alone. I told her Kelsey was on the game and brought clients back to the flat. I said I'd seen Leila hanging around the estate after dark and had sometimes taken her back to my flat and given her food. Sharon thanked me for my concern. She said she too was very worried about Leila and was gathering evidence to take to the social services. She felt the social worker wasn't doing enough, just monitoring Kelsey and Leila. We swapped numbers and she asked me to call her if I had any more evidence of Kelsey's neglect of her daughter.' Colin paused, took a sip of water from the polystyrene cup and carefully set it down again before continuing.

'It wasn't long before I had reason to call Sharon with more details of Kelsey's neglect of her daughter, and she suggested we meet in a coffee shop near where we both worked in town. I told her that Doris Goodman had had to give Leila dinner twice that week or she'd have gone hungry. Sharon was appalled by her sister's neglect of Leila. Then we began chatting about other things. After that we started meeting regularly, a couple of times a week, and got on really well. As well as discussing Leila, we talked about ourselves and the conversations became more personal. Sharon was an intelligent and attractive woman, not at all like her sister, and as the weeks passed, I realized I was falling in love with her.'

Colin Weaver stopped and took a deep breath while his solicitor continued writing, turning the page in her notebook as she went. Beth and Matt looked at Weaver, intrigued by his story.

'Our meetings grew longer and more regular,' he continued. 'And became more like dates. Then one evening I asked her why she'd never married – a lovely woman like her – and she said she was still looking for Mr Right. She said if she'd met someone like me, she was sure she would have married by now. It was what I needed to hear to be able to tell her how I felt. I told her I loved her, and to my astonishment she said she felt the same about me. I was elated, over the moon – I couldn't believe it. I'd never had a proper girlfriend before, and Sharon seemed right out of my league. We went to restaurants and the cinema and eventually to bed.'

'Where? At her place or yours?' Beth asked as she wrote.

'Hotels. She never invited me to her house and didn't want to come to my flat in case she bumped into Kelsey. She thought it was better she didn't know we were seeing each other. As we talked and got to know each other better, we found out we were both fed up with our jobs and would love a new start, a new life abroad. Sharon said the only thing stopping her was Leila. I thought that was admirable. I mean, not many people would put their own life on hold for the sake of their niece. I said it was a pity she couldn't achieve her dreams, but if she ever decided she could go abroad to live I'd certainly go with her. I was planning to ask her to marry me.'

Colin paused and rubbed his hand over his forehead in anguish.

'Do you want to take a break?' his solicitor asked.

'No.' He took another sip of water and continued. 'One day when we met, at the beginning of June, she was very animated and excited about something. We went to a restaurant and she ordered a half-bottle of champagne, to celebrate, she said. I had no idea what we were celebrating, but it crossed my mind that perhaps she was going to propose to me – women do that now.' He threw them a small, sad smile. 'But she began talking about Leila and said she'd thought of a way we could go abroad to live without abandoning Leila. She said Kelsey would never give Leila up and would continue to selfishly ruin her life, just as she had her other children's. She said she'd stood by long enough waiting for social services to act and wasn't prepared to wait any longer.

Her plan was that we'd take Leila with us to live abroad. But she needed my help. I was so in love with her, I would have done anything. She said if Leila just vanished, one of the first places the police would look would be in her house, so she wanted me to take Leila to my flat as I'd done before, but to keep her there. Then to hide out in Doris Goodman's cottage until the fuss died down and we could all go abroad to live.'

There was a short silence before Matt asked, 'Does Sharon know Doris Goodman?'

'Yes, a little.'

'It may seem crazy now, but couples do flee the country to evade the social services or a violent partner. I thought Sharon's plan would work and that I was going to spend the rest of my life with the woman I loved. To be honest, I wasn't fussed if Leila came or not, but I would have done anything for Sharon. I agreed to her plan and she took care of all the arrangements. She told me that when I took Leila, I should make it into a game so she wouldn't cause a fuss, and to buy her new clothes and cut her hair so she couldn't be recognized. When the day came for me to take Leila, she came back to my flat without a problem. I did as Sharon suggested and told her we were tricking her mother and teaching her a lesson for not looking after her properly. But almost straight away she began playing up.

'She was rude and demanding and not used to doing what she was told. The first night she made such a fuss about not having her bloody teddy bear that we had to go back to her flat for it. She had the key and let us in. Her mother had passed out, off her head again on whatever she'd taken. Leila got the bear and we left. Later, I got rid of the bear when you featured it in your missing person's appeal.'

Beth nodded. 'Go on.'

'We were supposed to stay in my flat until all the commotion had died down and then go to the cottage. But Leila made such a noise, someone was sure to hear, so we decided to move her the next night. I had drawn out all my savings by then, ready to start my new life abroad, and I left a suicide note, as Sharon had told me to. Leila slept for most of the journey, but when we arrived at the cottage I couldn't believe the state it was in. Doris Goodman had said the cottage was basic and that she no longer used it, but it was far worse than I imagined. There was no proper heating so the place was freezing. The roof leaked, there was no hot water and no television or Internet. Leila was used to watching television and didn't know how to amuse herself. She quickly grew bored and played up even more. Unbelievably, she missed her mother, though goodness knows why. I was pissed off and the only reason I stayed was the thought of spending the rest of my life with Sharon.

'Then one day, I think it was a Wednesday, I couldn't stand Leila's whining any longer and I left her in the cottage while I went into town to buy some more provisions and to download some films on my laptop for her to watch. It was the only thing that kept her amused. I told her to keep out of sight of the windows, but the cottage was miles from anywhere, so I didn't see a problem. I never for one moment thought she'd leave. I mean, where would she go? But when I got back, she'd escaped and stolen nearly two thousand pounds of my money. I spent ages looking for her in the fog and then gave up.'

'So you felt it was all right to leave an eight-year-old, lost on the moors in winter, when the temperature plummets to below zero at night?' Beth asked incredulously.

'I wasn't thinking straight. I was more concerned with what Sharon would say. To be honest, I'd had enough of the kid by then.'

Beth shook her head in disbelief. 'Then what happened?'

'I was about to leave the cottage when your lot turned up and arrested me.'

'Where were you planning to go when you were arrested?' Beth asked.

'To phone Sharon. I needed to tell her what had happened, and that we should bring forward our departure, change the tickets and meet at the airport. But there's no signal in the cottage – you have to go further up the lane. I was going to drive up the lane to phone her when your lot arrived. I thought Sharon would tell you what happened once she'd found out I'd been arrested, but she hasn't got in touch with me since. I don't think she had any intention of doing so. I now believe she used me.'

'What for?' Matt asked.

'So she could gain custody of Leila. She was obsessed with having the child, and she hated her sister. I didn't see it at the time. I've got no experience of families – I'm an only child. I thought she was just being nice – the caring aunt – but it was more than that. Something far deeper and darker. She was getting her own back.'

'For what?' Beth asked.

'I don't know.'

'Sharon has been very supportive of her sister,' Beth said. 'Why would she go to all that trouble of having you kidnap Leila when she could have just applied for custody?'

'Kelsey would never have agreed to Sharon having Leila had she not been pushed into a corner,' Colin said. 'After she disappeared, the social services took action and the choice became Sharon or a foster carer. For Kelsey, having Leila live with Sharon was the lesser of two evils, although she may live to regret that decision.'

'What do you mean by that?' Matt asked.

'Something happened when they were kids. I don't know what – Sharon would never say – but neither of them has got over it. Sharon appears respectable – regular job, nice home, goes to church sometimes – but I now believe that underneath she's more screwed up than Kelsey.'

'Colin,' Beth said, slightly changing the subject. 'You said Leila was very badly behaved. How did you deal with that?'

'I shouted at her, threatened her, even slapped her. I thought if the three of us were going to live together, she needed to learn to do as she was told. But nothing I tried did any good.'

'Did you sexually abuse her?' Matt asked.

'No! I'm not a paedophile! I keep telling you. It's Sharon you need to protect Leila from. Looking back, the signs were there, but I ignored them. I think she's unhinged.' He stopped and stared at them.

Beth sat back and surveyed Weaver across the table. 'Why are you telling us this now? If all this was true, surely you would have told us straight away, when you were first arrested?'

'Back then I thought Sharon loved me and would help me by admitting her role and that we'd acted in Leila's best interest. While I was on remand in prison, I came to realize that wasn't going to happen. She got what she wanted – Leila – and she has no need for me now.'

'When was the last time you spoke to Sharon?' Beth asked.

'November. I called her the day I took Leila. I've tried phoning her since and left messages, but she hasn't returned any of my calls.'

'What's Sharon's phone number?' Beth asked.

'I can't remember offhand.' Beth held his gaze. 'I'm telling you the truth!' he blurted. 'If you don't believe me, ask Doris Goodman. She'll confirm everything I'm saying.'

It took a moment for Beth to recover. 'Are you saying that Mrs Goodman knew of your plan to abduct Leila?'

'Yes. She was in on it. That's why I called her when Leila disappeared.'

Beth saw his solicitor raise her eyebrows, clearly this was news to her too.

'And what was in it for Mrs Goodman?' Matt asked sceptically.

'I've no idea. I've told you all I know. You'll have to ask her.'

'We will,' Beth said. 'Is there anything else you want to say, Colin?'

'No.'

'We'll be in touch once your client's new statement is ready,' Beth said to his solicitor.

FORTY-THREE

'What the hell do you make of that?' Matt said as he and Beth made their way back to the main office.

'It seems ludicrous, although there was a lot of detail.'

'Weaver's had plenty of time to concoct a story, and there's been no evidence that anyone else was involved in Leila's abduction.'

'I know, but we'll need to speak to Sharon and Mrs Goodman and see what they have to say,' Beth said. 'Do you remember when we interviewed Mrs Goodman after Colin was arrested at her cottage – you said you thought she might know Weaver better than she was admitting?'

'Yes. And he was willing to jeopardize his suicide story by phoning her about the cold. But her story stacked up, and Weaver's call data confirmed he only spoke to her once while he was at the cottage – complaining, according to Mrs Goodman. Since Leila is in the care of her aunt, we'd better make visiting her our priority.'

'I'll phone the social worker and see if he can meet us at her house,' Beth said.

'While you do that, I'll update the boss,' Matt said.

As Matt went to find their DS or DCI, Beth sat at her

desk, brought up Peter Harris's work contact details on screen and keyed in his mobile number. He answered straight away with a slightly terse, 'Yes, Peter Harris speaking.'

'This is Detective Constable Beth Mayes, working on the Leila Smith case.'

'Hello.'

'I need to ask you a few questions. Is Leila still living with her aunt – Sharon Kern?'

'Yes. In fact, I'm going there today, as soon as I can get away from my desk.'

'For a routine visit?'

'No. There's a problem with contact. I left Sharon and Kelsey to make their own arrangements, but Sharon is refusing to allow Leila to see her mother. She says Kelsey is always drunk and it's harming Leila. Kelsey has been on the phone too, very upset. She was expecting to see Leila this afternoon, so I've told her I'll go and talk to Sharon and sort something out.' He sounded stressed. 'Always something!'

'Can I and a colleague meet you at Sharon's in about an hour? We need to speak to her and Leila. Colin Weaver has been into the station today and changed his statement. He's now claiming Sharon knew all about Leila's abduction – in fact, according to him, she masterminded it. There's no proof of this, but we do need to speak to her and Leila.'

'Yes, of course. That's very worrying. Do you think there's any truth in it?'

'Probably not, but at this stage it's impossible to say.'

'OK. I'll meet you there. But I doubt you'll get much out of Leila. She's still traumatized from what happened to her.'

'We'll go easy. Were all the usual foster-carer checks completed on Sharon before you placed Leila with her, even though they're related?'

'Yes, we did the same checks as with any foster carer – police check, medical, work reference and so on – all clear.'

'Any mental health issues?'

'None came up.'

'Has Leila said anything about her abduction?'

'Only that it was Colin Weaver who took her. I've told Sharon not to push it. It may take months or even years before Leila is able to talk about what happened.'

'When you visit Leila, is Sharon always in the room with her?' Beth asked.

'Not for the whole time, no. When I visit any child in care, I see them alone for some of the time so they can speak openly about how they're being looked after.'

'And Leila is happy living with her aunt?'

'She appears to be, although obviously she's still suffering from the effects of her abduction.'

'Yes, of course. Does Sharon own or rent her house?'

'She owns it, I believe. I'd need to check. Why? You don't have to own your house to foster.'

'No. That wasn't my reason for asking,' Beth said. 'Colin Weaver is claiming Sharon was going to live abroad with him and Leila, and it's easier to give up your home if you rent – you just give notice.'

'That's highly unlikely,' Peter said. 'Sharon's said nothing to me about any intention to live abroad, and Leila hasn't even got a passport. Foster carers need permission to take a looked-after child abroad even for a short holiday. It's doubtful we would have placed Leila with her aunt if she'd had any plans to emigrate.'

'OK. Thank you. We'll see you in about an hour.'

Beth replaced the handset. She hadn't pointed out to Peter that if Sharon had wanted to get Leila a passport without him knowing, she could have done so illegally. With no sign of Matt yet, Beth used the time to check something else Weaver had said, and brought his call data on screen. He'd said he'd telephoned Sharon the day he'd taken Leila. Now

Beth could see that the only calls he'd made that day were to the pay-as-you-go phone they hadn't been able to trace. There were other calls to that number stretching back months. If that phone was owned by Sharon it would give weight to Weaver's claim they were in a relationship and Sharon was involved in Leila's abduction. But how to prove it?

Beth picked up her desk phone again and entered the number for the pay-as-you-go. Matt appeared. 'Won't be a second,' she said to him as she listened to the phone go straight to voicemail. She replaced the handset.

'The boss has given us the go-ahead,' Matt said. 'Visit Sharon first and then Doris Goodman.'

'Good.' Beth stood. 'Peter Harris is going to meet us at Sharon's house. He was going there anyway. I'll fill you in on the details as we go.'

Fifteen minutes later, Beth had updated Matt as he drove and had tried the pay-as-you-go number again without any success.

'I think it should be illegal to sell SIM cards without registering the owner,' Beth said, frustrated. 'We can only trace the phone by GPS if it's switched on.'

'The black market would take up the shortfall and reset stolen phones,' Matt said. 'It already does.'

Beth nodded sagely. He was right, of course. Drug dealers and terrorists relied on reset stolen mobile phones. 'I suppose it was asking a bit much for the owner of the phone to answer and identify themselves,' Beth said with a rueful smile.

'Yes. And if it was used in the abduction of Leila Smith, it's probably been dumped by now. The canal is awash with mobile phones used in crimes, if you'll excuse the pun.'

'Perfect timing,' Matt said as they drew up outside Sharon Kern's home – 86 Park Road. It was a modern terraced house on a small new estate of similar houses. Peter Harris was just getting out of the car in front. He saw them and waited on the pavement. They shook hands.

'Does Sharon know you're coming?' he asked as they began up the path to the front door.

'No,' Beth said.

'I'll need to explain to Leila why you're here. What reason shall I give?'

'Just say we've come to make sure she's OK,' Beth said. 'Don't worry, we won't push her if she isn't willing to talk to us. Then perhaps you could take her to another room while we talk to Sharon?'

'Yes, it would be upsetting for Leila to hear her aunt being questioned, and it will give me the chance to have a chat with Leila. It's a nice house,' he added as he pressed the doorbell.

A few moments later Sharon answered. Her shock at seeing Beth and Matt was obvious. 'Oh. You've brought the police with you!' she exclaimed.

'I didn't bring them,' Peter corrected. 'We arranged to meet here. They need to speak to you and Leila.'

'What about?' Sharon asked, clearly thrown by their arrival. She stood aside to allow them to enter.

Leila appeared at the other end of the hall, smartly dressed but looking at them very warily. 'Hi, Leila, how are you?' Beth asked, smiling at her.

Leila didn't answer but stared back apprehensively.

'Can we go into the sitting room?' Peter said to Sharon, pushing open a door on their left.

'Shall I send Leila to her room while we talk?' Sharon asked.

'No, we'd like to speak to her first,' Beth said.

Beth took in the modern L-shaped living room, with its cream leather sofa, matching chairs and pouffe, neatly framed prints on the walls and Smart TV. Tastefully furnished and immaculate. A large wooden toy box containing brand-new children's toys, puzzles and games was on a rug at one end, although there was no sign it was being used prior to their arrival. Peter had been right when he'd said it was a nice house – compared to Kelsey's flat, it was a palace.

'Matt and Beth have been investigating your disappearance,' Peter said gently to Leila as the adults sat down. 'Now they'd like to talk to you. It's nothing for you to worry about, and you don't have to say anything unless you want to.'

Standing just inside the door, Leila stared back at them cautiously.

'Come and sit down,' Sharon encouraged. 'Don't worry, I'm here with you.'

She did as her aunt said and perched on the pouffe beside her..

'She's not talking about any of it,' Sharon said.

Beth looked at Leila. 'Are you able to tell us anything about what happened to you while you were missing? It doesn't matter how small it is.'

Leila stared back and then shook her head.

'We know Colin Weaver took you to his flat,' Beth tried. 'Did anyone else come to the flat while you were there?'

Leila didn't reply.

'Did you hear him speaking to anyone on the phone?' Beth asked.

Leila shook her head again.

'What about in his car? It was a long drive to Heath Cottage. Did he speak to anyone during the journey?'

'I don't know. I was asleep,' she said in a small voice.

'OK, good girl,' Beth said. 'You were at the cottage for over two weeks. Did anyone visit you while you were there?' Beth glanced at Sharon for any sign that she might be trying to influence Leila. Matt was watching her too.

'I don't know,' Leila replied.

'Can you think of anything else that might be important?' Beth asked.

Leila shook her head and then began to look very worried. It was time to stop. 'That's fine, good girl,' Beth said. 'If you do think of anything, just tell your social worker.'

'Or she can tell me,' Sharon added.

'Yes, of course,' Beth said. 'We'd like to have a chat with you now. Can Leila go in another room with Peter?'

'They can go in the kitchen-diner,' Sharon said. 'He knows where it is.'

Leila dutifully followed her social worker out of the room. As the door closed, Sharon looked at Matt and Beth cautiously. 'What's going on?'

'We need to ask you a few questions,' Beth said as Matt prepared to take notes. 'We didn't think it was wise for Leila to be present.' Sharon nodded warily. 'How well do you know Colin Weaver?'

'Barely at all,' Sharon replied.

'You've never had a relationship with him?'

'Goodness me, no!' She looked shocked.

'He's saying you did.'

'He's lying.'

Beth paused. 'How many mobile phones do you own?'

'One. You have the number. I gave it to you when Leila first went missing.'

Beth took a sheet of paper from her shoulder bag and read out the mobile phone number Sharon had given to her.

'That's it,' she confirmed.

'And you don't own any others?'

'No. There's the landline, but I keep it unplugged.'

'Why?' Beth asked.

'Kelsey keeps phoning and it's very unsettling for Leila.'

Beth nodded. 'Does this number mean anything to you?' she asked, and read out the number of the unregistered SIM.

The colour drained from Sharon's face.

'So you recognize it,' Beth said.

'Yes, but I haven't used that phone in ages. I'd forgotten all about it.'

'It wasn't that long ago. The last time you used that phone was the night Leila went missing.' Beth held her gaze.

Sharon stared back, visibly shaken. 'Did I?' she asked at last.

'Yes. You received three calls from Colin Weaver on that night, which is a lot considering you say you don't know him.'

A small nerve flickered at the side of Sharon's eye and Leila's voice drifted in from the kitchen.

'I'm so sorry. I should have told you sooner,' Sharon said, rubbing her cheek. 'I do know him.'

'So why didn't you tell us?'

'It was difficult.'

'Colin Weaver is accusing you of being his accomplice in Leila's abduction. He says not only did you know all about it, but you organized it. He's claiming that the two of you were in a relationship and were going to flee the country with Leila.'

Sharon was shaking her head. 'No, that's ridiculous! Of course I wasn't involved with him. Not at all. Do I need a solicitor?'

'That's up to you. If you want to make a formal statement, we would need to go to Coleshaw Police Station.'

'I've got nothing to hide. I can tell you what I know.' Sharon drew a breath and shifted in her chair. 'It's true, I did know Mr Weaver more than I've admitted, but not in the way you're suggesting, and I had absolutely nothing to do with Leila's disappearance. I was as shocked and worried as everyone else. I first met Colin Weaver about nine months ago. He approached me as I was leaving Kelsey's flat. He said he was very worried about Leila because Kelsey was

271

neglecting her, which of course I knew. I was doing all I could to help them, but it wasn't enough.

'Mr Weaver told me he'd been keeping an eye on Leila and that he sometimes offered her shelter in his flat if it was raining and her mother was with a client. She's a prostitute, you know?' Beth nodded. 'I thought it was kind of him, and I knew Doris Goodman was also helping Leila, but clearly the situation couldn't go on forever. I told Mr Weaver I was very worried about Leila and I was gathering evidence to take to the social services, as I didn't think they were doing enough. I gave him my phone number – the pay-as-you-go one. I used it when my smartphone was in for repair. Later I was pleased I'd only given him that number because he kept calling me. Nothing to do with Leila – he became very personal and I realized he was infatuated with me. Obsessed. Like a stalker. I gave him no encouragement whatsoever, but he began waiting for me outside Kelsey's flat.' She stopped and grimaced.

'So why didn't you report him to the police if he was harassing you?' Beth asked, as Matt wrote.

'At the time I just thought he was weird and I could deal with it. Then, when I found out what he'd done, I didn't want my name linked to his in any way. Mud can stick. But I swear, I had nothing to do with Leila's disappearance. I was in complete shock when I found out what he'd done.'

'Why did he call you the night Leila went missing?'

'To tell me he loved me. It never for one moment crossed my mind that he might have taken Leila.' Sharon paused, visibly upset. 'The poor kid – goodness knows what she's been through, and it's partly my fault. I should have realized he was unbalanced. That night was the last night we spoke, and I haven't used the phone since. I got my smartphone back.'

'Do you still have the pay-as-you-go phone?'

'No. I dropped it and the screen shattered, so I threw it away. It was only cheap.'

'And the SIM that was in it?'

'It went in the bin with the phone. There was no reason to keep it.'

Beth nodded. 'Have you seen Mr Weaver since his release from prison?'

'No, he's not allowed to contact Leila, me or Kelsey. It's a condition of his bail.'

'Do you have any plans to live abroad?'

'What? No. I don't even have a passport and neither does Leila.'

'Are you still working at Elm & Co.?' Matt asked.

'Yes, of course. I've been there for ages. Why would I leave? They've been very good to me and have given me extra holiday while Leila settles in.'

'Why do you think Colin Weaver tried to implicate you in Leila's disappearance?' Beth asked.

'I've no idea, other than because he's obsessed with me. He's unhinged. Perhaps he thought he was doing me a favour by taking Leila. I really don't know.'

Beth gave a small nod. 'OK. Thank you. We'll need to take a statement from you at some point. Perhaps you could come to Coleshaw Police Station next week?'

'Yes. I'll do anything I can to help. I'm sorry I didn't tell you sooner.'

'One last question,' Beth said, returning the sheet of paper to her bag. 'How well do you know Doris Goodman?'

'Quite well. As I say, she helped Leila.'

'And Mr Weaver? Does he know her?'

'A little, I expect. I really don't know.'

'OK. Thank you. We'll say goodbye to Leila and Peter and then leave you to it. Let us know when you're coming to make your statement.'

'I will.'

FORTY-FOUR

'I believe Sharon,' Matt said as he and Beth returned to their car.

'So do I. It makes far more sense than what Weaver is claiming. He was obsessed with Sharon and found a way to get close to her through Leila. In his warped perception, he believed he was helping Sharon by 'rescuing' Leila. She has a steady job and owns her house – I checked the Land Registry on the way here. It's not rented. She clearly has no intention of leaving the country.'

'And all those calls on Weaver's phone log were one way – from him to her,' Matt said, starting the car. 'It's classic stalking behaviour – bombard her with calls, lie in wait to see her and not take no for an answer. It's a pity Sharon didn't report him at the time. We might have been able to stop him abducting Leila.'

Beth nodded thoughtfully. 'Unfortunately we haven't got the resources to check the CCTV at the restaurants and hotels Weaver claims he went to with Sharon. It would prove her story and that he's a fantasist and a liar.'

'Although there's enough evidence to convict him for the

abduction of Leila without it. You'd better update the boss and tell Peter Harris,' Matt said.

'Yes, I'll do that now. Can we stop off for a burger on our way to Doris Goodman? I'm starving.'

'Me too.'

As Matt drove, looking out for a fast-food takeaway, Beth phoned DS Scrivener and then Peter Harris's mobile. 'Are you still at Sharon's?' she asked.

'Yes. I'll be here for a while. I can go outside if you want to talk to me in private.'

'Yes, please.'

Beth waited a few moments until Peter came back on the phone. 'Go ahead,' he said.

'I thought you'd want to know the results of our interview with Sharon.'

'Yes, absolutely.'

'She has denied ever having a relationship with Colin Weaver, or playing any part in Leila's abduction. She's coming into Coleshaw Police Station next week to make a statement. There's no solid evidence to suggest anyone else was involved in Leila's abduction but Weaver. Did Leila tell you any more?'

'No, she's still too traumatized,' Peter said, 'but she seems happy with her aunt. Thank you for letting me know. I'll phone my manager and update her. I'm sure she'll agree that Leila should be allowed to stay with her aunt. Leila doesn't need any more upheaval now.'

'No. She's very quiet,' Beth commented. 'Not at all like the Leila I used to see on the estate when she lived with her mother. She could be quite lippy.'

'Sharon's a good influence,' Peter said. 'She's put boundaries in place, and Leila respects that. Plus, of course, Leila has been through a dreadful ordeal, so she's bound to be withdrawn for a while.'

'Yes. I'm sure you're right. I'll leave you to it then.'

'Thank you for the update.'

'You're welcome.'

It was nearly seven o'clock when Matt and Beth pulled up outside Doris Goodman's home, having picked up a burger and coffee on the way, which they'd eaten in the car. Mrs Goodman's Christmas lights were still sparkling brightly in her living-room window.

'I can't believe it's over a week since Christmas,' Beth said with a sigh.

'And it's a long time to the next holiday,' Matt said.

Looming to their right was the block of flats where Kelsey and Colin lived. Between the flats and Doris Goodman's flat was the play area. Mike, Jason and others were gathering in the shadows, ready for business as usual. As Matt and Beth got out of the car they dispersed, some running off and others on pedal bikes. 'Sensible choice!' Matt called after them.

'Fuck off!' came the reply.

'Leave it,' Beth said as Matt was about to go after them. 'I'd like to get home at some point this evening. It's been a long day.'

'I'll be back!' Matt shouted.

Doris apparently hadn't seen or heard the commotion and Matt had to press the bell, then knock, before the door was opened.

'Sorry. I was on the telephone,' she said, appearing flustered. 'Come in.'

'Happy New Year,' Beth said, as they went into her sitting room. A row of Christmas cards stood on the mantelpiece and a small decorated artificial Christmas tree was in one corner, but those and the fairy lights in the window were the only Christmas decorations. It looked a bit sad, Beth thought. 'Did you have a nice Christmas?' she asked as they sat down.

'Not bad. I had company, as usual. There's always at least one child on the estate who needs a meal and somewhere warm on Christmas Day. This time there were three of them.'

Beth tutted. 'Three kids whose parents couldn't be bothered even on Christmas Day. That was kind of you.'

Doris shrugged off the praise. 'It's company for me. How can I help you? I'm sure you didn't come here at this time of night to wish me a Happy New Year.'

'No.' Beth smiled and took a chocolate from the box Doris was offering. 'Thank you. How well do you know Sharon Kern, Kelsey's sister?' she asked.

'A little,' Doris replied, offering Matt the box. 'Sharon was very worried about Leila and knew I used to take her in sometimes. We chatted a few times, mainly about Leila. I was so relieved when she went to live with her aunt.'

'When was the last time you saw Sharon?'

'Hmm, let me think,' Doris said, closing the lid on the box. 'I can't remember exactly, but it may have been when Leila first went missing, around the fourteenth of November.'

'Have you spoken to her since?'

'Yes, on the phone. When Leila was found. I couldn't tell you the exact day. Why? Is there a problem?'

'No. We're just checking a few details, as Colin Weaver has changed his statement.'

'Has he?' she asked, clearly taken aback.

'Have you seen or spoken to Mr Weaver since his release?' Beth asked.

'No. Of course not! After what he did?' she replied, visibly affronted by the suggestion.

'Has he tried to contact you?'

'No. Why should he? I wouldn't have anything to do with him after what he did. If he's got any sense, he'll keep his head down. There's plenty round here who would give him a right going over if they got the chance.'

Beth looked carefully at Doris. You'd be hard-pressed to find a more respectable, law-abiding citizen, but – 'Mr Weaver is saying that you knew he was taking Leila to your cottage,' she said.

'What! That's ridiculous. Why would he say that? It's not true.'

'He's claiming that not only did you know Leila was at the cottage, but you and Sharon were involved in Leila's abduction. That you planned it together.'

'Ludicrous!' Doris cried, throwing up her hands in horror. 'Of course I didn't know Leila was there, nor did I have anything to do with her abduction. To say such a thing is madness. You surely don't believe him?'

Beth held her gaze. Seated here in this neat, warm, cosy living room, with a kind, elderly lady who took in children when their parents neglected them, Weaver's claims did seem just as Doris said – madness. Yet …

'Why do you think he would try to implicate you?' Beth asked.

'I've no idea. For the same reason he tried to implicate Sharon, I suppose.'

'I don't think so,' Matt said. 'Mr Weaver was obsessed with Sharon – you know, infatuated with her.'

'He told you that?' Doris asked.

'Yes.'

'Perhaps he thinks blaming others will make him appear less guilty,' Doris suggested. 'What is Leila saying?'

'Nothing at present,' Beth said. 'She's still too traumatized to tell us what happened.'

'I see. Well, I'm sorry but I really can't help you. Colin Weaver is lying, that's all I know.'

Beth nodded. 'Well, if you think of anything else that might help, please let us know. We won't keep you further. Thank you for your time.'

They stood and Doris saw them out. The door closed quickly behind them.

'You seemed a bit doubtful in there,' Matt said as they got into the car.

'Not really. It's just, I don't understand – what's in it for Colin Weaver to incriminate Doris Goodman in the way he has?'

'It's probably as she said – Weaver trying to spread the blame to make himself appear less culpable. Who better to accuse than Sharon, the woman who didn't return his love, and the owner of the cottage where he hid Leila?'

'Yes, when you put it like that it makes sense.'

Matt started the car and as they pulled away Beth looked up at the block of flats towering to their left. The lights were on in both Colin Weaver's and Kelsey Smith's flats. 'I hope Peter Harris sorts out contact soon,' Beth said. 'Kelsey must be devastated. Seeing Leila is all she has left.'

FORTY-FIVE

At the same time Matt and Beth were leaving the Hawthorn Estate, Kelsey was standing in her living room, phone pressed to her ear, shouting at Peter Harris. He'd just called her to explain why she wouldn't be allowed to see Leila for the time being.

'But Sharon's lying!' Kelsey screamed. 'It's not true. I don't keep getting drunk!'

'Kelsey, please be realistic,' Peter said patiently. 'I've seen the photographs Sharon took. They show you lying on your bed, fully dressed, unconscious from drink. Sharon said you drank a whole bottle of gin and had started on a second before she stopped you. It's damaging for Leila to witness you getting drunk and then attacking her aunt.'

'I didn't attack her!' Kelsey cried, even more angry and frustrated. 'I just went to bed like she said. And it was New Year's Eve, for Christ's sake! We were celebrating. I promise it won't happen again.'

There was a moment's pause before Peter said, 'But it has happened before, Kelsey, hasn't it? Lots of times. You drank a full bottle of vodka on Christmas Day.'

'Did Sharon tell you that?'

'Yes. I appreciate how difficult it is not to relapse. I really think you would benefit from joining a support group like Alcoholics Anonymous.'

'But Christmas Day was different,' Kelsey said in despair. 'Leila was missing. I thought she was dead. I was trying to blot out the pain. And Sharon wasn't even there when I started drinking, so how does she know how much I drank?'

'She found the empty bottle in the bin.'

'She searched my bin? The cow! I bet she didn't tell you she was the one who brought the gin on New Year's Eve. I'd been doing OK until then. My neighbour, Brooke, said it was wrong of her to give it to me.'

'Look, Kelsey, it's late and you're upset,' Peter said. 'It would be better if I visited you tomorrow to discuss contact and any other issues you have.'

'Bollocks! What is there to discuss? You're not going to change your mind about me seeing Leila.'

'I'm only suspending contact until I can arrange supervised contact at a family centre. If you were to arrive there under the influence of alcohol or drugs, contact wouldn't go ahead.'

'But I'm off the drugs and I only relapsed with the drink on those two occasions Sharon told you about.' Kelsey knew she was sounding desperate, but she couldn't help it – she *was* desperate.

'Sharon also found a used syringe in your bathroom on New Year's Eve. She removed it so Leila wouldn't hurt herself.'

'She's fucking lying!' Kelsey screamed. 'I'm clean – I haven't used in ages.'

'Kelsey, get some sleep and I'll visit you tomorrow. You will see Leila again before long.'

'No, I won't. You and Sharon will find a way to stop me. The pair of you have already made up your minds.'

Cutting the call, Kelsey dropped to her knees and wept. All hope had gone. Sharon was against her. Was Leila in on this too? It seemed likely – the two of them working together to cut her out of their lives forever. What use was she to Leila now she had Sharon? None at all. As Kelsey wept, her thoughts went to New Year's Eve, when Sharon and Leila had put her to bed. She remembered thinking she'd seen the flash of a camera as she'd passed out. When she'd woken the following morning they'd gone and, unknown to her, they had the evidence of her drunkenness on Sharon's phone.

But there hadn't been a syringe in the bathroom. She was sure of that. There were no syringes at all in the flat and there hadn't been for months. Sharon had lied about that and about other things to paint Kelsey in the worst possible light. But why? What had she ever done to Sharon to deserve this? There'd be no chance of Leila ever being returned to her now. Peter had said how well Leila was settling in with her aunt. The decision had been made. This was the end of the line for Kelsey. She wouldn't get in their way any more.

She pulled herself to her feet and, wiping her eyes on the sleeve of her cardigan, went into her bedroom. She took the last of Colin Weaver's money from where she'd hidden it under the bed. There was £180 left. Plenty to buy what she needed: the drugs to send her to oblivion, permanently. She felt a numb acceptance as she tucked the money and her keys into the pocket of her jeans and left her flat.

With the decision made, how simple everything had suddenly become. Jason and Mike should be in their usual place by now, dealing, and she would buy whatever they were selling. It didn't matter what, as long as it was enough to stop her pain once and for all.

Nothingness beckoned and Kelsey felt relieved. For her, life had been one long struggle, but not for much longer.

The night was bitterly cold and Kelsey dug her hands into her jacket pockets as she made her way towards the play area. She couldn't see any sign of Mike or Jason; they didn't appear to be in their usual place. But Kevin Bates was there, loitering with another guy. Undeterred (she had no fear of him now), Kelsey continued towards them.

'Well, look who it is!' Bates sneered as she approached. 'The slag of Hawthorn Estate.'

'I'm not looking for trouble,' Kelsey said. 'I just want some stuff. Where are Jason and Mike?'

'They had to leave,' Bates laughed. 'The police were here again. But my friend Sam can help you. He's got some good coke.'

The other lad stepped forwards. 'It's pure,' he said, showing her a packet of white powder. 'Forty quid a gram.'

'Give me four grams,' Kelsey said.

'Wow. You having a gang bang up there?' Bates guffawed.

'Just shut the fuck up, will you?' Kelsey hissed.

'Oh, someone's in a bad mood.'

Kelsey ignored him and gave Sam the money. He passed her the four packets of coke. She turned and headed back.

'How much for a blow job tonight?' Bates shouted after her.

Clutching the bags of coke, Kelsey continued across the play area and then in through the main door of the flats. Bates couldn't harm her now. No one could. She was beyond all of that. Four grams would do it. She'd dissolve it in water and drink the mixture since she didn't have any syringes to inject with. The result would be the same – an overdose, leading to death.

Slowly and heavily, Kelsey climbed the stairs to her landing and was about to round the corner when she heard a movement behind her. She turned. Colin Weaver stepped out of the shadows.

'What the fuck! You bastard!' she cried, going for him.

He grabbed her wrists to deflect the blow. 'I need to talk to you.'

'Let me go. You've done enough damage.' She pulled away and began towards her flat.

'No! Wait, please,' he called after. 'It's about Leila.'

She stopped and turned. 'What about Leila?'

'I heard you in your flat just now shouting and crying. I know why you're upset and it's not your fault.'

Kelsey stared at him. 'You don't know anything about me. You took Leila, you sicko, and now I've lost her for good. I hope they lock you up and throw away the key.'

'I did take her and I'm sorry, but it wasn't my idea. It was your sister Sharon's idea. She told me to do it.'

'What are you talking about? You don't even know my sister.'

'I do, very well. Or did. She and Doris Goodman persuaded me to take Leila.'

'Bullshit. You're lying. The police know it was you.'

'I've admitted my part, but Sharon was involved too. She planned it, although the police don't believe me.'

'Neither do I. You're just trying to get off lightly.'

'Think what you like about me, but believe me for Leila's sake.' He took a step towards her. Kelsey remained where she was. 'She's in danger, living with your sister. Sharon is obsessed with keeping Leila. She'd stop at nothing.'

'Tell me about it!' Kelsey said dismissively, and she turned and continued towards her flat.

'You need to believe me!' he cried down the corridor. 'You'll be sorry if you don't.'

'Yeah, I'm sorry for a lot of things!' she shouted back. Letting herself into her flat, she slammed the door shut.

She doubted Weaver knew Sharon, and even if he did, she was beyond caring now. It was no business of hers, and she hoped he got what he deserved. Going to the kitchen, Kelsey filled a glass with warm water and took it, with a teaspoon, into the living room. She sat on the sofa and placed the four bags of coke in a line in front of her. Her phone, on the sofa where she'd left it, now vibrated with an incoming call. She ignored it and opened the first packet. She didn't have to talk to anyone now or ever again, and this was strangely comforting. She carefully tipped the powder from the first bag into the glass of warm water and stirred. The white particles gradually disappeared, dissolving into the water.

Her phone buzzed again and she turned it over so she could see the caller display. It was from a mobile number her phone didn't recognize, so the person wasn't in her contact list. Probably a client, she thought, and carefully opened the second packet. No need for clients now or ever again.

She stirred in the powder. Only once she had dissolved the contents of all four packets would she start drinking the mixture. She'd drink it gradually so she wasn't sick and her body had time to absorb it. Then it would slowly shut down her organs and eventually stop her heart and that would be the end. No more struggling to get it right and failing. No more worries. Nothing.

The phone buzzed again and she glanced over. It was from the same caller. Someone must be desperate for sex. It could even be Bates, given his remarks about a gang bang. She'd never given him her number, but he could easily have obtained it from a client on the estate, and he knew she was in.

Kelsey concentrated on opening the third packet and tipped the powder into the now-milky-coloured water. Her phone bleeped with a text message. She glanced over and read the display as she stirred. *Mum its me Leila pick up i need to talk to you.*

Of course it wasn't Leila. Kelsey continued stirring the mixture. It was someone playing a sick joke. Bates? Leila was with Sharon and didn't have a phone, because the one Kelsey had bought for her was still in her bedroom here. The only other person who could be playing a joke like this, apart from

Bates, was that sick weirdo Weaver. Maybe, having stopped her on the stairs, he was now trying to mess with her brain and frighten her. Little did he know she was beyond that.

She opened the last packet and tipped the contents into the glass as her phone bleeped with another text message: *Mum its Leila why arent you answering?* Then her phone began to vibrate again with a call from the same number. Kelsey's anger flared and she grabbed the phone.

'Who the hell is this? What do you want?'

There was silence, then the sound of breathing, and a faint voice, barely audible, said, 'Mum, it's me, Leila.'

Kelsey's heart stopped as she fought to regain control. 'Leila?' It couldn't be.

'Yes.'

'Is that you? I can hardly hear you.'

'I'm whispering so Aunty Sharon doesn't hear me. I've locked myself in her bathroom. I want to come home. I don't like it here. She's horrible.'

'Has she put you up to this?' Kelsey asked. 'You haven't got a phone.'

'I'm using an old phone of Sharon's. I found it in a drawer in her bedroom. I wasn't supposed to be in there.'

Kelsey hesitated. Her throat had gone dry and her heart was racing. Was this a trick? 'How do I know you're telling the truth? Peter Harris told me you liked Sharon and you were getting on well.'

'No, I had to pretend when he came here. Just like I had to pretend to the police. Sharon told me to say nice things about her or she would be angry. She made up lots of bad things about you and now I can't see you any more.' Kelsey heard her whimper.

Was Leila telling the truth? She desperately wanted to believe her. She stared at the glass of dissolved coke she'd been about to drink.

'Did you know Sharon took a photograph of me on New Year's Eve after I'd passed out?' Kelsey asked. 'Were you in on it?'

'No, honestly, Mum, I saw it today for the first time when she showed Peter. I tried to tell him it wasn't your fault and Sharon got you drunk, but he didn't believe me. He said I was being loyal to you. She's made up other things too.'

'I know.'

'She won't let me speak to you on her mobile and she's unplugged the phone in the living room so you can't call. You know how we were so late arriving on New Year's Eve?'

'Yes.'

'That was her fault. She said you'd be so stressed by the time we arrived you'd be more than ready for a drink.'

'But why is she doing this?'

'To make sure I stay here. She said she doesn't need Colin Weaver any more.'

Kelsey's stomach contracted. 'Sharon knows Weaver?'

'Yes. I heard her talking to Mrs Goodman about him. That's how I knew she had another phone. I listened outside her bedroom door. I think Sharon had something to do with Colin taking me. I don't want to stay here, Mum. I don't trust her. You need to help me.'

'Yes, I'm trying to think how.' Kelsey's thoughts churned as she struggled to make sense of what was going on and formulate a plan. Who was going to believe her over a social worker and her respectable sister?

'You need to do something quickly, Mum,' Leila whispered. 'She's coming. I have to go.'

Kelsey heard a loud knock on the bathroom door together with Sharon's voice, hard and demanding, talking to Leila in a tone Kelsey had never heard her use. 'What are you doing in there? Come out now!'

The line went dead.

Kelsey's hand trembled as she stared at her phone and felt sick with fear. She couldn't call Leila back to make sure she was all right. If what she said was true then Sharon was sure to hear. Had Leila had time to hide the phone before letting her aunt into the bathroom? Would Sharon notice the phone was missing before Leila could return it? Would she check the call log? She had to believe Leila and act fast.

With all thoughts of suicide now gone, Kelsey stood and stared distractedly around the room. What to do for the best? Colin Weaver had said Sharon was in on Leila's abduction and Leila was in danger. She hadn't believed him, but now it seemed as if he was telling the truth. Leila needed help, rescuing, but it was an hour in a car to Sharon's house even if she had the money to pay for a taxi, which she didn't. She'd spent the last of the money on coke. Her only option, she quickly decided, was to call the police and pray they believed her. With her hand trembling uncontrollably, she pressed 999.

'Which service do you require: ambulance, fire, police or coastguard?' the call handler asked.

'Police and quickly.'

'I'm putting you through.'

'My daughter is at her aunt's house and is in danger,' Kelsey cried as soon as the call was connected. 'She needs rescuing now.'

'Calm down, please,' the officer said. 'What's the name and age of your daughter?'

'Leila Smith. Eight years old.'

A second's pause, then, 'Is this the same child who was missing last month?'

'Yes. She's living with her aunt – my sister – but I've just found out she was involved in Leila's abduction.'

'And the aunt's name?'

'Sharon Kern.'

'The address where the child is?'

'Eighty-six Park Road, LE31 5ZX.'

'And what makes you think your daughter is in danger?'

'She phoned just now, scared stiff. She'd locked herself in the bathroom to get away from her aunt.'

'All right, try not to worry. I'll send someone to look into it.'

'Thank you. Please hurry before it's too late.'

FORTY-SIX

'You little cow!' Sharon cried, grabbing Leila by the arm and pushing her back into the bathroom. 'I heard you. Where's my phone?'

Leila stared at her, petrified, then watched as her aunt began searching the bathroom, still holding her arm tightly so she couldn't get away. There weren't many places to hide things in the bathroom and within seconds Sharon had opened the small wall cabinet and spotted the phone concealed behind the shower gel.

'You need to learn to do as you're told,' she said, shaking Leila. 'Who were you talking to?'

'No one,' Leila said, her voice slight.

'Liar. I heard you.'

Slamming the bathroom door closed behind her, Sharon stood in front of it, blocking Leila's escape, and checked her phone. 'You called your mother! What did you tell her?' she demanded.

'Nothing,' Leila said, trembling.

'I don't believe you. But it won't do you any good. No one will believe a crackhead like her over me.'

'I hate you!' Leila shouted, made brave by defending her mother.

'You're just like her,' Sharon cried, her eyes blazing. 'You should be grateful I'm looking after you. No one else would.'

'I'm not grateful!' Leila retaliated. 'I love my mum. I hate you. I'm going home.'

'Over my dead body!' She glared at Leila, her face ugly from anger.

'Why are you being horrible and making up things about my mother?' Leila asked. 'She hasn't done anything to you.'

Sharon paused for a moment as though a connection had been made, a fuse lit, then, lowering her voice, she said, 'I'll tell you if you really want to know. You're old enough. It's time you understood. It goes back to when your mother and I were children. We were happy then, but our father died and our mother remarried quickly because she couldn't stand being alone. The man she married was evil and abused your mother in ways you don't want to know. He would have started on me too if it hadn't been for her. She was two years older than me and she kept him away from me by sacrificing herself.' Pain shot across Sharon's face and she stared distractedly around the room, which made Leila more afraid than ever.

'We told our mother what he was doing, but she didn't believe us,' Sharon continued. 'Kelsey could have left when she was sixteen, but she stayed to protect me. As soon as I turned sixteen, we both left, but the damage was done. Your mother married a thug and then took to drink and drugs to try to blot out the pain. I buried myself in respectability – a steady job, a house of my own, church on Sundays. But it was there in the background for both of us, gnawing away. Even though our stepfather hadn't abused me, knowing how your mother had sacrificed herself and suffered all those years was torture for me. I made the decision that I couldn't risk having children in case what happened to us happened to them. But your mother had children and I had to stand by and watch her lose them all. It wasn't fair. The abuse ruined both our lives – you see that, don't you?'

Scared further by her aunt's manic passion, Leila gave a small nod.

'I did what I could to help your mother keep you and so did Doris Goodman, even though your mother resented it. Doris is a good woman. Don't ever say anything bad about her, whatever happens. Do you understand?'

Leila nodded again.

'One day Colin Weaver approached me as I was leaving your flat. He said he was going to phone the social services with evidence that showed how badly you were being neglected. I knew you'd be taken into care and adopted so I'd never see you again like your brothers and sisters. I felt I'd failed, so I hit upon a plan to rescue you and get me the child I deserved but had been denied. I realized you'd be hard work because of the life you'd led, but I was prepared for that. Raising you would be like a penance to repay the debt I owed your mother for protecting me from our step-father for all those years. The weight of that debt was bringing me down.

'It didn't take long before Colin Weaver was willing to do whatever I wanted,' Sharon continued with a smile that turned Leila cold. 'He was in love with me and thought we were going to start a new life together – the three of us. As if! I knew your mother would never have agreed to you coming to live with me had she not been pushed into a corner. Once you were missing and the social services had taken out a care order, though, it would be easier.' She paused again as if remembering.

'Did you love Colin Weaver?' Leila asked, trying to distract her. Sharon had been so absorbed in telling her story, she'd dropped her guard and moved slightly away from the door.

'No, of course I didn't love him!' she said, with a sneer. 'I couldn't love any man after what our stepfather did. And neither were there any plans to live abroad. That was just what I led him to believe. The final stage of my plan was for me to make an anonymous call to the police and tell them there was a child matching your description living at Heath Cottage. But you ran away before that happened. As it turned out the result was the same. You're here with me and Colin has been charged.' She stopped, triumphant.

'I'll tell Peter Harris what you did,' Leila said, and took a step towards the door.

'And you think he'll believe you!' Sharon laughed.

'I'll tell him about the phone you've got hidden and all the lies you've told.' She took another step towards the door and then went to grab the handle, but not in time. Sharon caught hold of her by her jumper and pulled her back.

'Let go!' Leila shouted, trying to break free.

Suddenly a loud knock sounded downstairs, together with the doorbell ringing and a male voice shouting, 'Police! Miss Kern, open the door, please.'

Sharon froze.

'I told my mum what you've done,' Leila said. 'They've come to rescue me.'

The police banged on the door again. 'Police! Open the door now!'

'You won't say a word if you know what's good for you and your mother,' Sharon hissed. 'I can bluff this out. Just stay quiet.'

Grabbing Leila's hand, Sharon opened the bathroom door and began downstairs.

'I'm coming!' she shouted, dragging Leila behind her.

'Police. Open the door!'

Still tightly holding Leila's hand, Sharon unlocked the front door. Suddenly the hall was full of police, but not the ones who were here before, Leila noted. She looked at them expectantly and waited.

'Sharon Kern?' the lead officer asked.

'Yes, that's me, and this is my niece, Leila.' Sharon smiled sweetly. 'Is there a problem?'

Leila saw the officers taking in her aunt's clean, tidy, nicely decorated hall.

'Are you Leila Smith?' a female officer asked her.

Sharon squeezed her hand hard, warning her to be careful what she said. 'Yes,' Leila replied.

'There's nothing to be afraid of,' the officer said gently. 'My name is Petra and I'd like to talk to you and your aunt to make sure you're OK.'

'Yes, of course,' Sharon said, before Leila could answer. 'Shall we go into the living room?'

It seemed to Leila that even now, with the police here, her aunt was still in charge. Gripping Leila's hand, Sharon led the way into the living room. Petra and a male officer came in while two other police officers waited in the hall.

'Do sit down,' Sharon said politely, finally releasing Leila's hand so she could sit on the pouffe. 'You gave us quite a shock with all that noise. We were in the bathroom. I was just about to give Leila a bath.'

'Isn't she old enough to give herself a bath?' Petra asked, as if she might suspect something, Leila thought.

Sharon smiled. 'Yes, but I like to run the water to make sure it's not too hot.'

Petra seemed to accept this and turned to Leila. 'How are you? We hear you've been through a lot recently.'

She saw her aunt's gaze, mean and threatening. 'I'm OK,' Leila replied, her voice unsteady. Surely they would see through Sharon's act and know what was really going on here?

'Your mummy telephoned us,' Petra said. 'She's worried about you and thinks you may be unhappy.'

Leila saw the look in her aunt's eyes and knew she had to be very careful. She needed to give Petra some clues but not say so much that it would be bad for her if they didn't see through Sharon's lies and went away, leaving her here.

'I'd rather be with my mummy,' Leila said.

'Her social worker said that's normal and only to be expected,' Sharon put in quickly, smiling at Leila. 'He was here this afternoon, making sure she was being well looked after. He was satisfied, of course.'

'I believe two officers from Coleshaw Police Station were here too,' Petra said.

Leila's heart leapt. Perhaps they would help her.

'Yes, that's correct,' Sharon replied, unfazed. 'I'm afraid it appears my sister, Kelsey, has been making trouble again. I can understand why. She wants Leila back, but that's not possible. If you speak to the officers – DC Beth Mayes and Matt Davis – you'll see I was able to reassure them. Also, Peter Harris is aware of what Kelsey is like.'

Leila saw the way Petra and the other officer standing by the door were looking at her aunt – nodding, sympathetic, clearly believing her. Just as Peter had. This was her only chance. If she didn't act now, there may never be another opportunity. 'Can I say something?' she asked.

'Yes, of course,' Petra replied.

Sharon glared at her.

'I haven't been able to tell anyone what happened to me when Colin Weaver took me,' Leila said. 'But I feel ready now. I want to tell you what happened. Can we go in another room, please?'

'That's not necessary,' Sharon said, touching her arm. 'You're fine in here. There's nothing you can't share with me, love.'

Leila's heart sank. She looked at Petra and then at the other officer. Even if she could tell them the truth, it would be her word against her aunt's. They were sure to believe Sharon and, once they'd gone, she'd be in even more trouble, and so would her mother. It wasn't worth the risk, was it? How stupid of her to think she could get the better of her cunning, devious aunt. She'd fooled Colin, her mother, Peter Harris, and now she was fooling the police. She'd have to say she'd changed her mind.

Leila was about to speak when a phone began ringing from the pocket of Sharon's cardigan. Leila realized it was the phone she'd used to call her mother. Sharon had stuffed it into her pocket when she'd discovered it in the bathroom cabinet. She saw Sharon stiffen as she tried to ignore the call.

'Do you want to answer that?' Petra asked.

'It's OK. Whoever it is can leave a message. I'll deal with it later. Now, where were we?' She looked at Leila.

Another ring and the phone stopped, going through to voicemail. But almost immediately it began to ring again, the caller having redialled. Leila's heart missed a beat.

'I think you'd better take that,' Petra said. 'It might be important.'

To refuse would have made her look guilty, Leila thought. She watched as Sharon reluctantly slid the phone from her pocket and looked at the caller display. Leila saw a second's panic cross her face and then she recovered.

'I don't recognize the number. It must be a nuisance call,' she said and powered off the phone, returning it to her pocket. Leila saw the red flushes on her cheeks and wondered if the police had seen them too. She looked from Petra to the other officer, but it was impossible to tell what they were thinking.

'You were going to tell us what happened to you,' Petra reminded Leila.

Leila shook her head.

'If you've remembered something, you need to share it,' Sharon said, again touching Leila's arm. She moved away.

Surely Petra or the other officer would see through her aunt, even if Peter Harris hadn't? The police were trained to spot lies and catch criminals, unlike her social worker. He had taken her to another room to talk in private, unaware that Sharon was listening at the door.

Leila remained silent and saw her only chance of being saved slipping away.

'It's late and the police officers are very busy,' Sharon prompted her.

Leila looked at Petra, willing her to see the truth.

'Would you like to go into another room to talk?' Petra asked.

Leila gave a small nod and stood.

'I'll make us a tea while you talk,' Sharon said, standing. But Leila knew that from the kitchen Sharon would hear every word of their conversation, just as she had when Peter Harris had been here. It was hopeless. Sharon had outwitted the police, just as she had everyone else.

Leila heard the front door open and close, then one of the officers who had been waiting outside came into the living room.

'Did a mobile phone ring in here just now?' he asked, looking at Sharon. Leila held her breath. Sharon could hardly deny it. They'd all seen and heard it. 'Can I have that phone, please?' the officer asked.

A moment's hesitation, then Sharon took the phone from her pocket and passed it to him. There was silence as he switched it on and studied the caller display.

'What's going on?' Petra asked.

'They're all lying,' Sharon said.

Leila swallowed hard and hoped.

The officer with the phone looked up. 'DC Beth Mayes

just called this phone. They've managed to trace it to this address, and they called to check. It's a burner and it was used in the abduction of Leila.'

Leila watched as the officer quickly took the few strides across the room to where Sharon sat. Slipping a hand under her elbow, he drew her to her feet. As he snapped handcuffs around her wrists, he said, 'You are under arrest on suspicion of the abduction of Leila Smith ...'

Leila remained where she was, unable to believe what was happening, as the officer completed the caution and then led Sharon away. A tear escaped and ran down Leila's cheek. For the first time since she could remember, her mother had acted to protect her. Now, surely, she would be allowed to go home to live with her?

FORTY-SEVEN

Kelsey walked up the neat front garden path she was now familiar with, pressed the doorbell and waited. A planter of brightly coloured spring flowers stood to the right of the doorstep, and the sound of children's laugher floated from the house. Not just Leila's laughter, but that of Tyler, another foster child, and the carer's own child, Ellie. The three of them were close in age and got along well.

Leila had been living here for two months now and Kelsey was pleased she'd settled in and was being well looked after. Leila had arrived very late on the night of 2 January, after being removed from Sharon's house and brought here by the police. She had been distraught when she'd first arrived, so Sandie, the foster carer, had sat up with her all night, holding her hand and reassuring her until she'd finally fallen asleep around 3 a.m. Kelsey admired Sandie's dedication as a parent and carer and wished she could have been more like her when she'd had the chance of bringing up her children. But there was no point in yearning for what might have been. It was the present and future that were important, not the past.

Sandie opened her front door, smiling and welcoming as usual. 'Hi, love. Come on in. How are you?'

Leila ran down the hall behind her and fell into Kelsey's arms.

'Mum, I'm so pleased to see you. I love you!'

'I love you too,' Kelsey replied.

Sandie smiled.

'Come and see what I've made,' Leila said excitedly. Taking her mother's hand, she led her down the hall and into the kitchen-diner. The children were often involved in an activity when she arrived: cooking, arts and crafts or playing games around the table. When the weather was nice, they played in the garden, which had swings, a climbing frame, a see-saw and a sandpit.

'Wow!' Kelsey said, admiring the pizzas the children had made, which were about to go into the oven.

'You will stay for tea, won't you?' Sandie asked as she often did.

'Yes, please,' Kelsey replied.

'You'll love the pizza I made!' Leila exclaimed.

'We all made them,' Tyler, Sandie's other foster child, corrected.

'We all made them and we'll all eat them,' Sandie said, smiling indulgently.

Kelsey laughed. Sandie had a way with children and Kelsey couldn't help but like her, despite her having Leila.

'Do you want to take your mother into the living room and show her your schoolwork?' Sandie suggested to Leila.

'Yes, come on, Mum.'

Sandie always gave her and Leila some time alone, popping in every so often to check they were all right. Because Kelsey was cooperating with the social services and wasn't considered a threat to Leila's safety, Peter Harris had allowed contact to take place in Sandie's home rather than in the more formal Family Centre. Kelsey wasn't allowed to take Leila out without Sandie, but hopefully that would change in time, once she'd proved herself. Kelsey saw Leila every Monday, Wednesday and Friday after school from 4 p.m. to 6 p.m. Sandie's home was a twenty-minute bus ride away from Hawthorn Estate and Leila had continued to go to the same school. Kelsey was satisfied with these arrangements and felt included – even part of Sandie's extended family – cherished and valued in a way she hadn't done since before her father had died.

Seated beside Leila on the sofa in the living room, she smiled as her daughter proudly showed her the maths and English folders she'd brought home from school so she could do her homework. 'You can help me,' Leila said.

Kelsey laughed, embarrassed. 'I'm no good at schoolwork. Sandie will be able to help you much better than I can.'

'You're doing very well, Mum,' Leila said in her old-fashioned way, and kissed her cheek.

'So are you, love.'

'When do you think Peter will let me come home to live with you?' It was a question Leila had asked many times before. 'I like it here, but you're my proper mummy.'

'I don't know. But it won't be for at least a year – probably longer. I've got to stay clean for twelve months. I also have to attend counselling and parenting classes and then I'll be assessed.'

'Peter was here yesterday,' Leila said, resting her hand on her open maths book.

'Yes, he told me. He has to visit you every four weeks. How did it go?'

'He said the trial for Sharon and Colin starts on Monday. He wanted me to know in case I saw it on television or one of the kids at school said something.'

'That's right. But there's nothing for you to worry about. You don't have to go to court. You gave your evidence in that interview you had with Beth.'

'Do you think Colin and Aunty Sharon will go to prison?'

'Yes, I do. They're both pleading guilty, although your aunt's lawyer is saying she needs psychiatric care rather than prison.'

'Why?'

'Because she has mental health problems and only acted as she did because of what our stepfather did when we were growing up.'

'But he did that to you, not her,' Leila said.

'I think we both suffered in our own way and she needs help just as much as I do.'

'I'm getting help too,' Leila said brightly. 'I'm going to start play therapy because of what happened to me. Sandie said it'll be fun.'

'Yes. Peter told me.' Kelsey paused, reluctant to ask the question that had been on her mind since Leila had made her statement to the police. It was niggling her and she really needed to know for her own peace of mind. 'Leila, when you told Beth what happened, you didn't ever mention Doris Goodman, did you?'

Leila looked at her mother carefully and shook her head. 'No.'

'Sharon hasn't mentioned her either, but Colin is claiming she was involved in your abduction. Why would he say that?'

Leila paused then said quietly, 'Because it's true.'

'What!' Kelsey exclaimed, astonished. Then she lowered her voice. 'What on earth do you mean?'

'If I tell you, you must promise never to tell anyone,' Leila whispered.

'Yes, but what is it? You're scaring me.'

Leila moved closer to her mother so she couldn't be overheard. 'Granny Goodman came to see me while I was at Colin Weaver's flat. She talked to me and knew I was going to her cottage. She was really nice and said everything would be all right. She said I was in danger because you weren't looking after me and now I was being taken care of. I don't think she knew what Colin was really like – mean and bad tempered. I haven't seen her since that night, but when I was at Sharon's she said Doris was a good woman and that I must never say anything bad about her, so I haven't.'

Kelsey stared at her daughter, utterly astonished. 'She caused me a lot of heartache. I was worried sick when you were missing. I thought you were dead. She could have said something to me, at least.'

'But what could Granny Goodman have said to you, Mum?' Leila asked, her voice rising. 'She kept telling you to look after me, but you wouldn't listen to her. Back then you were always off your head on drugs or drink. She was nice to me, and she was right to tell you off, but you hated her for it. You're a different person now. I don't want her getting into trouble and neither does Aunty Sharon. Perhaps you could be friends with her?'

'That's asking a lot,' Kelsey said. 'I'm really shocked by what you've told me.'

'Please?'

The door opened and Sandie came in. 'Everything OK in here?'

'Yes,' Leila said.

'Fine, thank you,' Kelsey replied.

'Dinner won't be long.'

Once Sandie had left the room again Leila whispered, 'You won't ever tell on Granny Goodman, will you? She was kind to me and the other kids. Promise me you won't.'

'All right.'

'Good. Now you can help me with my maths homework.'

The two hours' contact flew by, and once they'd had dinner it was time for Kelsey to say goodbye to Leila and return to her flat. Parting was always difficult, but more so today – Friday – as she wouldn't see Leila again until Monday. She was allowed to phone on Saturday and Sunday, though.

'Speak to you tomorrow,' Kelsey said at the door, hugging Leila goodbye one last time. 'Be good for Sandie.'

'I'm always good,' Leila said, with a cheeky grin.

Kelsey kissed her daughter and then went down the front garden path. As she turned, she waved goodbye and Leila and Sandie waved back.

'Take care,' Sandie called.

'Love you, Mum.'

'Love you too.'

Kelsey headed up the road towards the bus stop, zipping up her jacket as she went. Despite the chill in the air, she always felt warm after leaving Sandie's, from seeing her daughter and being made to feel welcome. It gave her a frisson of hope for the future, that one day Leila might be able to live with her again. But in the meantime, she was satisfied that Leila was being well looked after. Sandie was a lovely person – none better, she thought.

Yet what Leila had said about Gawping Goodman was bothering her. It seemed incredible that Goodman, squeaky-clean and moral gatekeeper of the estate, would in any way be involved in anything illegal, let alone Leila's abduction. The police had interviewed Goodman at her home a number of times during the investigation. Surely they would have picked up on something if she'd been involved? But why would Leila lie? It didn't make sense. There was only one way to find out the truth and that was to visit Goodman and ask her outright.

Twenty minutes later, Kelsey alighted from the bus and made her way across Hawthorn Estate in the direction of Doris Goodman's home. At 6.30 p.m. the sun had just set and teenagers were hanging around the swings in the play area. Kevin Bates, Mike Doherty and Jason O'Leary were unlikely to appear. They hadn't been there dealing for some weeks now, not since the police had cracked down and cleared them out. Not that Kelsey would need them any more. The last drugs she'd bought – or would ever buy again – had been on 2 January when, consumed by despair and believing Leila would be better off without her, she'd intended to take her own life. When Leila had phoned, everything had changed. That time in her life had passed.

Kelsey arrived at Doris Goodman's door and faltered. What on earth was she going to say to the woman? Now her brain had recovered from the drink and drugs she could think more clearly and appreciated just how rude she'd been to her in the past. She could hardly come here now and accuse her of having played a part in Leila's abduction. Unless, of course, it was true – then she could.

Not giving herself any more time to think and change her mind, she quickly pressed the doorbell and waited, her heart drumming loudly and her palms hot and clammy.

'Oh!' Doris said, opening the door, clearly shocked to find Kelsey on her doorstep. 'What do you want?'

'I've come to apologize,' Kelsey said.

'Really? What for?' Doris looked even more worried and unsure.

'For being rude and not listening to you when you tried to tell me I wasn't looking after Leila properly. I've just come from seeing her.'

'Oh, I see. How is she?' She relaxed slightly.

'Good.' Children's voices came from inside the house.

'Do you want to come in? I've got Tilly and Freddie Miller here. They're just finishing off their supper.'

'Thanks.' It was like coming from one foster home to another, Kelsey thought as she went in.

'Have a seat in there,' Doris said, pushing open the door to the front room. 'I'll just check on the children and then I'll join you.'

Kelsey went in and looked around the spotlessly clean and meticulously tidy front room. It was the first time she'd been inside Doris's home, but Leila had been in plenty of times – to Kelsey's shame. She knew children weren't allowed in the front room – Leila had told her – and now she saw why. The light-beige furnishings, glass coffee table and display cabinets crammed with dozens of china ornaments were delicate and wouldn't stand boisterous and energetic children.

Kelsey perched on the sofa as Doris's voice floated in, telling Tilly and Freddie they could play now they'd finished their supper. 'If you want me, I'll be in the front room,' she said.

'Would you like a hot drink?' Doris asked a moment later, coming in.

'No, I'm fine, thanks,' Kelsey said. 'I had dinner at the foster carer's. You've got a nice place here.'

'Thank you. It's home.'

Doris sat in the chair opposite Kelsey and there was an uncomfortable silence before Kelsey said, 'The court case starts on Monday.'

'Yes, I know.'

'Leila's evidence has been taped. She doesn't have to go to court.'

'That's good.' Another awkward silence. Was it Kelsey's imagination or was Doris guarded, watchful, ill at ease? Hardly surprising with the grief Kelsey had given her in the past, she thought.

'Both Colin and my sister are pleading guilty,' Kelsey said.

'Yes, I know,' Doris said again.

Another silence as Kelsey prepared to say what she had come to. 'Mrs Goodman,' she began, taking a deep breath.

'Please, call me Doris.'

'OK. Doris, in the past you've always talked straight to me. Been honest, even if I didn't appreciate it. Leila has given me a good talking to and I can see the error of my ways.' She gave a little smile. 'There's something I need to know, something that doesn't make sense. If I ask you a question, will you give me an honest reply?'

'I'll do my best,' Doris said stiffly, her guard going up again.

'Colin Weaver is claiming you knew Leila was at your cottage and that you were in on planning her abduction. While Sharon maintains you had no idea.'

A long pause before Doris said, 'So I understand.'

'Leila didn't mention you in her video statement,' Kelsey continued. 'But when I saw her this afternoon she said you knew all along she was at your cottage and you visited her while she was at Colin's flat.'

'I see.' Doris nervously touched the corner of her mouth. 'Do you believe her?'

'Yes, I think so. There's no reason for her to lie. She made me promise not to tell anyone.'

Doris looked away and then back again. 'I suppose you have a right to know the truth. Goodness knows I've nearly confessed enough times. It's been weighing heavily on my conscience.'

Kelsey watched and waited, her senses tingling, as Doris prepared to speak again.

'I made a huge error of judgement,' she began. 'I've been paying for it ever since. I don't sleep at night, worrying about you and Leila. It's me who needs to apologize to you. I hope you can forgive me. I honestly thought I was doing the right thing.'

'So it's true?' Kelsey gasped. 'You were in on Leila's abduction?'

'Yes and no. I'll tell you what happened and then you can

decide what to do with the information. At the beginning of November last year, Sharon came to see me out of the blue. I'd never met her before. She was very agitated and kept saying it was only a matter of time before the social services took Leila and that would be the last she saw of her, just like all your other children. I sympathized with her because I knew you weren't looking after Leila properly. Sharon said she'd been denied the chance to have children of her own but wanted to save Leila at all costs; that drastic situations needed drastic solutions. She said she had a plan to save Leila but needed somewhere remote to hide her for a few weeks until she was allowed to officially foster her. She knew about my cottage from the advert I'd put in the newsagent and asked if she could use it. She said it was better if I didn't know all the details but promised me Leila would be well looked after – much better than she was being looked after by you, which wouldn't have been difficult.

'I wasn't sure to begin with, but Sharon convinced me it was the only way to save Leila, so I agreed to her using my cottage. I wasn't supposed to see Leila after Colin took her on the evening of the thirteenth of November, but the police were everywhere so I went to his flat to warn him. It was only then I realized it was Colin, not Sharon, who would be staying with Leila at the cottage, and it was clear he had no idea about looking after children. I was worried for Leila and phoned Sharon. Call me a foolish old woman but she persuaded me everything would be all right. It was only much later I realized Sharon had issues. I didn't hear any more from her until Leila disappeared from the cottage. That hadn't been the plan and I was worried sick. I was about to go to the police and tell them what I knew when Leila turned up at your flat. The rest you know. Obviously I did wrong and you have every right to go to the police, but I promise you I acted in good faith. All I've ever wanted to do is help children.'

Kelsey continued to stare at Doris, amazed by her confession.

'But didn't the police suspect you?' she said at length.

'I think Beth Mayes might have done for a while; she certainly asked plenty of questions. But they can't prove anything. There's no evidence that I knew Leila was at the cottage or I was involved in her disappearance – only what Colin Weaver is saying.' She paused. 'Do you think I should confess?'

Kelsey saw the humility in her eyes. This once-formidable woman, who'd so often chastised and lectured her on her morals and for being a bad parent, was now asking for forgiveness, and wondering if she should hand herself in to the police, which would very likely result in a prison sentence. Kelsey knew she held all the cards and Doris's fate lay in her hands.

'No,' Kelsey said after a moment. 'I don't see that you confessing now would do any good at all. Leila is safe. I've learnt a very difficult lesson the hard way, and I think you have too. It's better if you stay here and continue to look after the Freddies, Tillies and Leilas of the world. Sharon was the one who masterminded Leila's abduction, and you and Colin fell in with her plan. I know how persuasive she can be.'

Doris's eyes filled. 'Thank you so much. I don't think I'd survive prison at my age. I am sorry for the pain I've caused you.'

'I know.'

'Have you seen Sharon?' Doris asked, wiping her eyes. Tilly and Freddie's laughter drifted in from the other room as they played.

'Not since her arrest.'

'I have. She's full of regret and remorse. If you can find it within your heart to forgive her, I'm sure she would appreciate a visit.'

Kelsey sighed. 'I'm not sure. Maybe one day, after the court case.'

Doris nodded. 'And Leila is doing well with her foster carer?'

'Yes. She'd like you and me to be friends.'

'She's a good kid,' Doris said. 'Do you think we could manage that, for her sake? I would like it if we could.'

'Yes, I think so.'

FORTY-EIGHT

A month after the court case, in which Colin Weaver and Sharon Kern both received custodial sentences, Kelsey entered Silverlight Prison for women. The prison offered good psychiatric care, but it was over an hour's train ride from Coleshaw. However, it wasn't the journey that had delayed Kelsey from visiting, but the ordeal of seeing her sister again. Now she was here, unpleasant memories of her own two spells in prison for drug offences returned. With each security check, her feelings of guilt and unease increased, and she had to remind herself she had nothing to feel guilty about now. It was Sharon who'd done wrong and was in prison.

Having completed the final security check, Kelsey continued into the visiting hall. She stopped just inside the door and surveyed the rows of tables and chairs. It was a moment before she spotted Sharon – seated at a table on the far right-hand side. She seemed smaller now, less confident and authoritative. Kelsey made her way over. Sharon was looking out for her, and as Kelsey approached their eyes met.

'Hello,' Kelsey said quietly, sitting in the chair on the

opposite side of the table. 'I never thought I'd be visiting you in prison.' She laughed nervously.

Sharon managed a small smile. 'Thank you for coming. I was surprised you wanted to see me.'

Kelsey shrugged awkwardly. 'I bought you some chocolates, but I had to leave them in reception to be checked. I hope you get them in the end.'

'That was kind of you.'

'It's OK.' She stopped, unsure of what to say next. 'How are they treating you in here? It looks better than the one I was in.'

'It's not bad. I have therapy twice a week, in a group and one to one with the psychiatrist.'

'Is it helping?'

'I think so.'

Kelsey nodded. 'Doris said you could be out in a couple of years.'

'Yes. Thanks to you.'

'Why thanks to me?' Kelsey asked.

'It was your evidence that swung it for me in court. Mad not bad.'

'Oh, I see.'

'I know how difficult it must have been for you to stand there in the witness box and relive our stepfather's abuse. I'm very grateful.'

'It needed to be done,' Kelsey said dismissively. 'And you're not mad, Sharon, any more than I am. We just lost our way, only differently. I should have been there for you.'

'Whatever do you mean?' Sharon asked, confused. 'You were there for me right through our childhoods, protecting me.'

'No, I mean later. Since then. It never occurred to me that you were as damaged as I was, and suffering in your own way. Pity we didn't get the help we needed earlier. I'm seeing a counsellor as well as part of my rehab programme. And Leila's going to start play therapy soon.'

'Good. How is she? Doris said she was with a foster carer.'

'Yes, Sandie. She's nice. I didn't want to like her. I really resented her to begin with for having Leila, but she's kind and caring, and Leila likes her. I see her at Sandie's house three times a week and we speak on the phone in between. Leila can stay with Sandie until she's eighteen if I don't get her back.'

Sharon looked down, her face clouding. 'I hope you get her back. I expect Leila hates me,' she said quietly.

'A little. For the way you treated me. She's very loyal. She always has been. But she's young, she'll get over it.'

'Will you tell her I'm sorry?'

'Yes.'

There was another awkward silence and then they both spoke at once. 'Go on,' Kelsey said.

'I was just going to say that Doris told me you and she had become friends. I was surprised.'

'So was I!' Kelsey laughed, more easily this time. 'I've been to her home a couple of times and I've invited her to mine. She seems a bit reluctant to come. I told her it was clean and there wasn't a syringe in sight.' She laughed again.

Sharon looked at her carefully. 'She explained her involvement to you?' she asked, glancing at the prison officer keeping watch over the room. 'She said she'd told you.'

'Yes. But don't worry – your secret is safe with me. Leila thinks the world of Granny Goodman. She'd never forgive me if I told.'

There was another silence before Sharon asked, 'Have you heard anything about Colin Weaver?'

'No. Have you?'

'No, I wouldn't in here. I feel bad about the way I treated

313

him, used him as I did. You have too much time to think in here. I was a real bitch to you both.'

'You were ill. At least you admitted what you did in court,' Kelsey said. 'The judge said you would both have got much longer prison sentences if you hadn't told the truth. Weaver could be out on parole in three years with good behaviour. And besides, he didn't have to do what you told him.'

'I suppose not. Has Doris seen him?' Sharon asked. 'She said she might go. He hasn't got any relatives who can visit him.'

'She was going to, but I warned her off it. The prison authorities note who is visiting who, and she doesn't want to raise police suspicion now. She said DC Beth Mayes had asked her a lot of questions during the inquiry. I know what it's like being inside. She doesn't.'

'OK.'

With that out of the way Kelsey felt the conversation got easier, and when the klaxon sounded signalling the end of visiting hour, Sharon's face dropped. 'Will you come and see me again?' she asked imploringly.

'Yes, of course.'

'And please tell Leila I'm sorry.'

'I will.'

Blinking back tears, Sharon stood, and Kelsey watched her file out of the hall with the other prisoners, humble and remorseful. The little sister she had protected all those years ago was now in need of her love and support again. Kelsey was glad she'd come and said what she had. She would visit her again.

FORTY-NINE

At Coleshaw Police Station, the team of officers set up to find Leila Smith and catch those responsible for her abduction had returned to their usual duties – investigating burglaries, sexual offences, assaults and so forth. Bringing Colin Weaver and Sharon Kern to justice had been good teamwork, but DCI Aileen Peters had made a point of singling out and thanking DS Bert Scrivener, DC Matt Davis and DC Beth Mayes for the parts they had played.

Although the team was now working on other cases, today Beth had reason to retrieve one of the archived files on the Leila Smith case so she could add a piece of paperwork. Even though the case had been closed with the sentencing of Colin Weaver and Sharon Kern, good record-keeping dictated that such paperwork should still be filed. It was impossible to know if it might be needed in the future, possibly in connection with another crime or one that hadn't yet been committed. It was a mundane but necessary part of police work. Beth sat at her desk and opened the file with the letter that needed to be inserted.

The letter had arrived at Coleshaw Police Station the day before. It was a copy of Colin Weaver's letter of resignation, sent by Abby Conway, head of Human Resources at Sparks Electronics. On the attached compliments slip Mrs Conway had written: *Apologies for not sending this sooner. I have been off sick.* Beth had spoken to Mrs Conway on 27 November, when Leila had been missing for two weeks. However, illness wasn't the only reason the letter had taken four months to arrive at Coleshaw. She'd addressed it to the wrong police station and it had bounced around a number of police forces and now showed the franking stamps of West Midlands police, Devon and Cornwall, Humberside and the Met, before finally arriving at Coleshaw.

Beth turned the pages in the file – one of the many physical files relating to the Leila Smith case, in addition to those stored digitally – then picked up the copy letter of resignation, ready to insert it. The next letter in the file was Colin Weaver's fake suicide note:

To whom it may concern. By the time you find this I will be long gone. I've had enough of my life. Please inform Belsize Nursing Home. My mother is a patient there. She won't understand I'm dead, but the staff need to know.
Colin Weaver

Beth stopped and looked at the letter of resignation and then back again at the suicide note. Something was wrong. She placed them side by side. The handwriting looked different. The style of the letter formation wasn't the same. True, the suicide note had been written in blue biro and the letter of resignation in black ink, but apart from that the actual handwriting was strikingly different. The shape of the letters, the pressure used, the slope of the words. She didn't need a forensic handwriting analyst to tell her these two letters weren't written by the same person.

'Matt,' she said, standing and going round to his desk. 'What do you make of this?' She placed the two letters side by side on his desk. 'This is the suicide note we found in Colin Weaver's flat, and this is his letter of resignation. The handwriting is completely different.'

Matt looked at the letters. 'Perhaps he was pissed when he wrote one,' he joked.

'Seriously, Matt, pissed or not, and allowing for the fact that different pens were used, the writing just isn't the same, is it?'

'No. They do look very different. That one', he said, tapping the letter of resignation, 'reminds me of the way my gran writes. The slant forwards, the thin lines, all the letters perfectly formed with a loop in the L. I think it's the way they were taught at school back then.'

Beth nodded thoughtfully. 'You're right. It's quite spidery – like an elderly person has written it – while the handwriting in the suicide note is firmer, heavier, more pronounced. The letters are rounder. Pity I don't have another sample of Weaver's handwriting to compare it to.'

'I suppose if he was upset and his hand was trembling when he wrote his letter of resignation it could look like that,' Matt said.

'Maybe.'

'Does it matter?' Matt asked. 'The case is closed.'

'Probably not.'

Beth returned to her desk and looked again at the two letters, deep in thought. She had other things she should be getting on with, but this was really odd. She couldn't just file the letter away and get on with something else. It would play on her mind. In her line of work, she was trained to ask questions and seek answers. There must be a reason for the discrepancy in the handwriting, beyond Matt's suggestions that Colin was pissed or upset. The only person who would know for certain why they were different was Colin Weaver, the person who wrote them.

317

Tapping the keyboard of her computer, Beth found the number for Sleaseford Prison, where Weaver was serving his sentence, and entered it into her desk phone. 'Detective Constable Beth Mayes,' she said. 'Calling from Coleshaw Police Station.' Matt glanced up. 'Can I speak to the governor, Malcolm Wiles, please?'

'I'll see if he is in his office,' the operator said. 'What is it in connection with?'

'Colin Weaver. He's a prisoner there.'

Matt rounded his eyes.

'I'm connecting you now.'

The governor came on the line, 'Malcolm Wiles speaking.'

'Good afternoon, it's DC Beth Mayes here. Thank you for making time to speak to me. I'm tying up a few loose ends on the Leila Smith abduction case. A letter has arrived that was purportedly sent by Colin Weaver, but I have doubts about its authenticity. Would it be possible to speak to him?' Beth knew her request was unusual.

'All mail is checked before it leaves the prison,' Malcolm Wiles said.

'This letter isn't recent. It was sent last year, in November, but got lost in the post. It would be really helpful if I could speak to him.'

'I can ask Mr Weaver if he's happy to talk to you, but you know he has the right to refuse?'

'Yes, I appreciate that. Thank you.'

'I'll call you back if he agrees. What number can we reach you on?'

Beth gave him the number of her work mobile, thanked him again and set her phone on her desk. Matt was still looking at her, now with a smile.

'You've got a cheek,' he said. 'I bet Weaver won't talk to you.'

Beth shrugged. 'It's worth a go.'

She tried to concentrate on some other work but without success. Matt was right: the chances were Colin Weaver would refuse to speak to her, or insist his solicitor was present, and this certainly wouldn't merit a formal interview. Anyway, there was probably a perfectly reasonable explanation as to why his handwriting was so different. It was just that Beth couldn't think of it.

Twenty minutes later, Beth's mobile rang and she snatched it up. Matt looked up.

'DC Beth Mayes speaking.'

'Hello, Malcolm Wiles returning your call. I have Mr Weaver with me.'

'Thank you.'

'He has agreed to talk to you on the understanding that he may refuse to answer your questions and I remain in the room.'

'That's fine,' Beth said.

Colin Weaver came on the phone and said a subdued, 'Hello.'

'Thank you for agreeing to talk to me. How are you?'

'You wanted to ask me about a letter?' he said curtly.

'Yes, it's nothing to worry about, but I've just received a copy of your letter of resignation.'

'Why?' he asked guardedly.

'I requested it last year as part of our investigation, but it got lost in the post and has only just arrived. The reason I wanted to speak to you is because the handwriting in your letter of resignation appears to be very different from the suicide note you left in your flat. I wondered why.'

'Because I didn't write the letter of resignation,' he replied bluntly.

'You didn't. Why not?'

'It wasn't my idea.'

'So who wrote the letter?'

319

'Doris Goodman.'

'Mrs Goodman wrote your letter of resignation?' Beth asked in disbelief. Matt's eyes widened in amazement. 'Why?'

'Sharon told her to. She didn't want my employers becoming suspicious and alerting the police when I didn't show for work. The letter needed to come from Coleshaw in case the postmark on the envelope was checked. So she got Doris Goodman to write and post it.'

'And you didn't think to mention this when you were interviewed?' Beth asked, meeting Matt's gaze.

'No. Why should I? It didn't seem important.'

'It would have substantiated your claim that Mrs Goodman was involved.'

'Oh. I see. Does it matter now? It won't help me get out of here.'

'No, but it could help build a case against Mrs Goodman.'

There was a pause before Colin Weaver replied. 'I don't think I want that now. Doris got caught up in saving Leila and thought she was helping her, as I did. I'm not going to be responsible for putting her in prison at her age. It wouldn't serve any purpose. Essentially she's a good person.' He cleared his throat. 'In fact, now I come to think of it, it's possible I wrote that letter and forgot. I was very confused and under a lot of pressure at the time. So if you were to ask me again formally who wrote my letter of resignation, I would say I did.'

'I understand,' Beth said.

'Was that all you wanted?'

'Yes, thank you.'

'I'll say goodbye then.' The line went dead.

Beth slowly set down her phone and looked at Matt. 'Mr Weaver isn't sure if he wrote the letter of resignation or not, but he believes he did.'

'Really?'

'Yes, really. He was confused at the time.'

Taking a sticky label from the pad on her desk, Beth stuck it on the letter and wrote: *Authenticity of letter questionable*. Then she placed the letter in the file, ready to be archived.

Colin Weaver was right. No useful purpose would be served by prosecuting Doris Goodman, although they would be keeping a close eye on her in the future. If necessary, the letter could be retrieved and the handwriting analysed, but for now it would be returned to the archive. Beth's next case awaited.

Suggested topics for reading-group discussion

Are there any clues early on to suggest that Sharon has a plan of her own in respect of Leila?

Describe the characters: Kelsey Smith, Colin Weaver, Sharon Kern and Doris Goodman. What sympathy, if any, do you have for them?

Beth Mayes and Matt Davis have appeared in other Lisa Stone thrillers. How would you describe their working relationship?

Do you think Leila is ever likely to be returned to Kelsey? Give your reasons.

Many of us are aware of a run-down area like the Hawthorn Estate. Using examples from the text, discuss how the author captures its bleakness.

Leila has had to grow up fast and is streetwise. Discuss.

Lisa Stone thrillers are fast-paced narratives that can appear deceptively easy to write. Try writing a paragraph that could go at the end of the book after Beth has returned the file on Colin Weaver to the archive.

YOU THINK YOU'RE SAFE, BUT ARE YOU?

Someone is always watching...

Derek Flint is a loner. He lives with his mother and spends his evenings watching his clients on the CCTV cameras he has installed inside their homes. He likes their companionship – even if it's through a screen.

When a series of crimes hits Derek's neighbourhood, DC Beth Mayes begins to suspect he's involved. How does he know so much about the victims' lives? Why won't he let anyone into his office? And what is his mother hiding in that strange, lonely house?

As the crimes become more violent, Beth must race against the clock to find out who is behind the attacks. Will she uncover the truth in time? And is Derek more dangerous than even she has guessed?

AVAILABLE NOW